# Dark Healing

## BLIND CURVE

### THE CHILDREN OF THE GODS
#### BOOK SEVENTY-THREE

## I. T. LUCAS

Published by Evening Star Press

**EveningStarPress.com**

**ISBN-13: 978-1-957139-81-4**

# Kian

At two o'clock in the morning, Kian gave up on sleep and got out of bed.

His thoughts still racing with all the implications of what his mother had discovered the evening before, he was like a live wire, and even Syssi's soothing presence wasn't enough to calm him down.

The secret of the royal twins that Jade had been hiding for so long was much more profound than she could have ever suspected.

In his wildest fantasies and most extreme conspiracy theories, Kian could have never imagined that the twins were his mother's half-siblings, his aunt and uncle, and they were potentially more powerful than Annani and even the Eternal King.

They were nothing like Annani's other half-sister, who was a weak goddess who didn't pose a threat to anyone.

Not only were they the children of two extremely powerful compellers, but as twins, they might be able to combine their powers.

The twins' compulsion ability could probably encompass the entire planet.

No wonder the Eternal King had concocted such an elaborate plot to eliminate them. The twins could have thwarted any direct assassination attack, and blowing up the settler ship they'd been smuggled on might have caused another bloody war with the Kra-ell.

Jade had speculated that the malfunction had been arranged by the Eternal King's wife to save her only son from the assassins his father had sent to kill him, but perhaps the gods' queen had nothing to do with it, and the king himself had been behind the sabotage for a completely different purpose. A ship lost in space was not enough to cause war, and by the time the twins arrived on Earth, their mother would have been long gone, and they would have been forgotten. Killing them seven thousand years later on a distant planet with no communication with the home world was a much smarter move.

Still, the puzzle pieces did not fit well together, and he didn't know how to arrange them so the picture would become clear.

Leaning against the vanity, Kian let out a groan.

The sabotage must have also affected the communication ability on the settlers' ship, because if the ship had continued communicating, the gods could have found it, repaired it, and brought it back to Anumati or let it continue its track to Earth. But if the settler ship had ceased communicating during its voyage, which it must have done to avoid detection, the Kra-ell queen would have assumed the worst, which would have started a new war.

The Eternal King wouldn't have sabotaged the ship because he would have predicted what would happen. After all, it had to have been the king's wife who had arranged for the ship's malfunction. Perhaps she hadn't cared if her actions caused a war as long as she managed to save her only son's life by making the ship with his assassin arrive on Earth seven thousand years behind schedule. She must have also arranged the sabotage of its communication systems so it couldn't send any signals, couldn't be tracked, and couldn't be repaired and sent back to complete its mission.

When the ship was lost, the Kra-ell queen assumed that her children had been murdered and started a new war. The fallout had been so devastating that it had either crippled both civilizations or altogether destroyed them. Otherwise, either the king or the queen or both would have sent scouts to Earth to look for their people.

There was also a third option, but it was less likely than the other two.

Igor's mind could have been sending information to someone on Anumati even while in stasis, in which case they would have had proof that the ship hadn't exploded but had only suffered a malfunction.

Would the Kra-ell queen have believed the king, though?

The only way Kian could imagine her accepting Igor's transmissions as proof was if she had direct access to them. The receiver must have been someone she trusted implicitly.

With the ship still out there, the queen would have had no legitimate reason to start a war, and since she wasn't immortal, she would have died long before the ship had finally arrived.

When some of the trackers came back online thousands of years later, her descendants had proof that the ship had arrived at its destination, but to them, the twins were a distant memory, if that.

But wait, he had forgotten about the Kra-ell's scouting team that had landed in China and had influenced the Mosuo people's female-dominated culture.

Kalugal was still digging for what he suspected had been their life pod.

The estimate was that the scouts had arrived about two thousand years ago, and by then, the settler ship had been gone for five thousand years. So, either the estimate was wrong, and the scouts had arrived much earlier, or it had taken the Kra-ell that long to develop their own inter-stellar travel.

Trying to put all the puzzle pieces together was giving Kian a headache. There were holes in each picture he'd constructed, and he was too tired to come up with even a hypothesis for the missing piece that would complete the puzzle. If the picture was still as fuzzy by morning as it was now, he would call Turner and bring him on board. The guy's analytical brain was needed to solve this mystery, and if he couldn't solve it because too much information was still missing, he could at least provide several plausible scenarios.

So far, the only ones privy to the information about the twins were Annani, Jade, Kian, and the brothers. He'd instructed everyone to keep it quiet, so he hadn't told Syssi yet. It wouldn't be fair for him to share the information with his mate while forbidding others to tell their loved ones.

Naturally, she'd taken one look at him and immediately guessed that something was up, and he'd promised to tell her as soon as he could.

First, though, he needed to wrap his head around it to present it to her in a way that wouldn't sound like the end of the world was coming. Then he needed to assemble the council and inform them of this new threat.

Well, it was a potential threat, not a confirmed one.

Firstly, suppose the Kra-ell queen had felt the need to smuggle the twins out of Anumati. In that case, she must have feared for their lives, which meant that they weren't more powerful than the Eternal King or that there was a way to ambush them despite their incredible mental abilities.

Secondly, the twins might not be Ahn's children. If their compulsion ability came only from their mother, they were not as powerful as the Eternal King had feared.

It seemed that the king hadn't been sure that the twins were his grandchildren, but he'd suspected it. His actions were extreme enough to indicate that he'd had an excellent reason to believe they were.

Sex between the gods and the Kra-ell had been taboo in both societies, so the affair between Ahn and the queen must have been shrouded in secrecy. Somehow the king had found out about it, which given the gods' advanced technology shouldn't have been too difficult to do, no matter how careful and circumspect Ahn and the queen had been.

The forbidden affair had probably reinforced the king's decision to do away with his rebellious son and any offspring he might have sired.

When the twins were born several months later, the Eternal King might have gotten suspicious, but since the Kra-ell queen had a harem of consorts and was much more fertile than a goddess, the timing of the pregnancy alone wouldn't have been sufficient for him to conclude that the children were Ahn's. But when it became known that the queen had dedicated the twins to the priesthood and that they were veiled at all times, the king had seen that as sufficient evidence that his suspicions were correct.

Naturally, this was all speculation.

Kian was trying to piece the story together with too little information.

Yesterday, Annani had been too distraught to continue searching Igor's mind for more details, but she had already told Kian that she would give it another try today.

And while she was at it, he planned to ask Igor whether he could communicate with anyone on Anumati. Annani had said he couldn't, but Kian still wasn't convinced.

It could be that Igor hadn't been transmitting telepathically or thinking about it while Annani had been inside his head, so she assumed that he couldn't, but Kian needed to know the answer to that with absolute certainty or as close to certain as he could get.

Another possibility was that Igor wasn't aware of sending the information. His ability might be one-way communication, with him transmitting but unable to receive.

Assuming that the Eternal King was still around and that the gods and the Kra-ell hadn't destroyed each other, the gods must have sent other ships to investigate what was happening. It didn't make sense for them to just abandon the settlement and forget about it. They must have known about the settlers' eventual arrival on Earth.

But if the gods had known about Igor and his colony, why hadn't they done anything about it?

Kian could understand their lack of interest in the Kra-ell settlers, but surely the Eternal King wanted to find out whether his son and his grandchildren had lived or died?

Regrettably, he would have wanted that information for all the wrong reasons.

The king had to have sent teams over the years to check whether the ship had arrived and if his commands had been followed. Finding the missing pods and confirming that the twins were dead shouldn't have been too difficult for the gods' technology, and the king would have wanted to make sure that the threat to his throne had been dealt with.

Then again, if the signal from the trackers could travel all the way to Anumati, then the king would have known right away if and when the twins woke up from their stasis.

Unless they hadn't been implanted with trackers.

Had Ahn and the other exiled rebels been implanted similarly to the settlers?

That would explain how the king had known that Ahn was dead.

Clever bastard.

The Eternal King thought he wouldn't need to send teams to investigate because the trackers would tell him everything he needed to know.

His plans had been sabotaged, and his assassins hadn't made it to Earth when they were supposed to. The king had either sat back and waited for the rebel gods to finish each other off or, which was more likely, he had sent another team of assassins to complete Igor's mission.

It was possible that it hadn't been Mortdh who dropped the bomb on the assembly of gods, but a new team of assassins sent by the Eternal King to complete the task.

Alena had accused Kian of being paranoid, but that made so much more sense than Mortdh embarking on a suicide mission. Being an insane megalomaniac hadn't made Mortdh suicidal, stupid, or ignorant, and he must have known what would happen if he dropped the bomb from a light aircraft with limited speed and maneuverability.

# Vanessa

"Don't go," Mo-red murmured as Vanessa pulled out of his arms.

"I need to use the bathroom." She kissed his cheek. "I'll be right back."

"I'll be waiting." Smiling, he turned on his side and hugged her pillow.

She felt guilty about wishing he would be asleep when she was done in the bathroom, but she really didn't want to talk about what had upset her the day before.

Her conversation with Borga was still reverberating in her head and souring her mood.

Being as attuned to her as he was, Mo-red had sensed that something was off as soon as she'd returned to their little nest. When he'd asked her what was bothering her, Vanessa couldn't bring herself to tell him that the mother of his son resented him and was reluctant to do anything to help his case.

Evidently, Mo-red wasn't as keenly attuned to others as he was to her. He'd been so sure that Borga's view of him was positive that Vanessa wondered how he could have been so wrong.

Seducing him instead of telling him something that would have upset him had been the coward's way out, but she just hadn't had the heart or the energy to tell him last night.

After their marathon lovemaking, he had thankfully fallen asleep, and she'd been given a little more time to come up with a way to soften the impact of Borga's betrayal.

Well, betrayal might be too strong a word, and Vanessa reminded herself that she shouldn't judge people.

Stepping out of the shower and toweling off, she tried to imagine what she would have done in Borga's shoes. Would she have defended Jackson's father even if she believed he was guilty of a heinous crime?

Her situation wasn't the same because Jackson didn't know who his father was, so she didn't need to do it for his sake, but even if Jackson knew the guy, he wouldn't have wanted her to defend someone she believed was guilty.

The question was whether Borga's attitude resulted from resentment and spite or her belief that Mo-red could have done more than he had under the circumstances.

Vanessa had a feeling that it was the second one and racked her brain, searching for something that could convince the female otherwise.

Except, beliefs were not rational, and therefore difficult to change.

What she needed was an exorcist.

Fates, she really didn't want to tell Mo-red about it, but mates shouldn't keep secrets from each other. Honesty and transparency were fundamental tenets of a healthy relationship. They indicated trust and appreciation of one's partner's acceptance of whatever she needed to tell him and his ability to deal with it.

Wait, had she just referred to Mo-red as her mate?

"Is Mo-red my mate?" Vanessa asked her reflection in the mirror. "My one and only?"

Her one truelove destined for her by the Fates?

On some level, she'd known that for days but hadn't acknowledged it. It wasn't an easy admission to make, and Mo-red's impending trial was just a small piece in the big picture of all the difficulties they would face.

That she would have to face.

Mo-red's lifespan was finite, Vanessa's wasn't, and the thought of losing him one day was so terrifying that she couldn't breathe for a moment.

It wasn't a "what-if," a hypothetical. It wasn't a general fear for a loved one like what she felt for Jackson and Tessa and all the other immortals who were dear to her.

It was an immutable fact that Mo-red would not live long past one thousand years.

How was Phinas dealing with the knowledge that Jade wouldn't be with him forever?

Perhaps being a warrior, his concept of forever wasn't as infinite as Vanessa's. Warriors died in battle, even immortals, and few of them thought in terms of forever.

That was why she'd been so happy when Jackson had chosen entrepreneurship as his weapon and business as his battlefield. The pitfalls and dangers were less exciting but, thankfully, less deadly.

Taking a deep breath, Vanessa let it out slowly through pursed lips.

There was plenty of time to worry about Mo-red's lifespan. He had another nine hundred years or so; in the meantime, human genetic science might catch up to that of the gods. They might discover the key to immortality in time for him to benefit from it.

What she needed to focus on now was saving him from the guillotine.

After yesterday's interviews, she wasn't sure Lusha could pull it off. There was so much resentment among the Kra-ell females, and since they would be sitting on the jury, his prospects didn't look good.

What was she going to do?

Was there some ancient law that Edna could find that would force the clan to protect him?

What if Vanessa officially mated Mo-red with all the pomp and ceremony Annani could muster?

Surely there was a law that stated that mates belonged to the clan and therefore were subject to clan law.

The Kra-ell weren't supposed to know that the goddess was back in the village, but that was only temporary until Kian got what he needed out of Igor. Not that there was much more he could get out of the guy.

In Vanessa's humble opinion, it wasn't likely that Igor could communicate telepathically with someone on the home planet, but Kian wasn't taking any chances.

After Igor was in stasis, hiding Annani's presence would no longer be necessary.

Kian might have a problem with her using a technicality to get Mo-red out of jail and stir things up with Jade, but Vanessa didn't care.

She would do anything to save him, including breaking him out of the dungeon.

Not that she had a clue on how to go about that, but where there was a will, there was a way.

The Guardians were letting her take Mo-red to the pool and the gym because he had cuffs that would sound an alarm if he tried to leave a certain predetermined perimeter, but if she managed to convince William to help her, he could disable the cuffs remotely.

Would he do that, though?

William was not a rule breaker, but he was a nice guy, and Vanessa knew how to be persuasive. She would tell him how she felt about Mo-red and why she believed he was innocent of the crimes he was said to have committed, or that there were at least mitigating circumstances since he was under Igor's compulsion, and William would help her spring him free.

"I can't believe I'm considering this." She shook her head at her reflection.

Nevertheless, the seed of the idea had been planted, and she knew she was going to pursue it and make a contingency plan for breaking Mo-red out of the dungeon. It might not come to that, but if it did, she would never, not in a million years and under no circumstances, let Mo-red die if there was even the slightest chance that she could keep him alive.

# Annani

⁓

Kian's guest bedroom was beautifully appointed, maybe too much so. Between the queen-sized bed, the two armchairs, and the small round table, there was barely any space left for pacing.

Halting for a moment, Annani looked longingly at the bed that Oshidu had turned down for her. Her body craved the softness of the mattress and the silky feel of the bedding, but her mind was reeling, and she could not rest until she came to terms with what she had learned.

Had her father even known that the Kra-ell queen had borne him twin children? Was that the real reason the Eternal King had banished Ahn to Earth?

According to Jade, matings between gods and Kra-ell were taboo in both societies.

Why, though?

Was there a reason for it other than simple prejudice?

It could not have been due to fear of genetic anomalies or defects. Vlad was a perfect example of a child born to an immortal mother and a Kra-ell hybrid father, and there was nothing wrong with him. But then, both of his parents were half-human, so maybe their human side had been enough to shield him from whatever abnormalities a child born to a pureblooded god and a pureblooded Kra-ell would have been cursed with.

Was it possible that unions between gods and Kra-ell resulted in abominations?

Or that these unions produced creatures so powerful that both societies feared them?

Fates, what had her father and the Kra-ell queen created?

Finding out that she and Areana had a half-sister and brother had been shocking enough; the fact that they were half god, half Kra-ell, and incredibly powerful was even more so, but the most important point was that they were somewhere on Earth, frozen in stasis and waiting to be awakened.

Should she be glad or afraid?

Potentially, they were much more powerful than her, and that was a reason for concern. Who could stop them from doing terrible things if they were not good people?

The Eternal King had conceived a clever plot to do away with the powerful twins. Perhaps she should take notes from her evil grandfather and make a contingency plan in case her half-siblings turned out to be malevolent dictators.

No. Unlike her grandfather, she would give them the benefit of the doubt.

The difference between her and the Eternal King was that he did not care whether his grandchildren were good or bad or how they used their powers. He feared them and was willing to kill them for being potentially more powerful than him.

The truth was that taking away a person's will was almost always bad, which was why Annani had been reluctant to use her ability despite being born with it.

That said, if she was powerful enough to compel the entire planet, she might have been tempted to intervene more than she had, preventing wars and stopping humans from committing other evils.

Perhaps it was a blessing that she could only compel those within hearing range.

Still, even if she could somehow reach every person on the planet, and even if her intention was to prevent suffering, it wouldn't be right to take away everyone's free will.

With a sigh, Annani put on a robe and quietly opened her bedroom door.

The downside of staying in Kian's house was that she had to be mindful of its other occupants. Alena and Orion were sleeping in the bedroom next to hers, but the primary bedroom was on the other side of the house, so if she tiptoed to the living room, she would be in the clear.

When she got there, though, she found Kian in the kitchen.

Wearing a beautifully embroidered kimono, he stood next to the electric kettle, waiting for the water to boil.

"I see that you could not sleep either, my son."

If she had startled him, he did not show it. "I'm making tea. Would you like some?"

"Yes, please." She tightened the robe around her waist. "What a beautiful kimono."

He smiled. "It was a gift from Syssi. She has a matching one in pink."

Kian's was made from black silk, and it had white, red, and gold embroidery. The gold dragon that covered the entire back brought a smile to Annani's lips.

"It is lovely. The dragon is a symbol of power and prosperity and is often associated with royalty. Her choosing it to decorate your kimono shows that your mate thinks highly of you."

"Syssi's faith in me is both flattering and humbling." Kian took two glasses from the cabinet, dropped a teabag in each, and poured hot water from the kettle over them. "I know that you prefer your tea freshly brewed, but right now, that's all I have the patience for."

She took the glass he handed her. "I am not as much of a diva as you like to think."

"I know." He smiled. "It's the persona you project, and we all love that about you."

Annani knew that, of course, but she did not bother to acknowledge his statement. Instead, she climbed onto one of the stools, made herself comfortable, and sipped on her tea.

Sitting on the stool next to her, Kian adjusted the folds of his kimono. "Now I understand why you always do that."

She laughed. "I do it for a different reason."

Kian was no doubt nude under the robe, and he adjusted it to avoid accidentally flashing his mother. Her reasons for always fiddling with the folds of her gowns were the lessons in propriety and royal conduct instilled by her own mother millennia ago.

"I wonder if my father knew about the twins," she said.

Kian shrugged. "I bet Ahn was sent to Earth before they were born and had no idea. Jade should know the timeline of the exile and the twins' birth. We can ask her."

"I will. Yesterday, I was too distraught to think clearly."

Until now, Annani had not discussed what she had learned with anyone.

Alena and Orion had not been home when she and Kian had returned from the keep, so she had not needed to talk about it before she had time to process the information.

Putting his glass down, Kian swiveled his stool toward her. "I dread the day we find them. I know that you are excited about discovering two additional siblings, but if the Eternal King feared them, so should we."

Annani smiled indulgently. "We think alike, my dear son. The same thought kept me pacing the little space in the bedroom you have given me."

He grimaced. "The guest rooms are small. As soon as we are done with Igor, you can return to your own home."

"I did not mean to criticize. The room is perfectly fine." She took a sip from the tea. "My grandfather feared the twins' power and sent Igor to kill them regardless of how they used it. He did not care if they were good or bad as people; he just cared that they might prove more powerful than he was and therefore posed a threat that had to be eliminated." Annani put the glass down. "I am also afraid of beings more powerful than me because I will not be able to stop them from doing terrible things if they choose to. But the truth is that despite being the most powerful person on this planet, at least for now, I still cannot stop bad things from happening."

Kian tilted his head. "What are you trying to say?"

"It is no wonder that you do not understand what I am trying to express when I am confusing myself." Annani sighed. "A long time ago, I realized that my ability to help humanity was limited and that the best way to do it was to plant the seeds of ideas and let them grow organically. I was content with the slow progress and accepted the limitations. But when it comes to my family, things are different. I have you and Sari to take care of finances, and Guardians to keep us safe, but I also know I can shield my clan. I do not like the idea of two powerful beings who could potentially subjugate my family. I want to reserve judgment and see what kind of people they are first, but by the time we can see that, it might already be too late to mount any kind of defense against evil intent. That is why we need to come up with a contingency plan —something we could implement even if our wills are taken from us."

"If you have any suggestions for how to do that, I would gladly hear them."

She let out a breath. "For now, the only thing that comes to mind is Igor. He was built as a tool to eliminate the twins. What if we can change his programming and turn him into a tool we can use?"

Kian shook his head. "His first task was to eliminate the Eternal King's only legitimate heir. With Ahn gone, that's you."

"I know. But right now, he is the only one who can stop them, and there must be a way to turn him to our side. After all, he is not a machine, and there are methods to reverse brainwashing. That is why I do not think putting him in stasis is a good idea until we figure out a better way to protect ourselves."

Kian leveled his gaze at her. "Igor cannot be trusted, and even if we could trust him, we don't need him to protect us. We have the Odus. Your grandmother sent them to us for a very specific reason. We just haven't figured out what that reason is yet."

# Kian

After returning to bed, Kian still couldn't fall asleep. Talking with his mother had made him even more stressed than he'd been before, raising new questions and bringing about new realizations.

His main takeaway was that they needed to put deciphering the journals on a fast track and start building an army of Odus.

That had been his great-grandmother's plan, or at least that was what Kian suspected. She'd sent the Odus to Earth with instructions on how to build more of them to protect Ahn from the Kra-ell assassins, but until Okidu's reboot and his birthday present to Kian, those instructions had been hidden inside the Odu's brain. Now that they had the blueprints, they should follow the queen's plan and not squander the gift they had been given.

They needed an army of Odus to protect themselves from the twins.

The more Kian thought about it, the more convinced he became that the twins' presence on the settler ship had not been as well-guarded a secret as their mother had hoped.

Both the Eternal King and his wife had known about it and plotted accordingly.

The gods' queen, however, was a much better strategist than her husband. Her plan was so intricate, and involved so many moving parts, and yet Kian couldn't find one single thing she had done wrong or could have done better, given the circumstances.

That was why he felt compelled to follow her plan without delay.

He needed those journals deciphered yesterday.

Perhaps he should text William and tell him to call back the team of bioinformaticians who had worked with Kaia before. Hell, maybe they should even double the team's size, get them all to the lab in Safe Haven, and put the thing on a fast track to production.

Except, it was too early to text William. The guy was a light sleeper, and the incoming text would wake him.

He should wait for at least another hour and get some shut-eye as well.

Using the breathing exercises Syssi had shown him, Kian somehow managed to drift away into a restless sleep, only to wake up moments later with a start.

What the hell happened?

His heart was pounding as if he was in flight or fight mode, and his first instinct was to check on Syssi. A quick glance confirmed that she was sleeping peacefully, and he smothered the urge to pull her into his arms and shield her with his body. Instead, he carefully leaned in and kissed the top of her head ever so gently so as not to wake her up.

Next, he listened to the baby monitor and Allegra's rhythmic breathing. Reassured that she was also fine, Kian finally allowed himself a relieved breath. The sense of impending danger was still there, but it was a little less overwhelming.

Still too worrisome to ignore, though.

He needed to check on his mother, sisters, and even his entire clan.

Kian rose silently, put his robe on, grabbed his phone off the nightstand, and headed to his home office.

Sitting behind his desk, he turned his computer on and logged into the village security feed. Everything seemed as peaceful as ever, and the alert level hadn't been raised from the usual green.

Still uneasy, he called the security office. "Is everything all right?"

"Yes, sir," the Guardian on duty said. "Are we expecting trouble?"

Kian chuckled. "Always, but apparently, not tonight. Have a pleasant rest of your shift."

"Thank you, sir. Good night."

Kian ended the call and leaned back in his chair.

Other than the distant threat of the twins, there was no other impending danger, and he should relax and go back to bed.

He could practically hear Amanda telling him to stop being paranoid and blowing things out of proportion, and Alena would probably second the sentiment.

His mother, however, seemed just as worried as he was, if not more, which was probably what had made him so tense.

He hadn't seen Annani so concerned since the last World War, and if she, the most powerful being on Earth, was anxious, a mere immortal like him should shake in his boots, or slippers as was the case.

If that was the only reason, though, he would have been returning to bed already, but Kian knew what was at the root of his frayed nerves.

The sense of vulnerability that had been plaguing him since Igor's attack was pissing him the hell off. He should have gotten over it by now, but he still had nightmares about Igor commanding him to do terrible things. In one, he had killed Anandur; in another, he had choked Jade to death while she looked at him with immense sorrow in her enormous, alien eyes.

It didn't help that upon waking up, he realized it couldn't have happened because he couldn't overpower

Jade or even Anandur without a weapon in his hands, but the sense of helpless despair plagued him so badly that Kian found himself reaching for the whiskey bottle more often than usual.

Perhaps once the trial was over and Vanessa had more free time, he would ask her to help him rid himself of those nightmares. He had no doubt that they were affecting his ability to lead, at the very least with the same surety and command as before.

# Mo-red

Mo-red didn't need to be a mind reader or even particularly attuned to Vanessa to know that she'd gotten some bad news the day before, and he also had no doubt that it had to do with him. Otherwise, she wouldn't have employed evasive tactics to avoid talking with him about it.

Not that he had minded being seduced within minutes of her arrival or the marathon of sex that had followed, but he didn't like her to carry the burden of what she'd learned alone.

Pretending to sleep when Vanessa returned from her prolonged visit to the bathroom, he waited until she was cuddled against his chest and her breathing evened out to open his eyes and look at her.

He was so in love with this incredible female who was fighting for his life with the ferocity of a hungry *dubca* protecting her cubs.

It was so obvious to him now that the Kra-ell had been fed lies since the age they could understand spoken language and had been manipulated to believe that they couldn't feel love.

There had been so many dogmas he'd believed in as a young male and knew now to be complete falsehoods, such as love was just a silly word that the gods used to court their females or that the Kra-ell did not have time for love in their purpose-driven lives.

Then there were the more subtle ones.

Loyalty to the tribe was sometimes mistaken for love but was so much more important and significant than the soft feeling that only small children were allowed to feel for their mothers.

There were more, but he didn't remember them, and they no longer mattered. He was a long way from Anumati, the queen, the priestesses and their teachings, and his family, who would have been mortified by his love for a descendant of the gods.

"I can feel you looking at me," Vanessa murmured.

"I thought you were asleep." He leaned down and kissed her soft lips.

"I thought that about you." She opened her eyes. "Did I wake you up when I got in bed?"

"No, I was awake. I just pretended to be asleep." He brushed a strand of hair off her forehead.

"Why?"

"You looked like you didn't want to talk, and the only privacy I could give you was closing my eyes and pretending to sleep."

Her eyes softened. "How can you read me so easily?"

"You are the most important person in my life. I pay attention to every minute change in your expression, in the scents you emit, your posture. I love you."

She gaped at him for a long moment. "You said that you loved me."

Hadn't he told her before?

Shockingly, Mo-red realized that he hadn't. What if she didn't want him to say that? What if it made her uncomfortable?

"Is that bad?"

"No." She smiled and lifted her hand to cup his cheek. "I love you, too. I planned to tell you that last night after I came back, but I got distracted by this body of yours." She put her other hand on his chest. "If you wanted to talk, you shouldn't have greeted me shirtless. What did you expect me to do?"

Even though Mo-red had known that Vanessa loved him for a while now, he was still reeling over her admission. He'd never been told that by anyone, not even his mother.

His own admission had just slipped out spontaneously, and he was glad it had, but he didn't know what to say next.

Instead, he explained, "I was exercising. I didn't want my shirt to get sweaty."

"I'm not complaining." She dipped her head and kissed his chest. "It was a very welcome distraction."

For a moment, he debated whether to ask her what she'd needed distraction from, but perhaps he shouldn't do that right after she'd told him she loved him?

In the movies, right after a mutual declaration of love, the romantic hero would kiss the heroine and whisper sexy things in her ear. He wouldn't start talking about upsetting things.

But this was not a movie, and they were not teenagers. As much as he enjoyed basking in the feeling of love, he shouldn't let Vanessa carry the burden of worry alone.

"Distraction from what?" he asked.

She smiled sadly. "I'd rather talk about how much I love you and how much you love me back."

"That's indeed a much lovelier topic of conversation, but if something is troubling you, I don't want you to carry the burden alone. You don't need to shield me from unpleasant things. It's my job to shield you."

She chuckled. "For someone raised in a female-led society, that's a very chauvinistic statement."

Had he offended her in some way? Wasn't defending the tribe a warrior's job?

Kra-ell females could fight as well as the males, but they were too precious to risk in battle. It was the males' duty to defend them and the young.

Only if they failed, and no more able-bodied males were left standing, would the females bear arms and face the tribe's enemies.

"I don't see why you would think my comment was chauvinistic or unbecoming of a Kra-ell male. The females of our tribe led, and the males followed their commands. We were the first line of defenders because we were expendable. The females joined the battle only if none of us were left standing."

"That's terrible," Vanessa whispered. "You are not expendable, and I don't want you to ever think that." She cupped both his cheeks and looked into his eyes. "Do you know what my definition of love is?"

"What?"

"It's not very romantic, but it's real. It boils down to me having your back and you having mine. I will fight to the death for your life, and you will fight to the death for mine. We are a team, and neither of us is expendable. We are both smart and capable. You might be physically stronger than I am, but I will still fight to defend you. We are equals in importance."

"I like it." He leaned his head and kissed her on the lips. "Do you want to hear my definition of love?"

"Yes, please."

"We are partners, and we have no secrets from each other, not even when all we want is to spare the other's feelings."

She scrunched her nose, looking adorable. "Fine, you are right. But can this wait for the morning? I would rather spend more time exploring our physical definitions of love." Her hands left his cheeks to travel down his chest to where he was still hard for her despite climaxing four times before falling asleep. "The physical aspect is a very important part." She wrapped her hand around his length. "Pleasure given and received."

Obviously, she was once again distracting him with sex, and he was too weak to object.

# Jade

A tall glass of cranberry vodka in hand, Jade walked out into the backyard and sat on a lounger. Phinas was asleep, exhausted after the night of wild sex she'd put him through, but she couldn't close her eyes no matter how hard she tried.

The queen had lied to her and the entire Kra-ell nation. She might have had good reasons for that, but it still didn't absolve her of her crimes.

The same crimes that Jade was committing now to some degree.

Had the queen fallen in love with the rebel prince?

She hadn't been the queen at the start of the rebellion, just the heir apparent to her mother, but for the Eternal King's son to be the father of her children, the affair must have continued long after she had ascended to the throne.

Jade could imagine the two young heirs plotting to make life better for the Kra-ell, finding they had much in common and falling for each other.

Had the princess committed one of the worst transgressions a Kra-ell could commit out of love? Or had it been lust, curiosity, and the taste of forbidden fruit?

The young didn't care about taboos and traditions. They were impulsive and thought that they could change the world.

Before meeting Phinas and discovering how deeply she could feel for a male, Jade would have accused the queen of irresponsibility at best and treason at worst. But now she was much more sympathetic.

Love was real, it was powerful, and it was a travesty that the Kra-ell had been brainwashed to believe it was the gods' invention and that they should avoid falling into its trap.

It was true that love was also a weakness, clouded judgment, and made people do stupid things like get pregnant with doomed children, but it also provided an added dimension to life that was above duty and loyalty.

When the side gate creaked, Jade wasn't surprised. Drova kept odd hours, claiming to be studying with friends to catch up on the education she had missed while in Igor's compound, but Jade knew that wasn't true. Lisa and Parker didn't keep the same hours, and Drova had probably been hanging out with the young Kra-ell, who loitered around the playground at night.

"Mother, what are you doing out here?"

"What does it look like?" Jade lifted her drink.

"Is everything okay?" There was genuine concern in her daughter's voice.

"Why wouldn't it be?"

"I don't know." Drova sat on the other lounger. "Did you fight with Phinas?"

"Would you care if I did?"

"Yeah, I would." Drova lay back and put her hands under her head. "He's okay. I like him."

That was the first time Drova had admitted to liking Phinas.

"I'm glad. He likes you too."

"I know. But I don't know why he does. Maybe he's a masochist."

Jade chuckled. "He says that you remind him of how he used to be at your age."

Drova laughed. "I don't envy his mother."

"His mother wasn't around. He was taken from her at thirteen, induced into immortality, and placed in a brutal military training camp." She turned to look at her daughter. "He didn't get to hang out with his friends, shooting the breeze and complaining about this or that. He trained until he dropped, and when he was your age, he was already fighting in wars. Phinas didn't have much of a childhood."

"Poor guy. I'm surprised that he's so nice to me. I thought he had good role models, but he didn't."

Jade shrugged and took a sip from her vodka. "The people we look up to are not always the paragons of virtue we think they are."

Drova burst out laughing. "No one is, Mother. Do you think that Kian is so virtuous? Or that the therapist, with her understanding eyes and condescending smiles, is a pure angel? Everyone has their selfish motives."

"I guess we do. My selfish motive is to be the best leader for my community that I can be." She took another long sip. "It might not sound very exciting to you, but that's what motivates me."

Drova eyed her from under her long lashes. "You seem different tonight. What's going on?"

Should she tell her daughter about the twins?

There was no reason to keep it a secret anymore. Kian and the Clan Mother knew, and Igor had known all along. Kian had asked them not to tell anyone about the twins being Annani's half-brother and sister, but she could tell Drova they were hybrids without mentioning the Clan Mother.

"Do you know that I used to serve the Kra-ell queen? I was in her private guard."

"Yeah, you told me."

"When? I definitely didn't tell you while we were still in the compound. I didn't want Igor to know."

Drova flinched. "I heard you talking about it with Kagra. Is it a secret that I wasn't supposed to know?"

"Now that we are free of Igor, it isn't. Every queen's guard member had to vow eternal loyalty to her. I vowed to protect her, her consorts, and her children with my life."

Drova shrugged. "They are all dead by now, so your vow doesn't matter."

"Two of the queen's children might still be alive, but I'm not sure I owe them loyalty since my vow was extorted under false pretenses."

Frowning, Drova looked at the glass in Jade's hand. "How much have you had to drink?"

"I'm not drunk."

"You're not making any sense."

"The queen's twin children were half gods, and she smuggled them onto the settler ship so no one back home would ever find out about her transgression. It was a big-time taboo for gods and Kra-ell to join, and any offspring of such a joining was considered an abomination. The queen and her children would have been executed if anyone ever found out."

"Lovely." Drova grimaced. "I'm so glad we are not living on that barbarian planet."

"Indeed. I only found out about it tonight. Well, not about them being on the ship. I knew about that. I didn't know that they were half gods."

"How did you find out?"

"Igor told me."

Drova scoffed. "He lied to get a rise out of you. You should know not to believe everything he says."

"I know." She wasn't supposed to tell any of her people about the goddess's presence in the village, including her daughter, so she couldn't tell her how she knew that Igor hadn't lied. "He was under the influence of a truth drug. He couldn't lie."

Drova didn't react for a long moment and then shrugged. "They're probably dead. All those pods that never came online are full of dead bodies."

"Yeah, you're probably right. I just don't know how I feel about it. Should I be glad that they are dead? Or should I be sad?"

"Does it matter?" Drova asked.

It mattered if they were alive and so powerful that they could take over the entire planet, but that was another thing she couldn't tell Drova.

"Not really."

"Then don't give it another thought."

Jade smiled. "You are wise beyond your years, my daughter."

Drova laughed. "I'll remind you that you said that when you are sober."

# Karen

"Good morning." Darlene walked into Gilbert's room and handed Karen a cardboard tray. "I'm on my way to the pool, and I thought you probably need coffee and something sweet."

It was four-thirty in the morning, which was Darlene's usual time for a swim. It was insane, but if it worked for her, who was Karen to judge?

"You must have read my mind. Thank you." She took the paper cup from the tray and put the rest on the floor. "How did you know that I wasn't asleep?"

Gertrude had offered her a cot, but Karen didn't want to crowd the small room. Besides, when she felt sleepy, she climbed into bed with Gilbert and took a catnap.

"I was in your situation not too long ago, so I know how it is. I couldn't sleep during the first thirty-six hours." Pulling the round stool from under the counter, she sat down and rolled it right next to Karen. "It's hard just to sit here and feel powerless to do anything to help, but you need to trust Bridget. She hasn't lost a transitioning Dormant yet, and Gilbert is not going to be the first. So, every time you feel anxious, remember that."

"Yeah, I do. I just hate seeing him like this. You know how he is, so full of life and energetic. Our home feels like a ghost house without him."

"Come on, Karen." Darlene rolled her eyes. "Dramatic much? Gilbert started transitioning yesterday, and he's been gone from the house for much longer than that on business trips."

"True, but now even the kids aren't fussing, or fighting, or doing any of the other things that keep the chaos in our home going. It's like they are in a holding pattern. We all are."

"Oh, boy." Darlene let out a breath. "How is Cheryl handling it?"

"Great. She and Kaia have been babysitting ever since it started so I could be here. They brought the little ones to give hugs and kisses to Mommy and Daddy. Bridget says it's important to engage Gilbert even when he's unconscious. The sounds of his family might help him find his way back to us."

Darlene's lips twisted in a grimace. "It all sounds so depressing. Let's talk about you and your induction." She smirked. "That's much more exciting, and I have some ideas that will make you blush."

Karen groaned. "Do we have to?"

"Yeah, we do." Darlene got to her feet and closed the door. "Do you know if the camera is on?"

"It is, but without sound. You can speak freely."

Perhaps she should have lied and said that everything was being recorded so Darlene wouldn't share her scandalous ideas, but it had occurred to her too late, and now she couldn't retract her statement.

"Good. So here is the thing. Eric and I talked, and we figured out that what worked for us wouldn't work for you and Gilbert. Eric says that Gilbert is already too jealous and possessive of you to allow another guy to lust after you. When he turns immortal, it will become so much worse, and Eric thinks the best thing would be to ask Connor, Onegus's former housemate, to do the honors of biting you. He won't be sexually interested in you, so it won't trigger Gilbert's newly awakened crazy immortal possessive instincts and won't make you uncomfortable."

Karen frowned. "Of course, it will make me uncomfortable. I don't even know Connor."

"He's a very nice guy, and I'm sure he will be happy to help."

"Oh, he doesn't even know you are volunteering him."

Darlene smiled sheepishly. "There is no point in asking him before you and Gilbert decide whether you are okay with it. It would be very rude to ask him and then say 'no, thank you'."

"Yeah, it would." Karen put her coffee cup down on the floor so she could rub her temples. "I really don't want to think about that right now."

"Fine." Darlene reached into her purse and pulled out a tattered paperback. "I brought you some reading material. When Eric was unconscious, I read him a slightly erotic romance, and we are convinced that the book did the trick. He got aroused from my reading, and that's what pulled him out of the coma."

"Let me see." She took the book and flipped through the pages. "What is it about?"

"It's a retelling of *Little Red Riding Hood*. Sexy retellings of classic fairytales are all the rage right now. The wolf is a werewolf, and Little Red is not so little." Darlene winked.

Her future sister-in-law was doing her best to cheer her up, but the more effort she put into sounding cheerful, the more anxious and sadder Karen became.

Not wanting to repay the kindness with tears, she put the book in her lap and forced a smile. "It's not my usual cup of tea, but it sounds fun. Is that the same book you read to Eric?"

"No, it's a different one." She smiled. "Eric would be upset if I shared our special one. But this one is just as fun. Do you want me to start reading it out loud? Eric says I make a great narrator."

"I'm sure you do, but if anyone is going to read sexy books to Gilbert, it will be me."

"I get it." Darlene pushed to her feet. "I'll leave you to it then. Don't wait, though. Start right away. You need to keep stimulating him." She winked again.

"I will. Thank you so much for the early morning snack and the book."

"No problem. Enjoy."

When the door closed behind Darlene, Karen opened the book to the first page.

"Once upon a time, in a land far, far away, there lived a young woman named Red. Red was the color of her hair, the color of her riding cloak, and her fiery temper. One day, Red was walking through the forest when she felt someone's eyes on her. It wasn't the first time she'd experienced this sensation, but what was strange about this time was the sudden arousal that washed over her—"

# Vanessa

S till groggy from sleep, Vanessa popped a pod into the coffee maker, and as she waited for the device to start brewing, she was struck once again by the thought that she would never get to share a meal with Mo-red.

The most they could have together was coffee, tea, and booze. He could also tolerate certain juices in small quantities when mixed with alcohol, but that was it.

If she ever got him free and they moved in together, she would still cook just for herself or eat with the girls in the sanctuary. And that was another problem.

What was she going to do about that?

The fitness instructor she'd assigned to run the sanctuary in her absence was doing great, but she was a temporary fix, and she couldn't handle the traumatized new arrivals that would start pouring in as soon as the rescue missions resumed, which would happen when things got back to normal in the village and the Kra-ell situation was settled.

"What are you thinking about so hard?" Mo-red pulled her into his arms. "You look like the weight of the world is on your shoulders."

Should she tell him? She hadn't even told him about Borga yet. "I'm not much of a conversationalist before my first cup of coffee in the morning."

He chuckled. "I've noticed. Sit down, and I'll bring it over when it's done. Do you want a protein bar with it?"

She'd brought some to put in the fridge in case she got hungry, but she was in the mood for a hearty breakfast of an omelet, hash browns, and toast with butter and jam.

"No, thank you. I'll grab something in the village café."

When the coffee finished brewing, he pulled the mug from under the spout and brought it to her. "Do you want cream?"

The only thing she had there was the powdered kind, and she wasn't in the mood for that either. She should bring back a proper creamer so she could at least enjoy her coffee while she was with Mo-red.

After all, a female couldn't live on sex alone, although given her track record so far, she was doing pretty damn well on a diet rich in sex but poor in other nutrients.

"No, thanks." Vanessa patted the spot next to her. "I'll drink it black this time. Come sit with me."

Mo-red pulled the other mug from under the spout and brought it over with him to the tiny table. "Are you ready to tell me what got you in a mood?"

Vanessa nodded. "I interviewed Borga yesterday, and it didn't go as well as I expected. She is not going to be as helpful to your case as you thought she would be. I think she's jealous of our relationship."

His big eyes got even bigger. "There is nothing between us other than Pavel. The last time Borga shared my bed was fifteen years ago, if not more. I've been with many females since then, most of them were humans, but occasionally I've been with some of the other purebloods."

"Well, she might have been hoping for more, or maybe she never liked sharing you with others, but it wasn't socially acceptable for her to voice her displeasure. She might feel a special connection to you because you share a son, which is understandable, and she fears that I will take away her special status in your life."

As the mother of Mo-red's only pureblooded son, Borga felt like she deserved extra consideration from Mo-red, and she wasn't wrong. They would be forever connected by the son they had brought into the world. In the Kra-ell society, it was as close to a relationship as it got, and Vanessa was threatening it.

Mo-red shook his head. "That doesn't make any sense. If I am executed because she refuses to testify on my behalf, she's going to lose the connection anyway."

"Feelings are seldom logical. I don't think she will say anything bad about you because of Pavel, but don't expect her to sing your praises either."

"What exactly did she tell you?"

"She said that she shared your bed and that of Igor's other pod members not because she was coerced but because she had no other choice if she wanted to fulfill her duty as a Kra-ell female and bring children into the world. There were no other males to choose from. Then when I said that you are a wonderful male, she said that you know how to be charming when you want to but that you can also be cold and cruel. Did she have anything to base that on, or was it just spite?"

Vanessa hoped it was the latter, and as she waited for Mo-red's reply, her breathing turned shallow.

He sighed. "Sometimes, I had no choice but to turn cold. Otherwise, I wouldn't have been able to handle what I was told to do. But I was never cruel by choice."

She let out a breath. "That's a relief. I knew she was just being spiteful."

Mo-red shook his head. "It might have seemed like that to her." He took Vanessa's hand. "Is that what got you so upset? It's just one small setback."

"Borga's testimony is important, and not just because she has a son with you. She holds a lot of sway among the other pureblooded females, and they might follow her lead."

"What about Jade? Is she going to testify?"

"I don't think so. She's adamant about leaving it up to the females you and the others have harmed. She doesn't count herself as one of them, but then she was exclusive with Igor, so she has no beef with any of you."

"Kagra wasn't exclusive with anyone, and she has two sons. I don't think she holds a grudge against any of us."

"Who are the fathers of her sons?"

"She killed one, and the other one is Madbar."

"Madbar? He didn't mention having a son."

"He hasn't been involved in raising him. He was too scared of Igor to dare to get close to the boy."

"The next time I talk to Borga, I should point out that the others did much less for their children than you did, not because they didn't care but because they were too scared of Igor. You risked a lot to get close to your sons."

"Don't." He brought her hand to his lips and kissed the back of it. "Leave her be. We will find a different line of defense."

# Mo-red

"I can't just leave everything up to Lusha," Vanessa protested. "We need to be active participants in your defense, and any crumb of goodwill we can scavenge might be the tipping point. I'm unwilling to skimp on any effort to collect every last one of them."

Mo-red didn't want to worry Vanessa any more than she was already worried, but if even Borga had nothing good to say about him, he was doomed.

He put his coffee mug down. "I'm so tired of talking about the trial." He pulled her onto his lap. "Let's make love instead."

Letting out a breath, she buried her nose in the crook of his neck. "I'm starting to think that your best option is to run away. If nothing else works, I will have to break you out of here."

Mo-red tensed.

Vanessa had probably meant it as a joke, but the computer listening to everything they said and analyzing it for trigger words might not recognize humor and flag it as something that needed to be reported.

"Ha, ha. Very funny." Perhaps that would clarify Vanessa's meaning to the dumb bot.

It would be interesting to find out whether making light of something affected artificial intelligence the same way it affected people.

Governments all over the world had been hiding things from their citizens by simply ridiculing those who spoke up about them. It was almost as effective in silencing people as killing them, or maybe even more so. Destroying someone's reputation was a better way to discredit any claim they made than arranging their deaths.

"I mean it," she whispered into his neck. "The Guardians are lax with your security, and they let me take you out of here to go to the gym and the swimming pool whenever I want. I can speak with William about remotely disabling your cuffs."

"Shhh." He put a finger on her lips. "Someone might take you seriously." He rolled his eyes to emphasize. "You don't know which words this thing is programmed to flag."

Vanessa smiled. "Then it's good that we are experts at saying things in ways that do not trigger those alarms."

"We might be able to do that, but if we follow your plan, someone will listen to all the recordings and figure out what you did."

She shrugged. "By then, it won't matter. My people have no beef with you. If I take you away, they will not try to find us. We can move somewhere far away and live happily ever after."

"What about your son? Wouldn't you miss him?"

"He'll come to visit. And don't worry, no one will follow him to find us."

Vanessa was talking nonsense born out of desperation, and Mo-red didn't know whether he should humor her or talk some sense into her.

Humoring her for now would defuse the tension so he could make love to her before she had to leave for her appointments.

"Okay, let's think it through. How do you propose we do that?"

"Easy. Once William disarms your cuffs, I can smuggle you out of the gym. I'll stuff you into the laundry cart, cover you with dirty towels, and take you to my car."

He laughed. "And no one in security would wonder why the clan psychologist is doing the laundry?"

Vanessa shrugged. "Did you see the pile of dirty towels in the pool bathroom? No one has done the laundry in a while, and since we don't have a dedicated cleaning staff down here, everyone has to pitch in. If anyone asks, my contribution is doing the laundry."

Evidently, she had given it some serious thought.

"Are you sure no one would check the cart? And what about your car?"

"You'll have to hide from the cameras. You're flexible. I can stuff you in the back on the floor and cover you with a blanket or some of the dirty towels. No one checks in person. It's just the cameras."

"Okay." He nodded. "Where will we go from there?"

"I'll have to switch cars almost immediately because mine has the automatic pilot function, and it will take over as soon as they discover you are missing. I'll have to prepare an escape vehicle right outside this building. The best way to go about it is to buy a used car for cash and put a fake name on the registration. That way, the clan won't be able to track us."

"You've given it some thought, haven't you?"

She nodded. "I'm not letting anyone take you away from me. I'm prepared to do whatever it takes to save you."

Overwhelmed by the extent of Vanessa's love and devotion for him, a lump formed in Mo-red's throat. "I love you too much to agree to you giving up everything important to you for me. I'm not worth it."

She glared at him. "Yes, you are. I don't want to hear you speaking of yourself that way. To me, you are the second most important person in the world. My son will always come first, but you are next on the list."

Mo-red smiled. "I'm glad to be second. If you put me first, I would have been worried about your sanity. Although, to be honest, the crazy plan you've come up with makes me worry about it already. You realize that it's not doable, right?"

"If William refuses my request, it's not. But if I get him to say yes, then it's definitely a possibility. It's not going to be easy, but it's an option I'm seriously considering." She cupped his cheek. "It's not the only one, either. I have another one I'm working on, but since you think my ideas are crazy, I'm not going to tell you about it."

He much preferred it when Vanessa was in a playful mood. "I guess I will have to torture it out of you."

She affected a horrified expression. "Torture? What do you have in mind?"

He pulled her shirt over her head. "I will torment you with so much pleasure that you will beg me to stop."

Frowning, she lifted her hand to look at her watch. "You have a little under an hour before I need to shower and get dressed for meetings, and there is no way I'm going to beg you to stop that quickly."

He lifted a brow. "Is that a challenge?"

"You bet it is."

# Syssi

As Syssi waited impatiently for everyone in her unusually full house to get to the breakfast table, she glanced at her watch and shook her head.

At this rate, there was no way she and Amanda were getting to the university on time, and since they had a full roster of volunteers today, the postdocs would have to start the testing without them.

There was little she could do about it, though.

Annani was taking her sweet time getting ready even though she was usually an early riser. Alena and Orion were already there, enjoying the cappuccinos she'd made them earlier, and Kian was changing Allegra's diaper.

Amanda was on her way with Evie, and since she lived two houses over, that shouldn't take long, but even if she made it there in the next five minutes, they would still be late.

It was such a rare occasion to have nearly the entire family over for breakfast that it made it worth being late.

"Here we go." Kian put Allegra in her highchair. "It's much nicer to eat with a clean tush, don't you think?"

Their daughter looked at her father with a hard-to-decipher expression. "Daddy. Nini?"

"Nini is coming." Kian put the bowl of cereal in front of her. "Do you want to eat by yourself, or do you want me to feed you?"

"Spoo." Allegra snatched the plastic utensil before Kian could reach for it.

"Very well." He smiled at her. "Show Daddy how nicely you eat."

"Good morning, family." Amanda strolled in with Evie strapped to her chest. "What do you think about this nifty thing?" She patted the contraption holding her baby. "It's Prada."

"Of course, it is." Alena rose to her feet and freed Evie from the thing. "Come to Auntie, sweetie."

Pouting, Amanda pulled out a chair. "I wanted Dalhu to join us, but he was splattered in paint from head to toe, so I told him to clean up and then come. He must have gotten a spurt of inspiration in the middle of the night and attacked a fresh canvas with splashes of color. I've never seen him doing anything in the Impressionist style before." She looked around the table. "Where is Mother?"

"She's coming," Alena said. "Apparently, our brother and mother spent half the night talking, and Mother woke up later than usual. Perhaps Dalhu's nighttime inspiration has to do with what kept them up."

"I doubt it," Kian said.

"What's going on?" Syssi asked. "I've waited patiently for you to tell me, but I can't wait any longer. It's making me anxious."

He took her hand and gave it a gentle squeeze. "Let's wait a few moments longer for my mother to join us. It has to do with her, and I don't want to steal her thunder."

"Oh, okay."

Syssi got excited for a moment. Perhaps Igor had revealed more things about the gods' home planet? But then, why had Kian been so upset?

When Annani floated into the room a few moments later, all eyes turned to her.

She smiled. "Good morning. You should have started without me. Now I feel guilty for making you all wait."

Kian rose to his feet. "They are waiting to hear about what we learned last night." He pulled out a chair for his mother.

"Oh yes, I see." She sat down and adjusted the folds of her gown. "Yes, that is big news, and I want to share it with Toven as well." She turned to Syssi. "I hope you do not mind me inviting him. He will join us after breakfast."

"I don't mind at all, but I do mind if you want to wait with the news until he gets here. I don't think I can stand the tension any longer."

"Of course, my dear. I will not make you wait that long, but I would like a cup of coffee first. Would you mind making me a cappuccino? My Odus have not mastered the art yet."

Gritting her teeth, Syssi pushed to her feet. "Of course. Anyone else want a cappuccino?"

Naturally, Annani was stalling so Toven could get there before she started talking, but it wasn't as if she could confront the Clan Mother about her delaying tactics.

"I would love one," Kian said.

Amanda lifted her hand. "Me too."

Since Syssi could only make one at a time, that was going to take forever, and she was really starting to lose her patience.

Finally, when everyone who had requested a cappuccino had gotten one, Syssi sat back down. "Okay, now please stop stalling and tell us what got you two so rattled last night."

Kian looked at his mother, who waved a hand at him. "You can start, dear."

"As you wish, Mother." He turned to face the rest of their family. "By now, you have all heard about the royal twins, right?"

Orion nodded. "The Kra-ell queen's children, who Jade suspects were smuggled on the settler ship."

"Correct, but it's no longer a suspicion. It's a fact." He looked at Annani. "Do you want to take it from here?"

"Yes." She put her cup down. "Yesterday evening, I entered Igor's mind and sifted through his memories while Kian asked him questions to prompt him to bring specific recollections to the forefront of his mind. One of the questions was about the royal twins and what Igor knew about them. He answered that he did not know much, and what I saw in his mind confirmed it. He did not know what they looked like, and he had only seen pictures of them fully veiled. I transmitted that image to Kian, and his next leading question was whether the twins were supposed to conquer Earth and take over from the gods. Once again, Igor tried to make it seem that he did not know anything about such a plan, but his mind projected a picture of the two veiled figures sitting on two identical thrones."

"That doesn't mean much," Alena said. "He might have been influenced by Kian's question, and he also might have thought about them being their mother's heirs."

"That's why I asked him whether he was supposed to help the twins wrestle control from the gods." Kian lifted the spoon Allegra had thrown on the table. "The image Mother projected into my mind was of Igor standing behind the two thrones, dressed in a fancy outfit that looked like what you would expect a chief advisor to the crown in a fantasy movie would wear."

Annani sighed. "That wasn't so worrisome, but what Igor's mind showed me next was. It was a futuristic scene with the Kra-ell outnumbering humans and Igor ruling the entire planet. At that moment, I realized that Igor had been altered to be immortal, not just long-lived like other Kra-ell, and that he planned to become the absolute ruler of this planet after finding and eliminating the twins."

"Oh, my." Amanda leaned back with her cappuccino cup. "The plot thickens."

"It does," Kian confirmed. "But Mother hasn't told you the punchline yet."

As all eyes turned back to Annani, she lifted her cup, took a small sip, and put it back down. "Igor's task was to eliminate the king's children and secure the planet for the twins, but only temporarily until he gained their trust so he could kill them without them seeing it coming."

"Are they that powerful?" Orion asked.

Annani nodded. "Their power comes from both their mother and their father, and that made them potentially more powerful than the Eternal King, hence the very careful plot to take them out."

"Who was their father?" Syssi asked, although she had a feeling that she knew the answer to that.

Was it the Eternal King himself? Had he and the queen celebrated their peace treaty with a forbidden dalliance?

Annani closed her eyes. "The Kra-ell royal twins are my half-brother and sister. My father is their father as well."

# Toven

"**C**ome with me." Toven crouched next to Mia.

She had said she didn't want to go, but she'd put on a nice skirt and fixed her hair, which told him that she wanted him to insist.

Well, he could be wrong.

Females were complicated, and they did things for all kinds of reasons. She might have wanted to freshen up to look nice for him or herself, or maybe she just wanted to try out the new skirt with a new lip gloss.

The one thing Toven had learned over his very long life was to never assume he knew for sure what a female wanted.

"I don't know," Mia said in a tone that invited convincing.

"You need to get out of the house, sweetheart."

She put her drawing pad aside and cupped his cheek. "I've been out of the house for weeks and had a grand adventure. Now, I want to catch up on my book."

"You know that you don't need to work, right? You should do it only if it gives you pleasure, and letting it take over your life will soon make it seem like a chore rather than fun."

She sighed. "You are right. I no longer need to rush with submissions, and I can take my time. It doesn't matter when this book is ready."

Mia's publisher had managed to convince her that she wasn't a good storyteller and that she should stick with illustrations and let someone else write the story. Toven had disagreed wholeheartedly, and he'd made a wager with her that her story would do much better commercially than the story her publisher had commissioned for her illustrations.

That had finally convinced her to drop her publisher and go out on her own. Now, she could write the stories and illustrate them, and she didn't have to meet anyone's deadlines.

As a plus, she had complete artistic freedom, and she could take her time since she didn't need the income.

Still, he understood that she was eager to find out whether the children's book she was working on would succeed.

Toven placed his hand over Mia's. "So, does that mean that you're coming with me?"

She scrunched her cute little nose. "I don't know. Annani asked you to come over, not us. I don't want to show up uninvited, especially since it is in Kian's house, and neither he nor Syssi invited me."

So that was why Mia had been reluctant to accompany him. She thought she wasn't welcome.

"Nonsense." Toven pushed to his feet. "Annani knows that we are a team. If she invited one of us, she should also expect the other."

"It doesn't work like that." Mia turned her chair and followed him to the front door. "If anyone makes a disapproving remark or gives me a reproachful look, I'm telling them that it was your idea and that you dragged me along."

"Fine with me." He followed her down the ramp. "I wonder what Annani wants to talk to me about."

Mia's eyes widened with alarm. "We are not supposed to talk about her where we can be overheard."

Toven laughed. "Use your new immortal senses. Is there anyone nearby who can overhear us?"

"I can't hear anything over the noise the motor makes. Can you?"

Her chair ran on electricity, so it wasn't very noisy, but Mia's hearing wasn't as good as his.

"The nearest person is about five hundred feet away. From what I've noticed, most clan members are not morning people. There are a few runners who tend to leave their homes early in the morning, but most don't emerge until nine or later."

"Almost everyone I know works from home." Mia kept the speed of her chair steady. "Very few work in the city and need to get up early. But what about the Guardians that patrol the village? Or Kalugal's men, or the Kra-ell? They can't all be holed up in their homes."

"Apart from the Guardians, it would appear that they are." Toven stepped on the bridge that led to phase three of the village and waved hello at the hidden cameras. "Kian offered us a house here. I told him that I would check with you."

Mia shook her head. "I want to be next door to my grandparents, and he won't allow them here. Besides, I like being closer to the center of the village. If I open the windows, I can hear the children squealing happily in the playground, which lifts my mood."

"Yeah. That's one of the best things about the Kra-ell joining our community. We have so many more children now."

He knew that Mia couldn't wait to be a mother, but they hadn't started taking Merlin's fertility potions because the doctor wasn't sure if the potion was safe for Mia to take while regrowing her legs.

Since their return from the mission to liberate the Kra-ell, she'd been resting more. The growth had been so much more significant than Bridget had anticipated that she would have her legs back in about three months, which was much sooner than she had hoped for.

Toven didn't want to burst Mia's happy bubble, but he didn't agree with Bridget's optimistic estimate. Given that the growth rate fluctuated so greatly, it was anyone's guess how long it would take to regrow her lower limbs completely.

The feet in particular would take a long time because of all the intricate bones.

He was still giving Mia blood occasionally to speed up the process, but she was less and less willing to receive his transfusions because he was also donating his blood to other causes. He was helping her grandparents stay healthy and age at a much slower rate, and now that Gilbert was transitioning, he was helping him as well.

Last night, Toven had to pull off a Mission-Impossible style operation to give Gilbert a blood transfusion while Karen was in the room with them and the surveillance camera was on.

Heck, he'd gotten so good at it that he felt like a stage magician.

"What are you smiling about?" Mia asked.

He leaned closer to her. "I told you about last night. I pulled a pretty nifty trick to help Gilbert while Karen was beside him. She didn't notice a thing, and I didn't even use thralling or other mind tricks. It was all sleight of hand. I could have a career in magic." He winked.

She chuckled. "I think the trickster god title is taken. You'll have to be content with the title of the god of wisdom and knowledge."

"I'm very content." He leaned down and kissed the tip of her nose. "There is nothing I would change about my life."

She looked at her legs and sighed. "Mine will be complete when this stage is done, and I can finally start Merlin's fertility treatments. I want us to have a child together."

"We will." He lightly squeezed her shoulder. "When your horizon is forever, there is no need to rush. There is time for everything."

# Kian

Kian listened as Annani recounted yesterday's events for Toven, hoping to catch something she might have omitted before, but if anything, the version she was telling Toven and the rest of the family was shorter.

By the time she was done, Toven's forehead was creased with deep frown lines. "Let's hope that they don't wake up anytime soon, and in the meantime, you and I should practice our compulsion abilities. Maybe we can combine our powers without being twins."

Annani let out a breath. "I hate compulsion. I always thought of it as vile, and after meeting Igor, I am more convinced of it than ever. If I believed in the devil, I would have blamed him for this questionable gift and the temptation to use it."

Toven chuckled without mirth. "I won't argue that the temptation exists to use it for all the wrong reasons. But you have to admit that it is useful when you need to protect your loved ones, and that is what you and I will use it for. I have no wish to conquer lands or win political races. If I had such aspirations, I could have been elected president of any country whenever I wished, but I don't. Right now, providing people who have mobility issues with free access to the Perfect Match Virtual Studios is the extent of my involvement with humanity, and I don't intend to expand it."

Kian thought of all the riches Toven had accumulated throughout the millennia of his existence and wondered how much of it had been acquired with the use of compulsion. The god claimed that he'd been given all that gold as tribute, but Kian had no doubt that compulsion played some part in the savages' enthusiasm to honor Toven with such riches.

"Maybe you should run for President," Mia said. "The world would be a better place with you at the helm."

He snorted. "I have tried leading before, and unlike most elected officials, I actually had the best intentions of helping humans and preventing bloodshed, but I achieved the opposite. I'm never doing that again."

Kian was glad to hear that.

He'd thought long and hard about the favor he was about to ask of Toven, and the fact that the god had no delusions of grandeur and no aspirations to rule anyone made the decision so much easier.

Syssi rose to her feet. "Does anyone want another cappuccino before Amanda and I leave for work?"

They were already an hour late, and so was Kian, but this was important.

"No, thank you." Mia smiled at Syssi. "The cappuccino was amazing, but I don't want to keep you any longer."

Kian stood up and took Allegra into his arms. "I'll help you get her ready." He turned to look at Toven. "When I return, I would like a word with you if you have the time."

"I'm not in a rush to go anywhere." Toven cast a fond look at Allegra. "Have fun with Mommy at work, sweetie."

"Bye bye, Tata." Allegra waved at him.

"That's adorable," Mia exclaimed. "I think I'll start calling you Tata."

He grinned at her. "Tata means daddy in some Slavic languages. Are you hinting at something?"

As Mia's cheeks grew red, Kian laughed and led Syssi and Allegra to the front door. "I think Toven's comment was completely innocent, and Mia misinterpreted it. I think he meant to ask if she's hinting that he should become a father, as in them having a baby."

Syssi lifted on her toes and kissed his cheek. "Toven is very proper, but he's far from innocent. He meant exactly what Mia thought he did."

Amanda joined them at the door with Evie back in her Prada baby carrier. "Say your goodbyes, lovebirds. We need to go."

"Drive carefully," Kian warned. "You're transporting precious cargo."

Amanda's confident mask slipped for a moment. "Don't worry, I know. That's why I'm driving your wonder car and not a modified version of my Porsche."

The wonder car, as Amanda called it, was the model most clan members drove, and it was equipped with an array of sensors and autonomous driving that made it the safest vehicle on the road.

After another kiss to Syssi and Allegra, Kian closed the door behind them and returned to Toven.

"Would you like to join me for a cigarillo outside?"

Toven looked at Mia. "Would you mind?"

"Not at all. I'll stay here. Orion is telling me about the performance he saw in the sanctuary. Apparently, they have a very lively theater club."

"That sounds lovely." Toven smiled at Annani. "We should visit you and see one of the club's productions."

"You are always invited and can even participate in one of the plays. Call me, and I will arrange for one of my Odus to pick you up from the clan's airstrip."

"I might do that as soon as Mia is up to traveling again." He patted his mate's shoulder and followed Kian outside.

"I assume that smoking was not the main reason for your invitation. Do you want to talk to me about the twins?"

"It's related to them, yes, but not directly." Kian opened the box of cigarillos and offered one to Toven. "How familiar are you with the old language?"

"I'm very rusty, but with some effort, it will probably come back to me." He pulled out a cigarillo and accepted Kian's lighter. "Why?"

Kian lit his own and took a grateful puff. "I assume you know about Okidu's journals and our efforts to decipher them."

The god nodded. "Kaia is working on that, right? With William's help?"

Kian chuckled. "William has been so busy lately that he hasn't had time to sleep, let alone help Kaia with the research. I was thinking about calling back the group of bioinformaticians that were helping her before we had to evacuate Safe Haven so we could expedite the deciphering effort, but then it occurred to me that you could probably help Kaia progress much faster than any human bioinformatician. You are familiar with the gods' language, and although you are not a scientist, you are highly intelligent, and your father was a great scientist and engineer. You spent a lot of time with Ekin. You must have absorbed something."

"Something, yes, but not a lot. Why the sudden urgency? I thought that you were content to let it take as long as it needed to take. You were in no hurry to build more Odus."

# Toven

〰〰

"I wasn't in a rush before," Kian said. "In fact, I was reluctant to build them. But I realize now that the threat the twins represent might be mitigated only by the Odus, who are not susceptible to compulsion and are incredibly strong."

Being half god and half Kra-ell, the twins were probably as strong as the Kra-ell and healed as fast as the gods. It was a very dangerous combination.

Toven took a puff of the cigarillo. "I wonder whether the twins drink blood for sustenance or eat regular food like the gods."

Kian pursed his lips before answering. "If they can't subsist on blood, hiding their nature must have been incredibly difficult, and perhaps that was the reason they spent long hours in the royal gardens. The queen might have had fruit trees planted there for her children."

Toven chuckled. "As half Kra-ell, I'm sure they are carnivorous. They wouldn't survive on fruits alone. Perhaps the queen had animals in that garden for them to hunt."

"Yes, you're probably right. That would have been easier to explain."

"Not if they needed to cook them." Toven leaned back and leveled his gaze at Kian. "Why were you reluctant to build more Odus?"

Kian took a puff of his cigarillo. "It's a complicated and morally iffy issue. I think of Okidu and Onidu as sentient beings. The only reason the other five haven't evolved yet is that they didn't get rebooted. Frankly, I don't know how I feel about building more Odus, who could potentially become sentient, and exploiting them for my own purposes. Even if the journals include instructions about how to throttle their evolution and keep them non-sentient for an indefinite time, that still doesn't feel right."

For a two-thousand-year-old male, Kian was surprisingly naive.

"How is using the Odus to defend the clan different from what rulers all over the world are doing with their very sentient citizens?"

"What do you mean?"

Toven took a deep breath. "They draft the young to fight in senseless wars, sacrificing their lives for reasons that are soon forgotten, and neither the drafted soldiers nor their parents can do anything about it. If they refuse to go, they are imprisoned in some countries and executed in others. And don't get me started on mandatory taxes and how leaders frivolously spend their citizens' hard-earned money. I'm sure you will use the Odus more responsibly and conscientiously than most leaders use their people."

"Thank you for complimenting me and showing me a different perspective on the issue." Kian leaned back in his lounger. "We've speculated about who might have sent the Odus to Earth with the blueprints to build more of them and why, and we thought it was their maker or someone who disagreed with what was done with them. But now that we know about the Eternal King's plot to kill Ahn, we think that Ahn's mother sent the Odus to Earth. She wanted to help her son build an army to protect him from the assassins, and she gave him seven thousand years to do that by sabotaging the settler ship. Regrettably, things didn't work out as she planned, and Ahn perished anyway. Nevertheless, her plan is well thought out, and we can implement it to protect Ahn's daughter—who might be the only living legitimate heir to the Eternal King's throne." Kian took another puff of his cigarillo. "Even if the queen had more children, the king probably found a way to get rid of them as well."

"I see." Toven nodded. "You've realized that your great-grandmother knew what she was doing and that you should follow the plan she put in motion seven thousand years ago—hence your change of heart about building more Odus."

"Precisely. Will you help expedite the deciphering of the journals?"

Toven wasn't looking forward to poring over hand-written texts and schematics, but he had to admit that Kian's logic was solid. An army of Odus might be the only thing standing between them and Annani's half-siblings and their immense power, not to mention a team of assassins that had been enhanced by the gods to be even more dangerous than the Kra-ell.

Except, there might be a better way to deal with the threat.

"Wouldn't finding the other pods and getting rid of them before they wake up be easier to do?"

Kian huffed out a breath. "First of all, we don't know where to find them, and if they wake up before we do, we'd better have an army of Odus ready for them. Secondly, we are not murderers. Those twins might be the best of people and a blessing to us and this whole planet. I will not kill them in their sleep before finding out what they are about."

"That's very noble of you, but when it comes to your family's safety, nobility might cost you too dearly. I'd rather keep our families safe than do the right thing."

"Perhaps we can do both." Kian took another puff. "But the dilemma is out of our hands because we don't know how to find the twins or the other pods. They might be dead for all we know."

"They probably are." Toven extinguished his cigarillo. "But since we can't be sure of that, we need to build more Odus. I'll stop by William's lab tomorrow and look at those journals. If I can help, I will, but don't expect me to dedicate all of my time to it."

"Of course not. I'll let Kaia and William know that they can share the journals with you."

"I want something in return," Toven said. "I want a seat on the council."

He hadn't planned on asking for that before coming to Kian's house this morning, but he didn't want to be the last one to find out about what was going on, which seemed to be what was happening lately.

If the clan wanted his help, they needed to make him part of the decision-making process.

Kian frowned. "You didn't want to get involved before. What has changed your mind?"

"I get called to help left and right, so I am involved whether I want to be or not. I realized that I'd rather be one of the first to know what's going on than the last."

"That's understandable." Kian tapped on his cigarillo to dislodge the ash. "I'll have to put it to a vote, but I have no doubt that the council will vote to include you. Everyone holds you in the highest regard."

"Do I need to prepare a speech?" Toven asked.

He wasn't running for office and didn't want to make a big deal out of it, but he didn't want to offend the other council members by coming unprepared.

"The one you gave me right now will suffice. I'm calling a council meeting tomorrow evening to inform them about the new potential threat. I can present your bid for a seat either before or after that."

"What time is the meeting?" Toven asked.

"Six in the evening. Council meetings are held in the small assembly room in the village underground. Do you know where it is?"

"I'll find it."

# Annani

A nnani looked out the window of the SUV, not really watching the scenery they were passing by. Instead, the images she had collected from Igor's mind the day before were playing on a loop in her head.

Kian was next to her, the brothers were upfront with Anandur driving as usual, and Jade was behind her in the third row, quiet and contemplative, which was good since Annani needed some quiet time to collect her thoughts.

She'd had all day, but she had been busy with what? She could not remember.

Oh, yes. She had been on the phone with Emilia about a leaking pipe in one of the sanctuary's ponds.

Why did her people think that she even needed to know about that was beyond her? It was not as if she had ever fixed a leaking pipe or knew what to do about it. It was the Odus's job to take care of maintenance, and that was precisely what she had told Emilia.

Half an hour later, she got another call that the leak had been fixed.

The people of her sanctuary were not stupid or incapable, but it was human nature to turn to someone they considered an authority instead of trying to figure things out for themselves.

It was also human nature to fear someone perceived as stronger, smarter, or more successful. It was immortal and godly nature as well. Annani still remembered how she'd feared Mortdh and what he would have done to her if he had captured her. That fear had saved her life. So maybe it was not such a bad thing to be afraid, even when no direct threat had been issued.

But it was sad to think how many atrocities had been committed because of irrational fear and how many people had died horribly and painfully because others had feared them.

Annani was not going to succumb to the same primitive instinct and strike against her half siblings just because she feared them, but she was not going to be naive about it either. She would prepare contingencies, and as Kian had suggested, the Odus would be the main component of those precautions. The question was, how many Odus were needed to provide adequate defense?

Another seven?

Seventy?

Seven hundred?

Perhaps her brilliant grandmother had included the number in the instructions she had sent with the Odus.

Had she known about the twins, though? Or had she just planned a defense against the assassins?

Given her cunning smarts, she was always one step ahead of her husband, so she must have known about her grandchildren.

Did she think of them as abominations?

Annani turned to look at Jade. "I forgot to ask you about the timeline. Was the twins' mother already a queen when she had the dalliance with my father?"

"She was the heir apparent," Jade said. "Her mother was already elderly when the war started, and she stepped down to let her daughter lead the offense."

Annani nodded. "So, she led the battle while carrying the twins. Brave female."

"Yes. She was." Jade's lips tightened into a thin line. "She was also a betrayer of her people and a liar. I understand why she had to lie. I would have done the same thing to protect my children, but she forfeited her place in the fields of the brave."

Annani smiled. "No sacrifice is too great for a mother protecting her children's lives. Most would do anything in their power to save their offspring."

"But not the fathers," Jade said. "Not all of them. Igor was a shitty father, but he could at least blame his upbringing, or his programming, for his lack of emotions. What's the Eternal King's excuse?"

"Absolute power corrupts absolutely." Annani sighed. "I wish I knew more about my people and how the Eternal King became so powerful and held on to that power for hundreds of thousands of years. I don't even know his name or the name of my grandmother. Do you?"

Jade shook her head. "I only know them as the Eternal King and the Queen Mother, or the king's official wife."

"Do you know why she stayed with him despite what he planned to do to her son?"

Jade shrugged. "I guess she did that for the same reason I agreed to be Igor's prime. I detested every second of it. It was my personal hell and my punishment for failing my sons and the other males of my tribe. But it allowed me access to information I wouldn't otherwise have had, and knowledge is power. If I hadn't done that, I would have never stumbled upon Safe Haven's ads or recognized Emmett Haderech as a former member of my tribe. My people and I would still be suffering under Igor's rule. Therefore, I don't regret choosing hell for myself, and I also understand why the king's wife is still with him."

"Absolutely." Annani looked at the female with renewed appreciation. "You did well for your people."

Jade dipped her head. "Thank you, Clan Mother. I did the best I could."

# Kian

"Igor is loopy," Julian said. "I've dosed him just right for the Clan Mother. He's not so out of it that he can't think, but he's compromised enough to be easy to manipulate."

"He could fool you," Jade said.

"I doubt it." Julian shrugged. "But even if he's just pretending to be drugged, he can't do anything to the Clan Mother while chained to the bed and blindfolded."

Kian hoped this would be his mother's last visit to the dungeon to see Igor. Every time she got near the monster, his skin crawled.

"Thank you, Julian." Annani patted the doctor's arm.

"Before you go in." Kian stopped her with a hand on her shoulder. "It's imperative for me to find out whether Igor is communicating telepathically with someone on Anumati or anywhere else. Can you please look specifically for that? He might not even be aware that he's broadcasting."

His mother nodded. "I will do my best. What other questions do you want me to find the answers to?"

"Anything that can lead us to the twins. I'm sure he would have found them by now if he knew where to look, but maybe we have more resources than he could have commanded."

Annani smiled indulgently. "With his compulsion ability, Igor could have gotten any resources he needed, but I will check."

"Thank you."

"You will need to ask him the questions, Kian."

"Yes, I know. Let's do one last check of the earpieces before we go in."

His mother let out an exasperated sigh, but she did as he asked.

Jade didn't need reminders, and she didn't need encouragement. She knew how crucial the earpieces were and checked the fit diligently.

Kian waited for Magnus to open the cell door, and then the six of them crowded into the vestibule while Magnus unlocked the bars and stepped back.

"Let me check on him again before you go in," Julian said.

They waited until the doctor gave them the thumbs up to enter. They assumed the same positions they had the day before, with Annani sitting on a chair next to the chained prisoner and the rest of them standing next to her and behind her.

Igor sniffed. "The silent female doctor is back. Say something to me, doctor. I want to hear your voice."

Annani did not respond.

"She is not going to talk to you," Kian said. "She's here just to observe. Are you communicating with anyone telepathically?"

"Who, me?"

"Yes, you."

"I don't have a telepathic ability."

That was an interesting answer. "Do you know anyone that has it?"

"Of course. Many gods can do that."

"Can your handler speak to you telepathically?"

"I've never heard him in my head, so I assume he can't." Igor chuckled. "I should be thankful for that. Having him jabbering in my mind would have been annoying."

Annani shook her head instead of projecting anything.

"Who do you know personally that can communicate telepathically?" Kian asked.

"I don't know anybody like that. I've just heard of them."

Annani shook her head again.

"What other talents do the gods have?" Kian asked.

"Ask the gods you know."

This time his mother projected several talents that Igor was thinking about, all having to do with telepathy and compulsion, which apparently ran in families. Evidently, Igor deemed other talents unimportant.

Kian was about to ask another question when his mother lifted her hand to stop him and put it on Igor's chest.

The guy flinched as if he had been touched by a live wire but then quieted as if what she was doing was calming him.

Kian closed his mouth and waited until his mother let out a breath, pushed to her feet, and walked out of the cell.

Had she discovered another terrible secret?

As the rest of them followed her out, Kian waited for Magnus to close the cell door behind them before asking, "What did you see?"

Annani shook her head. "Igor does not know much more than he has already revealed. I calmed him down so his mind could wander aimlessly, and I could follow along. He does not know where the other pods are and thinks the other settlers are dead, including the twins." She looked up at Kian. "I think you can put him in stasis. We are not going to learn anything more from him." She turned to Jade. "That should make you happy. I am sure you cannot wait to be done with him."

Jade nodded. "I would have loved to find out where he stashed the rest of the money that he took from me and the others, but I can live without that."

Annani's eyes widened. "You should have told me. I would have gotten it out of him."

Behind them, Julian cleared his throat. "I don't think he can remember the long sequence of numbers and letters when he is drugged."

"He is a machine," Jade spat. "I'm sure he can."

"I can go back and get it," Annani offered.

Jade looked hopefully at Kian, but he shook his head. "I'm sorry, but Julian is probably right, and I don't want to waste my mother's time."

Annani glared at him. "It will only take a minute, and it can provide Jade and her people with money to support them for decades. I am going back." She took the earpieces out of her pocket and put them back in.

Knowing that it was futile to argue with his mother, Kian motioned for Magnus to open the door and put his earpieces back in as well.

As all of them crowded the cell again, Kian asked, "What's the seed phrase to the bitcoin you stashed Jade's money in?"

Igor laughed. "What will you give me in exchange for it? My life?"

# Jade

Igor was smart. He'd figured out that his days were drawing to an end, but the drugs made him too loopy to care.

Was he also too loopy to remember the seed phrase?

As the Clan Mother rose to her feet and walked out of the cell again, Jade and the others followed her.

"Did you get it?" Kian asked.

"Yes." She took out her earpieces and smiled at Jade. "The phrase he chose is a Kra-ell children's poem that you should know by heart. I just hope spelling will not be a problem."

"I hope so too. Thank you, Clan Mother." Jade dipped her head and turned to Kian. "I assume Roni knows what to do with that phrase?"

"He does." Kian regarded his mother with somber eyes. "Are you sure we are done with Igor, and there is nothing more we can get out of him?"

The goddess shrugged. "I am not sure, but I do not wish to delve into his mind again. It is not a pleasant place."

Jade scoffed, "I bet. If he has a soul, it's ugly."

"He has a soul," the goddess said. "Even a blade of grass has one. It is just very minimally aware."

"If you don't mind," Kian said. "We can discuss the matter of souls and who has them on the way home."

His expression indicated that the last thing he wanted was to get into a philosophical discussion about souls, and Jade was right there with him.

The priestesses back home used to preach about the eternal soul and its journey through the valley of the shamed. Those whose transgressions hadn't been too grave would get another chance and be born again. Sometimes more than one chance was granted before a Kra-ell secured their place in the fields of the brave. But those who had been rotten to the core, like Igor, didn't get a second chance.

It didn't matter that he had been made to be the way he was and that he hadn't chosen to be born evil. The same was true of naturally born people. They came into the world with a genetic predisposition, but what they did with that was up to them and their free will. Everyone had traits that weren't perfect, and they had to learn to work around them.

The important thing was to do no harm.

Except, that was a good motto in theory but very difficult in practice.

Sometimes what had seemed just and necessary at the time seemed harmful and cruel in retrospect.

Jade was well aware of every bad decision and action she'd committed, and that it had taken suffering in captivity for her to realize that she hadn't been a good leader to all her people and that she could have done much better.

She should have been more mindful of the way hybrids had been treated in her compound.

Hell, she should have been more attuned to the needs of all the males of her tribe. She shouldn't have taken it for granted that the way the Kra-ell society had functioned for hundreds of thousands of years was just.

Sometimes traditions needed to be changed, but one had to be very careful not to make things worse like Igor had done.

It was good that she was still young and had many years to compensate for her past misdeeds. If she worked hard on doing her very best, perhaps she could still gain admittance to the fields of the brave.

Then again, the whole thing about the valley of the shamed and the fields of the brave could be a fairytale made up by the priestesses. Religion was a powerful tool to control people with.

As they got into Kian's car, Jade again slipped into the third row of the SUV, and Kian and his mother sat in the middle.

She was surprised when Kian swiveled the seat to face her, and a moment later, the goddess did the same.

"I did not know I could do that." Annani was as giddy as a little girl who had discovered a new game, swiveling the chair back and forth until Kian put a hand on the seat to stop her.

"It needs to be locked in position during the drive."

"Oh." The goddess looked disappointed. "Well, I prefer to lock it facing Jade." She gifted her with one of her brilliant smiles.

Jade dipped her head. "Thank you, Clan Mother. You honor me."

Kian nodded his approval. "I want to discuss Igor's stasis and entombment with you. Do you want it done in a public ceremony, so your people can watch and have closure, or do you prefer it done away from the public eye?"

Did he really need to ask?

Her answer should have been obvious to him. "I definitely want it done publicly, and I want it done with as much pomp and ceremony as possible. I would prefer to take his head off, but this will have to do."

Kian nodded. "We need to discuss logistics. It will be done in the catacombs, which are under the keep. You can attend in person, but the ceremonial chamber is small and can only hold a few people. You can bring one more person with you, and we will probably use a couple of the young purebloods as additional security, but the rest of your people will have to watch the ceremony from the village. We will broadcast it live so everyone who wants to witness the ceremony will have access to the televised event."

"I have an idea," the goddess said. "Igor's stasis and subsequent entombment should be the starting point of the trial."

# Kian

For once, Kian was grateful for his mother's penchant for drama and her instincts for manipulating public opinion.

Her idea was brilliant.

Igor's public entombment would satisfy the Kra-ell's need for vengeance and retribution, putting them in a more lenient mood toward Igor's pod buddies, who would stand trial next.

As someone who had been under Igor's power for mere moments and still struggled with the effects, Kian was much more sympathetic to their plight than he'd been before the incident. Given Edna and Vanessa's favorable impressions of the prisoners, he wanted them to get absolved, at least from the murder charges.

Perhaps he should testify as well and describe his experience. As a respected outsider who had no stake in the outcome, his testimony might be the tipping point of the trial.

He should let Vanessa and Lusha know that he was willing to go on the witness stand so they could incorporate it into their defense strategy.

Jade regarded his mother with a challenging look. "That could go either way, Clan Mother. On the one hand, it might satisfy my people's need for revenge and make them less antagonistic toward the other prisoners, but on the other hand, it might just whet their appetites and make them more bloodthirsty."

Annani's expression was benevolently condescending. "I know that your people tend to be harsh, but I hope their time in the village has softened them. It is a new era for the Earth-bound Kra-ell, and I think they are all aware that the bloodthirsty way of the past should be abandoned."

"My mother is the quintessential optimist," Kian said. "She always believes that people will rise to the occasion to be the best version of themselves."

"I do not," Annani protested. "I know when that hope is justified and when it is not. That is why I said Igor should be put in stasis immediately. I know he will not redeem himself, and I do not wish to grant him a second chance. He has already proven that he has no regard for others."

Jade let out a breath. "Thank you, Clan Mother. I just wish we could put Valstar in stasis as well. Maybe not indefinitely like Igor, but for a couple of years."

Kian shook his head. "According to Edna and Vanessa's evaluations, Valstar was as much Igor's victim as the other prisoners."

"I think he just outsmarted them." Jade looked at Annani. "Perhaps you could take a peek at his mind as well? He might know more than he's revealed, and we might learn something useful from him."

"I do not mind." Annani looked at Kian. "You can arrange for Valstar to be lightly sedated while I probe his recent memories."

Kian wasn't happy about Jade's suggestion. He was glad that his mother was done with Igor's interrogation, and he didn't want her to return to the keep.

"What Valstar might know is not important enough for you to bother with."

"You never know, and it is worth a try." Annani jutted out her chin. "Please call Julian and inform him that I will visit Valstar tomorrow."

He knew better than to argue with her when she got that stubborn expression on her face. "As you wish, Mother."

He quickly texted Julian, informing him of the Clan Mother's wishes.

"When do you want to hold the trial?" Jade asked him when he was done. "I suggest sooner rather than later.

Especially since we want to tie it in with Igor's entombment, we shouldn't delay that."

"I need to check with Vanessa and Lusha. Lusha said she needed time to prepare her defense, and I don't want to rush her when people's lives are at stake."

Jade's lips twisted in a grimace, but she nodded. "I hope she's ready soon. It's like my people's lives are on hold while waiting for the trial. I want us to start living."

"I understand." Kian returned his phone to his pocket. "We need to discuss another issue. There are two options for putting Igor in stasis, and I need to know your preference."

"What options?"

"The cruel way is to just entomb him without the benefit of venom. He will eventually suffocate and enter stasis. The other is more merciful, and it involves one of our males injecting him with venom until his heart slows down to almost nothing, and only then placing him inside a sarcophagus. In either case, Igor will need to be chained and sedated, so it won't be as satisfying to you because he won't be fully aware of what's happening to him."

"Oh, he will." Jade crossed her arms over her chest. "He was aware even when the Clan Mother thralled him. Everyone in that chamber will have to wear the earpieces that filter out compulsion, and the broadcast will have to go through a similar filtering process as well."

"Of course." Kian nodded. "I would not chance him compelling people to come to his rescue or to attack each other."

Jade looked out the window for a moment. "I want him to suffer, but his daughter will be watching, and I don't want her to have nightmares. Igor was indifferent to Drova, but he didn't abuse her. For her sake, I'll show him a mercy he doesn't deserve."

# Vanessa

L usha trotted next to Vanessa, trying to keep up. "What if Kian expects me to show him what I have so far?" she asked. "He didn't give me time to prepare anything."

The closer they were to Kian's office, the more nervous Lusha was getting. She'd only seen him once since her arrival, and he'd been nicer than usual to her. However, Kian's nice was still intimidating as hell.

Vanessa put her hand on the girl's shoulder. "Relax. He doesn't eat humans. He probably just wants to hear about our progress, or maybe he has something for us."

Lusha let out a breath. "He scares me. I don't know why. He was polite when I met him the first day I got here. It's just that I feel like he has all that pent-up energy stuffed inside of him, and if I say one wrong word, it will explode in my face."

Growing up surrounded by Kra-ell purebloods and hybrids, Lusha wasn't easily intimidated, and it surprised Vanessa that Kian had such an effect on her.

He was indeed too tense most of the time, but he had no reason to be upset with Lusha.

"I've never seen him explode." Vanessa knocked on Kian's office door.

She'd heard of some epic fights between him and Anandur back in the day, but none had been serious enough to last beyond a few minutes. The two were like brothers and would literally die for each other.

"Come in!" Kian's gruff voice had Lusha wince.

Patting the girl's back, Vanessa opened the door and walked in. "Good afternoon, Kian."

"Good afternoon, Vanessa, Lusha." He rose and pulled out two chairs next to the conference table. "Please, take a seat."

"Thank you." Vanessa smiled at him before sitting down.

Lusha did the same.

"How are your preparations for the trial coming along?" he asked without much preamble.

"They are going well," Lusha said with only a slight tremble in her voice.

"What I mean is, how close are you to being ready? I want this trial to commence as soon as possible but without compromising the accused's defense."

Vanessa's stomach twisted with unease. "Did anything happen? Do you have any new information for us?"

Kian and Annani had visited Igor earlier in the day, and maybe they had learned something pertinent to the trial.

"I don't," Kian said. "Well, not directly. I have some ideas that might help your case, and one of them is somewhat time sensitive. If you are ready, I would like the trial to start this Saturday."

Hope surged in Vanessa's chest. "Anything helpful will be greatly appreciated, but Saturday is too early. Lusha and I have so much material we need to go through."

Lusha shifted in her seat. "Actually, I can be ready by Saturday. I don't think we need to interview any more of the Kra-ell, and the people are getting impatient. We don't want them to be in a pissy mood at the trial." She looked at Kian. "So, what are those things that might help our case?"

Evidently, the girl was no longer intimidated by Kian and had returned to her usual confident self. It was great, but Vanessa would have preferred that she stall and say she wouldn't be ready by Saturday. It was too soon, and it didn't give Vanessa enough time to prepare things for her contingency plan.

"I no longer need to keep Igor awake," Kian said. "I want to put him in stasis as soon as possible. I discussed it with Jade, and she agreed that having it done with the proper pomp and ceremony and televised for the benefit of her people would give them closure. I thought it would be a great start to the trial. The prisoners can be on the stage in the big assembly hall. At the same time, the ceremony would be broadcast on a big screen behind them. The Kra-ell, along with any clan members who wish to witness the proceedings, will be in the audience. Jade will show him mercy on account of their daughter watching, and he will be put in stasis with the help of venom before being entombed. Once it's done, and Igor is put to rest in the catacombs, we will have a break to allow Jade and Kagra time to get back to the village, and the trial will commence as soon as they are back."

In Kian's usual manner, he'd skipped over many of the details, but Vanessa had no problem filling in the blanks.

Jade and Kagra would attend the entombment ceremony in person while the rest of their people would watch from the village.

Lusha cleared her throat. "Are you hoping the Kra-ell will be satisfied with Igor's so-called demise and won't demand the prisoners' heads?"

"Yes," Kian said. "Am I wrong in my assumption?"

"No, I think you are onto something." She turned to Vanessa. "What do you think? You are the psychologist."

She'd been trained to deal with humans and had applied that to immortals, but the Kra-ell were different, and she was still learning what motivated them and why.

"It can go either way. It might calm them or incite them. I think a lot will depend on the testimony they will hear once the trial begins."

"Precisely," Kian agreed. "That's why I believe my testimony will be beneficial. I'll leave it up to you whether you think I should go first or last."

Vanessa frowned. "You weren't there when the crimes were committed, and you are not close to any of the prisoners to testify as to their character."

"I'm going to be honest and tell them how I felt when Igor had me under his compulsion. I'm a neutral outsider who is not trying to influence the trial one way or another, just sharing my experience of being controlled by a compeller and how it has shaken me to my core." Kian took a deep, calming breath. "He could have ordered me to kill Anandur, Brundar, or Jade, and I would have done it because my body would have obeyed his commands, not mine. I still have nightmares about it. The bottom line is that I know how these males felt; their lives were hell. They didn't suffer terrible losses like the females, and they weren't sexually exploited, but they were forced to do despicable things that probably haunt them to this day."

That was unbelievably generous of him.

Kian was not the kind of male who shared his feelings freely or admitted to carrying emotional scars.

Tears of gratitude misted Vanessa's eyes. "Thank you, Kian. I know it's not easy for you to share your feelings, not in private and certainly not in public, but your testimony will be immensely helpful." She looked at Lusha. "Right? You know the Kra-ell better than I do."

Lusha nodded. "The Kra-ell respect authority, and a testimony from the mighty leader of the immortals' clan will carry a lot of weight."

For the first time in days, Vanessa felt hopeful, but she was still moving forward with her plan B.

She wasn't leaving Mo-red's life in the hands of his people or even the Fates. Well, maybe the Fates were guiding her to take those extra precautions. It certainly sounded less blasphemous.

Besides, the last thing she needed was to offend the Fates.

## Karen

"He's doing fine," Bridget reassured Karen after checking Gilbert's vitals. "I'm going to the office building, but Gertrude is here, and if anything requires my attention, she will let me know."

Karen wasn't happy about the doctor leaving, but Bridget had to take care of her other job, which was no less important than transitioning Dormants. The rescue missions were resuming next week, and the doctor had a lot of planning to do.

"Thank you." Karen lifted her phone. "I have your number right here, and if anything looks even a little off, I'm going to call you."

"No problem." The doctor smiled. "But he's doing remarkably well for a guy his age." She shook her head. "I don't know what it is, but all the Dormants have been transitioning fantastically well lately. Maybe they are all closer to the source than I estimated."

That wasn't likely, given how long it had taken Kaia to speed up her healing ability after transitioning. But Karen wasn't a doctor, and if that was what Bridget thought, who was she to argue?

"Yeah, that must be the explanation."

Once the door closed behind Bridget, Karen walked up to the bed and kissed Gilbert's scratchy cheek. "I should give you a shave. Although I like you looking a little rugged." She ran a finger over the white prickly hairs covering his jaw. After the transition, the white would turn brown again, and the laugh lines around his eyes would smooth out.

Would it be difficult to adjust to his new youthful looks?

Nah, he would still be the same goofy Gilbert who made her laugh with his absurd jokes and big-fish stories.

She would look like his mother, though, and that would be a major bummer.

Sitting on her chair, she pulled out of her purse the romance book she'd been narrating to him and opened it to the last page she'd read before Bridget's visit, but instead of reading, she stared at the book blankly while her mind traveled back to the conversation she'd had with Darlene earlier that day.

Did she really need to wait for Gilbert to wake up to decide about the best way to induce her transition?

He would respect any decision she made, even if it was asking for Connor's help. He might not like having a male lust after him to produce venom to bite her, but she could convince him that it was necessary and that it would be less upsetting to him than having a random immortal male lust after her.

The question was whether Connor would agree to help.

If she was into women and someone asked her to perform a service of that kind, would she be offended?

Not at all, but then not everyone was the same, and Connor might find it offensive, especially given how Gilbert would most likely react.

"Oh, sweetheart." She got up and cupped his cheek. "You're such a goofball, and you like to exaggerate and make bombastic statements. Sometimes I'm not sure what to expect from you. What would you do if a hot guy got turned on thinking about you? Would you feel flattered or threatened?"

If another woman found her attractive, Karen would have felt very flattered, more so than if a man was attracted to her. But that was because women were more discriminating than men, and getting attention from another female would have felt more special.

Gilbert was the jealous and possessive type, and since he would get even more so after his transition, it wouldn't be safe to bring in someone like Max to bite her. Eric, who was much more open-minded and sexually adventurous than Gilbert, had nearly demolished the bedroom when Max had bitten Darlene.

"Maybe we should get another couple?" She sat on Gilbert's bed and took his hand. "Not a bonded couple or even a romantically involved one because the male would be repulsed by me, but just a random immortal couple. Maybe one of the former Doomers and a clan female who are in a friends-with-benefits kind of relationship. Once the guy gets aroused by his partner, he can have sex with her but bite me instead. That way, we wouldn't have to worry about anyone being attracted to you or me."

Laughing, she glanced at the camera mounted on the wall. "I'm so glad that Bridget turned off the sound recording. Imagine how scandalized she would be if she listened to my prattle."

Or maybe not.

The immortals were not shy about sex; her little trip into fantasy land wouldn't have shocked anyone.

"It's such a hot and kinky idea. I actually think it might work." She put the book aside. "I can do better than the werewolf story." She kicked her shoes off and lay next to Gilbert. "Let me tell you how this is going to play out."

# Vanessa

After parting ways with Lusha, Vanessa walked into the café, bought two large cappuccinos and two Danishes, and then hunted for a table that would afford her some privacy.

What she needed to discuss with Edna wasn't for public consumption, but it wasn't something she wanted to talk about on the phone. She needed to see Edna's face when she told her about her plan. The judge would be sympathetic, but she needed to find precedence in the ancient or modern laws to work. Proof of legitimacy was needed, and it could only be obtained if similar circumstances had resulted in a similar legal outcome before.

When the occupants of the table she'd been eyeing got up, she rushed over and put her tray down to stake her claim.

"I'm sorry." She smiled apologetically at the Kra-ell females who looked at her with twin frowns on their faces. "This is the only table in the shade." She waved a hand over her eyes. "I don't tolerate direct sunlight well."

"Ah." Understanding washed over the one who could speak English. "Your eyes. They hurt in strong sun."

"Yes." Vanessa pulled out her sunglasses and put them on.

She wasn't as sensitive to sunlight as some of those closest to the source, but it was a good excuse.

"Enjoy your coffee," the female said with a forced smile.

Her friend smiled and nodded, looking just as uncomfortable.

"Thank you." She gave them an encouraging smile back.

The Kra-ell were making tremendous efforts to learn not only the new language but also the way immortals and humans interacted in this part of the world. Smiling just to be polite was an effort for them and saying things like 'have a nice day' or 'enjoy your coffee' sounded fake to them.

Melding their separate cultures was not going to be easy, but as long as everyone made a conscious effort toward integration and was tolerant of the differences, it was doable.

Vanessa removed the lid off her cup and took a sip, then lifted the Danish and took a bite. It was delicious, like all the pastries Jackson was manufacturing in his Mega Bakery, as he liked to call his new modern bakery. The title was a little presumptuous, but that was Jackson's way.

Her son dreamt big, and he made his dreams a reality.

One day he would build a bakery the size of one of those Giga car production lines.

"Hello, Vanessa." Edna pulled out a chair next to her. "Is this for me?" She pointed at the coffee.

"Yes, and the Danish too. I thought you'd be peckish after driving home from your downtown office."

Edna had a thriving law practice in the city that served human clients, and that was in addition to handling the clan's legal matters and occasionally utilizing her alien probe talent when Kian needed her to determine someone's intentions.

"I'm not, but I can't say no to Jackson's pastries. They are the best in town, and I'm not saying that because he's your son."

"Thank you. I think so too."

Edna took a small bite from her Danish and regarded Vanessa with her shrewd eyes. "What did you want to talk to me about?"

Vanessa wouldn't be surprised if the woman had guessed her intentions. The judge did not need to use her alien probe to see into people's souls.

She looked around to make sure no one was eavesdropping and leaned to whisper in Edna's ear, "If I officially marry Mo-red, would that automatically make him a clan member?"

Edna didn't look surprised by her question. "It's not as straightforward as that. Technically, the answer is yes, but it depends on whether Kian and the council accept the union. If they don't say anything against it, the union stands, and the person becomes part of the clan, but they can veto it. Imagine a clan member who brought in a human wife or husband and demanded they become part of the clan. That's an extreme example, but you get what I mean."

Kian might refuse to accept Mo-red because he didn't want to antagonize the Kra-ell, especially not before the trial. If they found out about the marriage, they might turn against the other prisoners.

Vanessa did not plan to make her union with Mo-red public until after the verdict, so that shouldn't be an issue, but Kian might still object.

"What if the Clan Mother presided over the wedding?"

Edna smiled. "Then no one can contest it. Are you thinking of doing what I think you are?"

Vanessa nodded. "I need a plan B in case things don't go as well as Lusha and I hope they will."

Edna nodded. "I understand that the Kra-ell are almost equally divided between those who want the prisoners dead and those who don't."

Should she tell Edna about Kian's offer to testify?

Yeah, she should.

Since human rules did not apply, Lusha wasn't obligated to inform the judge or the prosecutor of who they were planning to call to the witness stand, but Edna was going to preside over the trial, steering it in the right direction so it was as fair and as civilized as possible, and she needed to be aware of every witness and every speaker ahead of time.

"Lusha and I haven't interviewed every Kra-ell, but they seem equally divided. However, I'm much more hopeful after speaking with Kian today. He offered to testify and share his horrifying experience of being under Igor's control for a few minutes. The attack left a profound impression on him, and he believes that sharing it will drive home the point that Mo-red and the others were just as much victims of Igor as the rest."

"I'm sure it wouldn't make things worse." Edna smiled and leaned closer to Vanessa. "Your plan B might not work, though. It doesn't matter if, under clan law, your mate belongs to the clan. It's what the Kra-ell law says that matters. Kian will not force the issue with the Kra-ell if they object."

"Right." Vanessa blew out a breath. "I should check with Lusha about that. She should know if there are any Kra-ell loopholes I can use."

"You should check with Jade. Lusha is not an authority figure for them."

"I don't want Jade to know beforehand. I'll tell her once it is done."

Edna trained her intense blue eyes on her. "You also need to check with the Clan Mother whether she's willing to marry you, and you need to talk to your son. He might want to be there when you tie the knot."

The truth was that Vanessa hadn't considered inviting anyone because she hadn't thought of it as a real wedding. She had yet to tell Mo-red about her latest idea. But she and Mo-red were in love, and the wedding would be official, which meant that Jackson had to be there.

"Of course. I would never do that without my son."

Edna nodded. "Good luck, my friend. I wish you all the best."

It occurred to Vanessa that she should invite Edna as well, and not just because she was the judge. They hadn't been close before, but they had become closer lately.

"Will you come to the wedding? I mean, you're the judge. It will make it more official."

A grin split Edna's typically austere face. "I would be honored to witness your wedding. I can be your matron of honor."

# Annani

"Of course, you can come over." Annani was delighted that Vanessa wanted to talk to her. The therapist might bring some juicy gossip to brighten her day. "Alena and Orion are visiting Toven and Mia, Syssi and Kian are not home yet, and I cannot leave the house because I need to keep my presence in the village a secret. I am bored, and I would love some company."

"Thank you, Clan Mother. I will be there in a few minutes."

"I will tell Ogidu to brew some tea for us."

Alena and Orion had wanted her to come with them to visit Toven and Mia, and Annani had been tempted. She could shroud herself so no one saw her on the way there, but she had been too agitated to bother with a shroud. Perhaps what had kept her home was a premonition that Vanessa needed her.

Several minutes later, the doorbell rang, and Okidu walked over to open the door. "Hello, Mistress Vanessa. The Clan Mother is expecting you."

"Thank you." The clan's therapist walked in, her spiky heels making clickety-clack sounds on the granite floor. "Good afternoon, Clan Mother." She bowed her head.

"Please, call me Annani." She patted the spot next to her on the couch. "Come sit with me."

"Thank you." Vanessa put her satchel on the coffee table and sat beside her. "I spoke to Kian earlier today, and he said you don't wish to visit Igor anymore. Did what you see in his mind upset you?"

Annani smiled. "It was not a pleasant place. Not that I expected to find rainbows and unicorns going in, but I had exhausted what was available in Igor's recent memories, and I could not access his long-term memories. I am also tired of hiding in Kian's home, and he does not want my presence to be known to the Kra-ell until Igor is in stasis." She sighed. "Despite my assurances, Kian still thinks Igor can transmit information telepathically."

"I see." Vanessa crossed her feet at the ankles. "Kian wants the trial to commence on Saturday, and he wants it to open with the ceremony of putting Igor in stasis."

"Yes. That was my idea." Annani smiled. "It will give the proceedings a dramatic flair and put the Kra-ell in a good mood." She leaned over and patted Vanessa's knee. "That is good for your male. His chances of acquittal will get better."

"I hope so." Vanessa let out a breath. "But I would like to hedge my bets. I want to marry Mo-red before the trial so he becomes a clan member and falls under the clan's jurisdiction. That way, the Kra-ell won't be able to sentence him to death if the trial doesn't go as well as we hope."

"That is a brilliant idea, child." Annani clapped her hands. "Would you like me to marry you and Mo-red? Is that what you came to talk to me about?"

"Yes. Edna said that according to clan law, Mo-red will become a clan member when I mate him, provided that I get approval from Kian or from you. If you preside over our wedding, that's approval, right?"

Annani laughed. "Of course. This is so clever. How about the Kra-ell laws? Will they accept it as a valid claim?"

Vanessa nodded. "I checked with Lusha, and she said that according to the legends and myths that Jade taught the kids, a female could pardon a male from an enemy tribe by claiming him as her consort. That's similar enough."

Annani waved Ogidu over with the tea tray. "When would you like to have the ceremony?"

"As soon as possible. The only remaining obstacle is getting Kian's approval. It will have to happen in the keep, which means another trip for you, which means another trip for him, and he might not be too keen about my plan because it might antagonize the Kra-ell."

"Do not worry about a thing." Annani accepted a teacup from Ogidu and waited for Vanessa to take hers. "Kian and I have plans to visit Valstar tomorrow, so we will be in the keep. I will bring a change of clothes, so I will have something appropriate for the ceremony, and we can have it either before or after my visit with Valstar." She took a sip from the tea and put the cup down. "Did you tell Jackson?"

"Not yet. I wanted to speak to you first. I didn't know whether you would agree, and without you, my plan wouldn't have worked."

Annani waved a dismissive hand. "You should have known that I would agree. I love weddings, and I love stories of forbidden love." She leaned closer to Vanessa. "My love for Khiann was forbidden, but I pursued him anyway and convinced him to ask for my hand in marriage." As always, talking about Khiann brought about a wave of longing and enormous guilt.

If she had not pursued Khiann, he and the other gods would still be alive.

Then again, maybe not.

No one knew the Fates' grand plan.

When Vanessa looked lost for words, Annani put down her teacup and forced a smile. "Call Jackson and invite him to the wedding. Is anyone else coming?"

"Edna said that she would like to be there, and if Jackson comes, Tessa will come as well." The therapist looked down at her hands. "This is not how I wanted my mating ceremony to be." She looked at Annani with wistfulness in her eyes. "Maybe someday, when this is all behind us, and Mo-red is free, we could reserve a date on a future wedding cruise and get a proper ceremony."

Annani chuckled. "I am still unsure that the first wedding cruise will ever happen. A village square wedding is a safer bet."

Vanessa nodded. "I wouldn't mind that. The weddings we had here were beautiful. Would you be willing to preside over ours twice?"

"Of course. I love weddings, and the more the merrier. Are Mo-red's sons going to attend both?"

Vanessa frowned. "I would love for them to attend, but Kian is keeping your presence in the village a secret from the Kra-ell. He's not going to authorize that."

"I will speak with him." Annani patted Vanessa's hand. "Go talk to your son, and I will take care of everything else. It will give me something to do."

# Vanessa

J ackson let out a sigh and hung his head. "That's not how I imagined your future mate. I hoped to meet the guy, get to know him, maybe throw a few threats about how I would cut off his nuts if he mistreated you, and then laugh about it over a couple of beers. I've never met Mo-red, and I know nothing about him except that he's on trial for murder."

"I know," Vanessa said quietly. "Don't you think I wish this could have happened differently? I would have loved the scenario you've described, maybe minus the threats about nut cutting, but the getting to know him and laughing over beers. Perhaps we will still get to do those things, but right now, I'm mating Mo-red to save his life."

"Do things look so bad for him?" Tessa asked.

"No, actually, I had a piece of good news today. Kian said he was going to testify on behalf of the prisoners. He will share his experience of being compelled by Igor and how helpless he felt. It's very courageous of him to open up to a crowd about being vulnerable, and I appreciate it tremendously."

"It's therapeutic to let it all out," Tessa murmured. "Keeping things bottled up inside just makes them grow into monstrous proportion. But I'm not brave enough to do it."

"You don't have to." Jackson wrapped his arm around her. "You're doing great."

"You are," Vanessa confirmed. "Therapy is not one-size-fits-all, and what works for one person does not work for another. For some, it's good to talk about their trauma in public; for others, it's better to share it only with one or two trusted people."

The last thing Tessa needed was to think she wasn't brave enough. With Jackson's help, she'd clawed her way out of paralyzing fear and embraced life again. It was a tremendous achievement, and she should feel proud of herself. In fact, Vanessa had told her so in the past, but perhaps she needed a refresher.

"You should be proud of all that you have achieved, Tessa. Jackson and I are awed by you."

Tessa smiled. "You are too nice to me." She leaned her head on Jackson's shoulder. "So where and when is the mating ceremony happening?"

"Tomorrow at two o'clock in the afternoon at the keep. Kian said that we could use his office. You don't have to come if you don't want to." She leveled her gaze at Jackson. "But if you decide to come, please don't threaten Mo-red. He might take you seriously."

True to her word, the Clan Mother had talked with Kian and arranged the time and place for the ceremony.

"Great." Jackson grimaced. "My mother is mating a guy with no sense of humor."

"Mo-red has a great sense of humor, but we come from two very different cultures, and he's under a lot of stress. He doesn't need my son to add to it with threats to his reproductive organs."

"Ugh, Mom." Jackson lifted his hand. "Please, I really don't want to hear about that aspect of your intended. Gross."

Vanessa laughed. "You started it."

Tessa's lips lifted in a smirk. "Jackson, can you make us some tea, please?"

He frowned at her. "What's your game plan? Do you want to have a girls' talk with my mother and need me to leave the two of you alone?"

"What if I do?"

"Nothing." He rolled his eyes. "Just be upfront about it."

"I am. And I also want some tea, and your mom could also use some calming chamomile."

"Fine," he said in a softer tone. "You have five minutes to talk about everything you don't want me to hear."

For a tiny female who seemed so fragile that a gust of wind could topple her, Tessa had backbone, and she had no problem bossing Jackson around.

"So, Mo-red." She was still smirking. "Is he handsome?"

"Very. Do you want to see a picture?"

Tessa's eyes sparkled with excitement. "Sure."

Vanessa pulled out her phone, opened her photo application, and handed it to Tessa.

"Oh, wow. What great hair. I love long hair on a male. I wish Jackson would grow his out, but he wants to look professional and says that long hair would make him look like a wannabe rocker. Which I remind him he wanted to be before he decided to be a pastries mogul." Tessa flipped to the following picture. "How tall is he? It's hard to tell. He's either very tall or that couch is very low."

"Mo-red is about Dalhu's height, just not as bulky." Vanessa took the phone back.

"He has kind eyes." Tessa glanced in the direction of the kitchen. "Don't worry about Jackson. He just needs to get used to the idea. Tomorrow he will meet Mo-red, they will shake hands, and everything will be okay."

"I hope so."

"Do you have a dress?" Tessa asked.

"I have many dresses, but I haven't decided which one I will wear. It's not the kind of ceremony to wear a wedding dress to."

"No, I guess not, but that doesn't mean you can't look amazing. Do you want me to help you choose?"

Vanessa felt some of the stress leave her shoulders. "Yes, please."

Tessa jumped up to her feet. "Let's go."

"What about the tea?" Jackson walked into the living room with a tray.

"It needs to cool a little." Tessa grabbed Vanessa's hand. "I'm helping your mom choose a dress for the ceremony."

# Mo-red

"What's all that?" Mo-red took the paper bags from Vanessa's hands.

"Things to celebrate with." She kissed his cheek.

"What are we celebrating?"

She wrapped her arms around his neck. "Our engagement."

As she pulled him to her and kissed him for all he was worth, Mo-red tried to figure out what she meant. Engagement could mean many things, and it wasn't the first meaning that had popped into his head.

Vanessa let go and leaned back with a smile. "Will you be my mate? To have and to hold and to cherish for as long as we both shall live, which I hope is forever?"

Was Vanessa proposing to him like he'd seen humans do in movies?

Why?

As far as he knew, most immortals didn't bother with the human custom. Matehood didn't require any special ceremony or an official certificate. The Guardians he'd talked to had told him that Magnus was married to his mate, but that was probably because she'd lived as a human before discovering she was a dormant carrier of the godly genes, and she'd wanted to follow the customs she was used to. Most of the other couples in the village were happy to just acknowledge their bond with each other.

He swallowed. "If I get the chance, I will spend the rest of my life at your side, holding and cherishing you and doing everything I can for you, but I don't understand what brought this about. I thought that immortals didn't believe in marriage."

Cupping his cheek, she kissed him lightly again, took his hand, and pulled him down to sit on the couch with her. "I don't need a ceremony or a certificate to validate our bond. This is just a contingency. I will mate you in an official ceremony that will be recorded, so we have proof. Once you are officially my mate, you become a clan member and fall under the clan's jurisdiction. The Kra-ell can no longer do whatever they want with you, so they can't execute you."

Hope fluttered its wings in his chest and landed heavily in his gut. "My people will not accept it, and I doubt your boss is willing to risk the alliance to accommodate your wishes."

"Not true. The Kra-ell need the alliance more than the clan does, and they will be willing to compromise. Secondly, Lusha checked the Kra-ell law, and a similar rule exists. Suppose a male from an enemy tribe is captured, and a female from the capturing tribe decides to take him as her consort. In that case, he belongs to her, and his ties to his former mistress are severed. She no longer has a say in his life. We can extrapolate from this custom that Jade, who could be considered your mistress because she's the leader of your tribe, has to relinquish her control over you to me."

Mo-red scoffed. "Warriors fight to the death. They are rarely captured. It's the ultimate shame; no female would take a shamed male as her consort."

"What if he was gravely injured? It's not shameful to get medical treatment and survive, right?"

"Well, that might be the only exception," he conceded.

"The bottom line is that there is a precedent, and if any of the Kra-ell try to argue, we can bring it up. Hopefully, there will be no need to evoke this clause because you will be exonerated."

There was little hope of that, and Vanessa's contingency plan might just be the thing to save his neck.

Mo-red had never imagined taking part in a mating cere-mony, so he shouldn't feel disappointed that it would be held in such unromantic circumstances, but now that the possibility had become real in his mind, he wished it wasn't going to be held in a dungeon and done out of necessity rather than love and devotion.

On the other hand, what other reason would Vanessa have to do this?

Her offer to mate him was a way to save him, and it was the ultimate show of love and devotion.

"Thank you." He lifted her hand to his lips and kissed it. "My gratitude to you is endless."

"I don't want your gratitude." She reached for one of the paper bags and pulled out a bottle of whiskey. "I want your eternal love." She pulled out two shot glasses. "I'm not doing this just to save your neck. This ceremony is the real deal. It's a promise of forever that's unbreakable." She opened the bottle and poured whiskey into the two glasses. "Are you ready to commit to me forever?"

"Yes, yes, and a million times yes." He took the glass she handed him. "But I don't want you to think even for a moment that I accepted your proposal to save my neck. This is for real for me as well."

Mo-red wanted to pull Vanessa into his arms and celebrate by making love to her, but he didn't know what the custom was in such circumstances, and he didn't want to spoil this moment for her. If drinking whiskey was what immortals did as part of a proposal ceremony, he would drink whiskey with her, and if it involved serenading the intended, he would do that too.

He would do whatever made Vanessa happy.

Lifting her glass, she looked into his eyes. "I know. I wouldn't have offered it otherwise. To us." She clinked her glass with his and then downed it in one shot.

"To us." He followed her lead.

# Kian

Valstar was so loopy from the drug that Kian doubted he would even understand his questions, let alone bring up memories for Annani to sift through.

"How much did you give him?" he asked Julian.

"Less than half of what I pumped into Igor. I didn't expect him to be so strongly affected. He and Igor are about the same height and weight."

"Evidently, Igor is more machine than male," Jade said. She pulled a folded piece of paper from her pocket and handed it to Kian. "I made a list of questions I would like to ask him. Do you want to look it over first?"

"You can ask him whatever you want. In fact, you can go first."

The truth was that Kian didn't think Valstar would have answers to his questions, but he was going to ask them anyway—just in case.

Jade glanced at Annani. "I don't want to waste your time."

His mother waved a dismissive hand but said nothing.

Last night, it had occurred to Kian that maybe Valstar was the one with the telepathic connection to Anumati, so he had instructed his mother to remain silent during the visit—just in case.

All the doors to the other cells were closed, so no one saw Annani arrive, and they wouldn't see her leave, which was why she hadn't bothered with much of a disguise this time. She had a ceremonial robe on, and the thing had a hood, so she could cover her hair, but it was such a fancy garment that it attracted as much attention as his mother's unearthly beauty.

Well, almost.

Nothing could compare to that.

Kian wondered how the gods regarded each other. Did they even see the beauty? Or were they so accustomed to perfection that it no longer registered?

In a way, it was like the extravagant diamond ring he'd bought for Syssi. At first, she'd looked at it with awe, then she'd locked it in a safe, and when he'd told her that she could safely wear it in the village, she'd started wearing it around the house, and after a while, neither of them spared it another look.

Was it a good comparison, though?

Probably not.

Still, he was curious about life on Anumati and the way the gods interacted with each other when there was no one else around to impress.

"You said that you weren't there when my sons were murdered. Is that true?"

"Yes. I did not kill your sons. I was with the humans." He smiled. "I forced myself not to look at the children. If any of them were hybrid boys, I was supposed to bring them to Igor, but since I didn't look, I could say that I didn't see any, and it was the truth. I hope I saved some."

Jade looked at Annani, who nodded.

"He might believe his own lies." Jade didn't sound sure about that at all.

"Were there any hybrid boys among the humans?" Kian asked.

He'd only known about Aliya, who had still looked human back then, and she had told them that there hadn't been any other hybrid children aside from her, but now that Kian thought about that, he realized that it didn't make sense. The Kra-ell were much more fertile than immortals, and the humans were much more fertile than the Kra-ell. There must have been more hybrid children among the humans Valstar had released.

Jade shrugged. "I didn't keep track of the hybrid children until they started manifesting Kra-ell features. I was only aware of Aliya because she was a girl, which was rare."

"Great. So, there might be lone hybrids roaming around China and beyond."

She nodded. "They must have learned to hide well like Emmett and Vrog did. They don't bother anyone."

Even if they did, Kian wasn't going to worry about it. Finding a few hybrids hiding in China or elsewhere was impossible. If the Fates willed it, they would be found. If not, oh, well. There was only so much he could do.

"Do you know anything about the royal twins?" Jade asked next.

"Yes, they were always veiled," Valstar said. "I assumed that they were deformed. They are long dead by now."

Annani concentrated for a few moments, her forehead creasing with a frown, but then she shook her head and mouthed, "Nothing."

Jade acknowledged with a nod. "Do you know how much money Igor has in bitcoin?" she asked Valstar.

"Money is not important," Valstar mumbled. "Life is important."

Kian was surprised when his mother projected Sofia's image into his mind.

Valstar seemed much more interested in his granddaughter's life than she or anyone else had suspected.

Jade let out an exasperated breath. "Try to focus, Valstar. An army cannot march on an empty stomach; it takes money to feed an army. Wasn't that what you used to say all the time?"

"Yes, money is good. Also, people. With no army, there is no one to feed."

Annani chuckled, but Valstar was too loopy to notice the sound or even that there was another person with them in his cell.

Jade tried to ask several more questions about the bitcoin and other supposed treasures hidden in the compound, but after a while, she gave up. "He's all yours. I have no more questions."

After everything that Jade had asked, Kian had only one question left.

"Can you or anyone you know communicate telepathically or in any other way with anyone on Anumati or any of its settlements?"

Jade chuckled. "You should break that question into smaller chunks. I don't think he's capable of understanding it in his state."

Given Valstar's vacant expression, Jade was right.

Kian repeated the questions, this time, one at a time.

The answer was still a vacant gaze.

"I assume that's a no." Kian turned to Annani.

She nodded. "He is out."

# Mo-red

For some reason, the doors to the cells were locked again. Mo-red suspected that it had to do with the big boss's visit.

Vanessa had told him that Kian would testify in the trial and tell the Kra-ell about his brief experience with Igor's compulsion and how Igor's attack had made him feel like a helpless automaton, forced to do whatever he was told.

The clan leader would probably choose different words to describe his experience. Since he wasn't Kra-ell, he wouldn't need to make himself look unaffected or indifferent. Perhaps he would manage to pierce through the Kra-ell's thick skulls and make them realize that Igor's pod members had no choice but to obey his commands.

As in any group, some were worse than others, and a few had enjoyed the power he'd given them over other settlers. Those pod members were dead, killed by Jade and Kagra with the help of the immortals.

As the door opened and Vanessa walked inside, looking even more beautiful than Mo-red thought was possible, he pulled her into his arms and smashed her against his body. "I can't wait to be mated to you. I know it won't change anything between us, but I'm excited nonetheless."

"I'm excited too." She pushed on his chest. "I spent a lot of time doing my hair and makeup, so don't mess it up. I want to look good for you." She smiled. "And on the recording. Who knows, maybe we will show it to our children one day."

He looked down at the borrowed jeans and T-shirt he was wearing. "I wish I had something nice to wear."

She frowned. "I would have gotten you something, but I didn't have time to stop by a store. The dress I'll wear has been hanging in my closet forever." She lifted the garment bag she was holding. "It's not much fancier than what I wear every day. Besides, you look good no matter what you have on." She gave him an appreciative once-over.

"Thank you for the compliment, and the same goes for you. You are the most gorgeous to me when you are in my arms in bed with no makeup, your hair mussed up, and not a stitch of clothing on you."

Vanessa's smile was brilliant. "Well, I can't get married wearing nothing. It would be scandalous."

"Who is marrying us, your boss?" Mo-red motioned at the closed door. "Is he here interrogating Igor again?"

"I think it's Valstar this time. Kian is not the one who will marry us, but he'll witness the ceremony."

"The judge, then?"

"Not the judge either. But Edna is coming as well."

Mo-red frowned. "Then who? Do the immortals have clergy?"

"They don't. It's a surprise, so stop asking because I won't tell you."

Vanessa seemed excited and happy, so perhaps the person marrying them was someone she cared about.

"Is anyone else coming to the ceremony?" He looked at the small cell and wondered where everyone would fit.

"My son and his mate. The ceremony will be in Kian's office, which is much larger than this place."

Mo-red's gut clenched with unease. He was about to meet Vanessa's son, who probably disapproved of his mother's choice. That was going to be awkward at best and hostile at worst.

He chuckled nervously. "I hope your son doesn't plan on getting rid of me even before the trial."

Vanessa's hand flew to her chest. "Fates forbid. Jackson would never even think of such a thing. He might not be happy about me mating a guy he doesn't know, but he would never do anything violent. That's not the kind of male he is."

"I'm glad to hear that." It occurred to him that Pavel was on duty in the dungeon, and if Vanessa's son could attend, his son should also be there. "Can I invite Pavel to the ceremony? I didn't tell him about it because you asked me not to, but he's here today, and I can ask him to keep it a secret if you wish."

Vanessa made an apologetic face. "I'm sorry. I asked Kian if I could invite your sons, but he said no. It's not because he's mean, though. He has a good reason for it, and once we are in his office, you will understand why."

Mo-red didn't like surprises, and what Vanessa was saying and not saying had him worried, but this was her game plan, and she was in the driver's seat. All he could do was try to enjoy the ride.

When the door's mechanism hissed, and it started to open, Vanessa quirked a brow. "I wonder who this is."

"It's me," Alfie said as he pushed through the opening with a garment bag in his hand. "I was told to bring this to you." He handed the bag to Mo-red.

"What's in there?" Vanessa asked.

"Open it and take a look." Alfie grinned.

Mo-red was sure that the Guardian had opened the bag and searched every centimeter to make sure no one was trying to smuggle weapons to him.

"Who brought it?" Vanessa asked the Guardian.

"Your son. He said that Mo-red needed something decent to wear."

"Oh, that's so sweet of him." Tears appeared in the corners of Vanessa's eyes. She wiped them with the tips of her fingers, careful not to smear her makeup. "You see? I told you that Jackson was a sweetheart and that he supported my decisions."

She hadn't said those exact words, but Mo-red wouldn't point that out. He also hoped that the outfit inside the garment bag wasn't laced with itching powder or, worse, with poison.

# Vanessa

lfie observed their exchange with a smile, but as
Mo-red reached for the zipper to open the
garment bag, the Guardian lifted a hand to
stop him. "It's bad luck for the bride and groom to get
ready in the same room. Which one of you wants to
come with me?"

Mo-red glanced at her. "Do you want me to go with
Alfie?"

She shook her head. "It's a silly superstition. We can both
get dressed in here."

"With everything that's stacked against us, we shouldn't
sneer at superstition." Mo-red turned to the Guardian.
"I'll go with you. Do you have a nice cologne I can
borrow?"

"I'll get you some."

Mo-red cast one last smile at her before following Alfie
out, leaving her alone.

The first thing Vanessa did was text Jackson and thank him for getting Mo-red something nice to wear for the ceremony. She didn't know what was in the garment bag, but she suspected it was a suit, and she wondered whether Jackson had brought Mo-red one of his.

Jackson was tall but not as tall as Mo-red, but hopefully the suit would fit well enough not to look strange.

When her phone pinged with a return text, she read it and smiled.

*It was Tessa's idea. We borrowed it from Dalhu, so it will fit lengthwise, but it will be loose on Mo-red. See you in a bit.*

So that was why Tessa had asked how tall Mo-red was.

She was such a sweet girl.

As more tears accumulated in the corners of Vanessa's eyes, she wiped them away with her fingertips and wondered why she was so emotional.

So yeah, it was a big deal to get mated with the Clan Mother presiding over the ceremony and her son being there with his mate, but they were only doing it as a contingency in case Mo-red's people decided to sentence him to death.

She wouldn't have thought about officially mating him without that hanging over their heads. There was no need for that.

Dalhu and Amanda had a child together and had yet to bother with a ceremony.

Except, they were bonded mates, and Vanessa doubted the same was true for her and Mo-red. There was love, and it was strong, but it wasn't the whole fated mate thing.

The truth was that she valued what she and Mo-red had more because no supernatural force held them together. It was a choice, and it wasn't an easy one, which made it even more precious.

Grabbing her garment bag off the back of the chair, Vanessa glanced at the door Alfie had left open. Not bothering to close it, she took the dress to the bathroom and changed there.

It wasn't white, but then she would have felt silly about wearing a white dress even if the ceremony had taken place in the village square in front of the entire clan. The dress was hot pink, and the only reason she had chosen it was Tessa's insistence that she looked like a bombshell in it and should go for it.

The truth was that Vanessa had originally bought the dress because she looked fantastic in it, but she hadn't worn it even once because the color was too bold for work, the cut too conservative for clubbing, and the fabric too luxurious for casual wear.

Hence, the perfect dress for the occasion.

She even had matching stilettos in the same hot pink color.

After checking her hair and applying a glossy layer of lipstick to match the dress, Vanessa was ready but stopped short of walking out the open door.

Should she take her satchel with her?

It was too big and didn't fit the occasion, but she had nowhere to put her phone. The dress didn't have pockets, and she wasn't about to stuff it in her bra.

Chuckling nervously, she just held the device and walked out. The cell doors were still closed, even though Kian and Annani should have been done with Valstar long ago. As she made her way to the elevator, no one was patrolling the hallway.

She should have asked Jackson to meet her at the dungeon level and escort her to Kian's office. It was awkward to make those final steps as a single lady alone.

Exiting the elevator on the level of Kian's old office, she strode toward the double glass doors at the end of the corridor and wondered whether Mo-red was already there.

Was Annani?

As the doors opened and Jackson stepped out, Vanessa smiled and looked him over. "You look like you belong on the cover of a magazine."

He had a new suit on, and it fit him as if it had been made for him. But knowing Jackson, he would rather splurge on new equipment for his bakery than on a fancy, custom-made suit.

"Thank you." He offered her his arm. "You look amazing. I'm glad Tessa convinced you to wear this dress." He led her inside the office that looked nothing like it usually did.

"Oh, wow. Who did all that?"

Large bouquets of flowers and balloon arrangements lined the walls, and rose petals covered the floor.

"Tessa and Jackson," Kian said. "They arrived over an hour ago with all this and commandeered my office."

The damn tears were once again threatening to ruin her makeup. "Thank you." She leaned to kiss Jackson's cheek.

"Lipstick!" He leaned away.

Vanessa laughed. "As much as things change, some never do. You've always hated when I kissed you with lipstick on."

He didn't seem to mind when the lipstick was on Tessa's lips, but that was natural.

"This was all Tessa's doing. I was just the muscle carrying things over. The Guardians helped carry some of it too."

"Where is Tessa?"

"Right here." Tessa walked out of Kian's private bathroom with a small flower arrangement in her hands. "The flowers needed a little sprucing up." She handed the bouquet to Vanessa.

"Thank you. You thought of everything. Even an outfit for Mo-red."

Tessa beamed. "It was my pleasure."

As Vanessa took the flowers, she handed Jackson her phone. "Can you keep it for me? I don't have pockets."

"Of course."

Clutching the flowers, she asked, "We are missing more than the groom. Where is the Clan Mother?"

Anandur was grinning like it was his own wedding, and if he was present, Brundar was probably with Annani.

"My mother likes to make a grand entrance," Kian said. "She is in another office, waiting for everyone else to arrive first."

# Mo-red

"How do I look?" Mo-red turned in a circle.

There was no mirror in the control room, where Alfie had brought him to change.

"You look good." Alfie pursed his lips. "You're missing a flower for your lapel, but I don't have one. Maybe you can get it later." He pulled out his phone and snapped a picture. "Here, take a look."

Mo-red had to admit that he looked...presentable.

The suit was the right length, which was a relief, but it was at least two sizes too wide, and he was swimming in it. The shirt underneath was no better, but at least it was tucked in, so it wasn't as noticeable.

He'd pulled his hair into a ponytail like he usually did, and one of the Guardians had gifted him a cologne sample that he'd sprayed over himself. The shoes were the same boots he'd arrived in, but he'd given them a quick polish with a wet towel, and they were passable.

148

"Are rings customary in clan weddings?" he asked.

Alfie chuckled. "Nothing is customary. We make up the rules as we go. The first wedding since the clan's inception was Kian and Syssi's, and that was only a few years ago."

"Did they exchange rings?"

The Guardian shrugged. "I don't remember." He took his phone back and glanced at the time. "We need to go." He slanted a look at Mo-red's cuff and smirked. "You don't have a ring to give Vanessa, but you have two cuffs. You can offer her one of those."

"Not funny," Mo-red rumbled.

"I thought it was." Alfie led him down the hallway.

"Where are we going?" Mo-red asked.

"The elevator. It's at the end of the corridor." Alfie pointed.

"Did you remember to update the restrictions on my cuffs? I don't want to end up twitching in pain on the floor instead of standing by Vanessa's side."

"Don't worry." The Guardian pressed the button for the lift. "Everything has been taken care of. Magnus is very detail-oriented, and he doesn't forget anything."

Magnus was the Guardian in charge, a suave fellow who was always meticulously dressed, soft-spoken, and polite. All traits that Mo-red appreciated and admired. If he ever got a ticket out of his crappy situation and could finally be the male he'd always wanted to be, he would like to be like Magnus. The guy also had a family, a mate and her two children, who he had adopted, and Mo-red liked that about him too.

When they stepped out of the elevator mere moments later, nervous butterflies filled his chest. It wasn't because he was unsure about mating Vanessa. He had never been more sure about anything in his life. It was because he feared that he wasn't good enough for her and that her son wouldn't like him despite his kindness, making sure Mo-red had a suit for the ceremony.

"It's the double glass door at the end of the corridor," Alfie said. "This was Kian's office before we moved to the new location."

"Why did you move?"

"Safety, of course. That's always the reason for us changing locations. We are small fry compared to our enemies and need to hide."

Vanessa had told him about the ancient feud and their enemy's tactics to produce an army of immortals. The guy had a lot in common with Igor, including the compulsion ability. Thankfully, he was not as powerful a compeller as Igor, or the clan might not have survived.

When they reached the doors, Mo-red saw Vanessa through the glass, and his breath caught in his throat.

Wearing a tight-fitting, knee-length pink dress and matching heels, she was stunning, and the smile she gave him through the glass was so full of love that his heart gave a happy flip.

Alfie opened the door and gave Mo-red a slight shove to get him going.

"You look good, my man." A redhead, who was nearly as tall as him and twice as wide, grinned. "I can see what Vanessa sees in you."

"This is Anandur," Vanessa introduced the guy. "Kian's personal bodyguard. And this is Kian." She pointed at a guy who Mo-red would have easily guessed was a direct descendant of the gods.

His near perfection gave him away. He was tall, broad-shouldered, and had the bearing of a warrior. This wasn't a dandy demigod who hid behind his bodyguards, but even he was no match for Igor, or for any other Kra-ell warrior for that matter.

"It's a pleasure to finally meet you." Mo-red dipped his head. "I've heard a lot about you."

"Good things, I hope." Kian offered him his hand. "Congratulations, Mo-red."

The gruff, raspy voice was a shocker. Mo-red had expected the cultured, melodic voice gods were known for. Kian sounded like he was chewing on gravel. Had he gotten injured as a child?

Perhaps the immortals were less resilient than their godly parents and didn't recover fully from certain injuries.

"Thank you." Mo-red schooled his expression as he shook Kian's hand. "And thank you for allowing Vanessa to take me as her mate."

The guy nodded. "I hope you prove worthy of her love."

"If given a chance, I will spend my life proving it every day."

"Good." A handsome blond man pushed to his feet. "I'm Jackson, Vanessa's son." He offered his hand to Mo-red.

"I can see the resemblance." He shook the young immortal's hand. "Thank you for the suit."

"Don't thank me. It was all my mate's doing, including the lovely decorations that transformed Kian's drab office into a wedding chapel." He turned and motioned for a petite female to come closer. "This is Tessa, the love of my life and the driving force behind everything I do."

The female rolled her eyes. "He doesn't need a driving force behind him. He has enough horsepower inside of him to launch a space shuttle into orbit." She put her tiny hand in Mo-red's. "Congratulations. I wish the two of you the best of luck."

"Thank you." He shook her hand with utmost gentleness. "It was very kind of you to decorate Kian's office for us and find a suit for me."

She smiled. "I wish I could have gotten you dress shoes as well, but I didn't know your shoe size, and besides, no one wants to wear borrowed shoes. Clothes are fine, but shoes are a different story, right?"

"I couldn't agree more."

As the door creaked open behind him, Mo-red turned to look at the new arrivals and gasped.

# Vanessa

As Theo escorted Pavel, Elias, and Vasily in, Vanessa arched an eyebrow at Kian.

He shrugged. "I made an exception to make things fair. She who must be obeyed will ensure that they keep quiet about it."

Mo-red was too busy hugging his sons and clapping their backs to hear the exchange, and other than him and his boys, everyone else knew who Kian was referring to.

If Annani heard him call her that, though, she would be upset. The goddess had nothing to do with the story about the immortal witch, but Sari's mate had met the goddess many lifetimes before, and in his current life, he had mixed up Annani with the witch in his dreams. When he'd met Annani again in this lifetime, he'd been terrified of her.

Everyone had long forgotten about that short-lived episode, but the nickname had somehow stuck.

As Anandur started humming the wedding march, Vanessa noticed the other changes to Kian's old office. The desk and the conference table had been pushed against the back wall, clearing the center, and the chairs surrounding the table were arranged in a semicircle around the vacated area.

"Thank you," Mo-red sounded choked up as he shook Kian's hand again. "Having my sons here means the world to me. I owe you a life de—"

"Stop." Kian lifted his hand. "It is nothing that deserves such an oath. Please don't complete what you were about to say because it would make me uncomfortable. I know how seriously the Kra-ell take their vows."

The pained expression on Mo-red's face indicated that his feelings had been hurt by Kian's refusal, but he didn't have a choice but to nod. "It's not an official vow, and it's not binding, but I owe you a debt of gratitude in my heart."

"I can live with that." Kian clapped him on his back.

Vanessa waited until Mo-red was done with another round of hugging and back-slapping before saying hello to his sons. They all knew her, but they didn't know Jackson other than as the guy who was in charge of the vending machines.

As she made the introductions, she caught Mo-red wiping his eyes discreetly. She diverted everyone's attention to herself by asking who was getting married next and teasing Pavel about his friendship with Drova.

"Yeah, he's asking for trouble," Vasily said. "Jade will cut off his nuts if he dares touch her underage daughter."

"For the millionth time, I'm not interested in Drova like that. We are just friends."

"Co-conspirators, you mean," Vanessa teased. "Are you planning a revolution?"

The smile slid off Pavel's face. "What did you hear?"

So, her hunch had been correct.

Vanessa smiled. "The village is a hive, and nothing is a secret. Besides, it's the nature of things for the young to want to make changes and for their parents to try to keep things the way they are."

Kian snorted. "Not in my case. I have a hard time keeping my mother out of mischief. I've spent many sleepless nights worrying about her."

"She's a goddess, right?" Pavel asked. "You are a direct descendant."

Despite the village's rumor mill, most of the Kra-ell had been left in the dark about Annani. They knew about Toven, and some even knew that Kian was the son of a goddess, but they didn't know who she was or where she was.

None of them had met her.

Kian nodded. "Yes, I am."

"Is your mother still around?" Pavel asked hesitantly.

"Very much so, thank the merciful Fates."

"Are we ever going to meet her?" Elias asked.

Kian nodded again.

"When?" Pavel asked.

"Don't pester Kian with questions." Mo-red put a hand on his son's shoulder. "He's in charge of everyone's safety and needs to keep some things a secret."

"Yeah, I get it." Pavel let out a breath. "So, who are we still waiting for?"

"The guest of honor, of course," Kian said. "Since everyone is here, we can start." He pulled out his phone and typed up a text.

"Wait." Vanessa's eyes darted to the doors. "Edna said she would come. Let me check what's keeping her."

"She's here," Kian said. "She joined you know who." He winked.

Vanessa stifled a chuckle. She'd never seen Kian wink before.

He must be in a good mood.

They all were.

# Mo-red

When the doors to the converted office opened, and a tiny female wearing a fancy cloak floated in, Mo-red didn't need to be told who she was.

This was the goddess, but not just any goddess.

An incredibly powerful one.

Other than Tom, he hadn't met any gods up close. Still, before getting on the settler ship, he'd seen them on televised broadcasts and holograms. Although they were all physically perfect like the redheaded one before him, he'd never felt awed by them.

He was awed by her.

Bowing his head, he waited for her to acknowledge him.

"What a lovely gathering," she said in the melodic voice gods were known for.

Regrettably, the son hadn't inherited his mother's voice, and yes, Mo-red knew without a shadow of a doubt that this was Kian's mother.

"Clan Mother." Vanessa dipped her head. "Mo-red and I are grateful and honored to have you preside over our mating ceremony."

Had he heard correctly?

Was Kian's mother going to marry them?

As Mo-red sucked in a breath, the goddess released a string of laughter that sounded like gentle bells.

"I see that no one has told you, my poor dear." As she floated nearer to him, Kian immediately stepped forward to intercept, but she just gave him a look that froze him in his tracks. "We are among friends, my son. No need to worry." She took Mo-red's hand and turned it palm up. "You have soft hands."

Was it a compliment or an insult? Was he supposed to have the soft hands of a scholar or the rough hands of a warrior?

Since Mo-red didn't know the answer, he said nothing.

"You can look upon my face, Mo-red." It was a command, not a permission.

He lifted his eyes and gazed at her perfectly beautiful face. Her expression differed from the other goddesses he had seen on broadcasts. Where theirs had been bored or haughty, hers was intelligent, insightful, and compassionate.

"I'm honored beyond words, Clan Mother. No one told me you would preside over Vanessa's and my mating ceremony."

"Yes, I realize that. They wanted to surprise you, but you do not like surprises. You like to be prepared."

He forced a smile. "You are very insightful, Clan Mother."

She laughed. "I am very old. I have seen every expression under the sun and the moon. It is not difficult to read people, and pureblooded Kra-ell are not as different from other people as they think."

The goddess turned to look at his sons, who stood speechless behind him. "You must be Pavel." She motioned for him to come forward.

He bowed his head. "I'm honored to meet you, Clan Mother."

"I've heard a lot about you." She put her hand on his arm. "You are a good son."

"I try to be."

"You are the oldest sibling, correct?"

He nodded. "I'm thirty-two. Vasily is twenty, and Elias is seventeen."

The younger boys bowed their heads respectfully.

The goddess smiled at them warmly and then turned her gaze back to Mo-red. "Your sons are good males, which tells me that their father is a good person as well."

"I wish I could take the credit for how they turned out, but it should go to their mothers. I didn't have as much contact as I would have liked with my boys during their formative years. When they were older, I was allowed to take up their training, and that was when we got closer."

The goddess's smile got even brighter. "Oh, my dear Mo-red. What you have just said, crediting the boys' mothers with how they have turned out, speaks even better of you as a person." She shifted her smiling eyes to Vanessa. "You have chosen well. Let us take our positions and start the ceremony." She turned to the blond male who had arrived with her. "Brundar, you are in charge of filming."

He dipped his head. "Yes, Clan Mother."

"Edna, music, please."

The judge pulled out a phone and a small speaker from her purse and turned both on.

As the music started playing, Mo-red didn't recognize the artist, and the song's significance was not clear to him. It was something about a kiss from a rose on the grey, and the melody was lovely.

Vanessa threaded her arm through his. "This is my favorite song."

"Then, from this day on, it is my favorite too."

## Annani

Mo-red seemed like a fine male, and although Annani had very little to base her favorable impression on, she prided herself on being a good judge of character. She knew she was not wrong about this male that Vanessa had chosen for herself or that had been chosen for her by the Fates.

It was strange to deliver her speech without a podium and to have to look up at Vanessa and Mo-red, who were both so tall. Perhaps she could ask them to sit down, so she would not have to crane her neck?

In days past, she could have asked them to kneel, but the practice had fallen out of favor, and for a good reason. She wanted people to admire and love her, but she did not want them to worship her.

"We need a podium for the Clan Mother," Tessa said. "Any ideas of what we can use?"

Annani waved a dismissive hand. "It is fine, child."

"We can all sit down," Vanessa suggested.

"Yes," Mo-red echoed the sentiment. "I don't feel comfortable towering over the Clan Mother. I feel like I should be kneeling."

"Please." Annani lifted her hand. "No kneeling. But you can sit down if you so wish."

In moments, two chairs were brought for the couple and one for her while the rest of the invited guests sat in a semicircle around them.

"Well, this is definitely unusual." Annani sat down and arranged the folds of her gown. "But then nothing about this wedding is usual."

Edna turned off the music, and as silence blanketed the room, Annani addressed the two lovers. "Love is the most powerful force in the universe. Some think it is light, gravity, or even information, but although those are the building blocks, love is what gives them meaning. It is the bond that ties us to family, to clan, to tribe. Love holds us tethered to this world and keeps us wanting to stay alive." She smiled at Mo-red. "Different cultures have different names for love, but they all mean the same thing. Some call it friendship and loyalty, others call it affinity or duty, but all those words describe the same feeling. The feeling of being part of something, belonging, and not being alone."

As everyone in the room nodded in agreement, Annani continued, "Love is about caring, closeness, and protectiveness." She smiled at Kian and then turned to the couple holding hands. "Love is also attraction, affection, and trust." She paused for effect before continuing. "Love is happiness, excitement, satisfaction, even euphoria at certain peak moments." She winked at the couple. "It is the most important emotion, that transcends cultures, and even species."

She thought about the royal twins and their mother's love for them. She thought about her grandmother and the clever machinations she had employed to save her son that had failed, nonetheless.

Did she know that he was gone?

A shiver rushed through Annani as she imagined how devastated her grandmother would be when she found out that all her excellent planning had not saved her son.

Shaking herself out of it, she forced a smile and continued, "We are gathered here today, family and friends of Vanessa and Mo-red, to celebrate their joining and witness their commitment and devotion to each other. Their love paves the path for the future of our combined communities and promises a life of cooperation and equality that, for some reason, could not have been achieved on Anumati. At least not before the settlers' ship left the planet over seven thousand years ago. The gods were set in their ways, and so were the Kra-ell, and instead of celebrating their differences and combining their talents, they chose to quarrel and discriminate, each in their own way. The gods sneered at the Kra-ell's traditional ways, and the Kra-ell sneered at the gods' quest for genetic perfection." She smiled at the couple. "You two are much smarter than the Eternal King and the Kra-ell Queen. You figured out that the greatest treasure in the universe is love. Please rise and declare your love loudly and clearly for everyone here to witness."

Mo-red seemed panicked, but Vanessa took his hand and smiled. "Don't worry, my love. I have it covered. You don't have to search for the right words."

"I love you," he said. "And if I'm given the chance, I will devote my life to your happiness."

"I couldn't ask for more." She leaned and kissed his cheek. "As someone who was raised to believe that love was a myth, you shouldn't have known how to love me so perfectly, and yet you do. You are willing to be vulnerable with me. You want to be with me, and you always listen to what I have to say. Your love for me is unconditional, and so is my love for you."

Someone started clapping, and then everyone in the room joined in.

Annani waited until they were done and motioned to Brundar to come forward. "Can I have the rings, please?"

He bowed and handed her the matching rings.

"These rings are a gift from my future son-in-law, Orion. They are antique and quite valuable, not just because they are old, but because their former owners had a long and happy marriage and imbued these rings with love."

Annani held a ring in each hand and lifted them to show to the small crowd. "A circle has no beginning and no end, and therefore symbolizes eternity." She shifted her eyes to the couple. "Please face me and offer me your ring fingers."

When they did, she put a ring on each and then joined their hands. "With these rings, you are officially mated. You can go ahead and kiss."

# Vanessa

ᕦᕳᕤ

After the kiss Vanessa and Mo-red had shared to celebrate their mating, she was in a state of dreamy haze, and she barely heard the toasts and congratulations that followed as Anandur poured champagne for everyone and whiskey for Mo-red and Pavel.

All she wanted was to grip Mo-red's hand, take him back to their cozy cell, and celebrate their mating with a very thorough consummation of their vows.

After all, Mo-red had promised to spend the rest of his life making her happy, and she was eager to collect on that promise right away.

"Congratulations." Kian offered her his hand. "I wish you two many happy years together. I'm afraid that I need to leave and take my mother with me. I have a council meeting starting in an hour, and I still need to prepare my speech."

"Thank you." Vanessa pulled him into a tight embrace. "For everything."

Kian wasn't a hugger, and she knew that, but she was overwhelmed with emotion and couldn't help herself.

"You're welcome." Stiff as a broom, he awkwardly patted her back.

After they said their goodbyes and thank-yous to the rest of their family and friends, she and Mo-red were escorted by Alfie to the elevators, but instead of stopping in front of the lower level bank, he took them around to what used to be Kian and Amanda's private elevator to the penthouse level.

"Where are we going?" Mo-red asked.

Alfie grinned. "To your honeymoon suite, courtesy of Kian."

Vanessa's eyes misted with tears of gratitude. "I thought the penthouses were rented out."

"They were, but both leases expired last month and weren't renewed." He ushered them into the elevator. "The Saudi prince who rented both went home, naturally taking his four wives and thirteen kids with him, and Kian decided not to rent out the penthouses again just yet."

As the doors opened to the vestibule, Mo-red gasped. "This is beautiful." He walked over to the round table and sniffed the huge flower arrangement in the center of it. "Real flowers. How I've missed the smells of nature."

168

Vanessa couldn't believe Kian was willing to be so lax with security. She'd abandoned the plan to break Mo-red out of the keep and live on the run with him, but when such an opportunity presented itself, how could she let it go?

She hated that it would be like a stab in the back to Kian, and that he might never trust any of his people again, but as the saying went, all was fair in love and war, and saving her male came before her loyalty to Kian. Besides, breaking him out would not hurt anyone except ruffle the feathers of some bloodthirsty, vindictive Kra-ell.

In the grand scheme of things, she would be in the right, and they were in the wrong.

Alfie walked over to the double doors on the left, but instead of opening them, he leaned his back against them. "Just so we are clear. The elevator is programmed to stop only at the dungeon level and here. So don't entertain any thoughts of going on unsanctioned excursions. Also, your neighbors to the right are Guardians, and every time your front door opens, an alarm alerts them to the fact." He lifted his finger to the ceiling. "The vestibule is under constant watch, and if any of the cameras suddenly stops working, Guardians will be out here in seconds. Bottom line, your only option is to go out the window, and since it's sheer glass all the way down, I wouldn't recommend that."

"I'm not going anywhere." Mo-red took Vanessa's hand. "All I want is right here."

Shrugging, Alfie opened the door. "Just in case you decide to take Vanessa and run, you should know that losing her would be much more painful to the clan than losing you."

Vanessa winced.

Without her, there would be no one to help members of the clan who had emotional issues to deal with, and those who suffered from phobias would have no one to turn to. But everyone was replaceable, and some young members of the clan would take it upon themselves to study psychology and take her place.

It would only be a temporary void, so if she wanted to run away with Mo-red, that shouldn't stop her.

"Look at this view," Mo-red whispered next to her, pulling her by the hand to the sliding doors. "Can I open them? I haven't been out in the fresh air for so long."

"Go ahead," Alfie said. "Just don't expect fresh air. This is downtown Los Angeles."

Vanessa's gut clenched with worry.

Why was Kian revealing their strategic location to Mo-red? Did he know for a fact that Mo-red wouldn't be a security problem for long?

Was that why he had made such a grand gesture and offered them the penthouse to celebrate their mating?

Alfie must have seen the panic in her eyes because he put a hand on her shoulder. "Everyone in the village knows where the keep is. If Mo-red is released and in time gains the right to come and go as he pleases, his knowledge of this location won't be anything to worry about."

"I know that, but I also know how paranoid Kian is. It's not like him unless he thinks..." She swallowed. "You know what I mean. I can't even say that out loud."

"I know. But it's not what he was thinking. Trust me."

# Mo-red

As Mo-red slid the door open and walked outside, he tilted his head up and closed his eyes. Feeling the warmth of the sun on his skin was incredible. It was like his skin had been thirsty and was now absorbing the healing light.

The air was polluted, smelling mostly of gasoline fumes and other fainter smells of garbage and food cooking. It was nothing like the crisp air of Karelia, but after spending so long underground, inhaling recirculated air, Mo-red was grateful to just be outside and breathe the air, even if it smelled faintly of garbage.

Vanessa joined him after a few moments. "I have a feeling that we are going to spend all of our time out here." She put her arm around his middle and leaned her head on his shoulder. "We can skinny-dip in the pool. The terrace is very private, and the area of the pool is not visible from the other buildings."

Wrapping his arm around her back, he tucked her closer to his body. "I'm not a great fan of pools, but if that's what you want, that's what we are going to do."

She laughed. "It's so good to have a husband who answers everything with yes, dear. The pool is only three feet deep, so you don't have to worry about drowning. It's called a lap pool."

He turned to look at her. "You seem to know the place well."

"I do. It belongs to Kian, and he lived here for many years. Then he decided to move everyone to the village and rent his penthouse out. The penthouse on the other side belongs to his sister."

For a moment, he was seized by jealousy, imagining something between Vanessa and Kian, but then he remembered what she'd told him about clan members being forbidden to each other and about dormant carriers of the godly genes, who had been found during recent years, becoming life mates to a small number of lucky clan members.

"It's very kind of him to let us use it. Did he specify how long we can have it?"

Vanessa shrugged. "Alfie said it's for our honeymoon, which implies a month, but since the trial is scheduled to start this Saturday, I don't think we will have that long here."

"What about our things? Can we get them from the dungeon?"

He didn't have much, just a few borrowed pieces of clothing, the books that Vanessa had brought him, and toiletries, but he needed to return the borrowed suit and put on everyday clothing.

"It's all already here. Alfie collected everything from our cell and brought it up during the ceremony. The refrigerator is stocked with food for you and for me, and the bar has an excellent selection of whiskeys and other spirits." She put a hand on his cheek and turned his head toward her. "You look a little shell-shocked. I think a drink would help loosen you up."

He nodded. "I'm overwhelmed. I didn't expect to be so happy or enjoy a luxury like this. Not in this lifetime."

"Oh, Mo-red." Vanessa leaned in and kissed his lips. "Allow yourself to hope. The Fates wouldn't bring us all this only to yank it away from us."

He chuckled. "I know that you don't trust those Fates as much as you profess to. I saw your expression when Alfie brought us up here. You were checking out the security features because you were thinking about breaking me out again."

"Busted," she admitted. "But after his little speech, I'm no longer entertaining the idea. And it's not that I don't trust the Fates. I just don't expect them to deliver everything on a silver platter. I fully expect to work for what they offer, and that includes being open to clues they throw my way. What if running away was what the Fates wanted us to do? What better way to nudge us in the right direction than to offer us this opportunity? If I didn't examine all the angles, I would be remiss."

"I see." He shifted his stance, leaned, and lifted her into his arms.

Wrapping her arms around his neck, Vanessa laughed. "What are you doing?"

"I should have carried you over the threshold when we came in, but I was too stunned to think straight." He stepped inside the professionally decorated living room. "Which way is the main bedroom?"

The living area of the penthouse deserved more than the cursory look he'd given it, but he would get to it later. Right now, he was much more interested in how the bedroom was furnished, particularly the bed.

"Go that way." Vanessa pointed toward the hallway. "I think it's the first set of doors to the right. The primary bedroom has sliding doors that lead to the terrace. We can go skinny-dipping straight from there."

# Kian

Kian arrived at the small assembly hall a few minutes early to verify that everything was ready. He'd sent Okidu to clean the place that morning, and Shai had arrived a few minutes before him to check the recording equipment.

Sitting down, Kian pulled out his phone to look at his notes. Usually, he didn't prepare for meetings, but since a lot of what he was going to tell the council was speculation, he wanted to make sure that it all made sense, and listing things in order helped him to organize his thoughts.

As Toven walked into the room, Kian rose to his feet and offered the god his hand. "Good afternoon, Toven. You are a little early."

Kian had planned to leave the vote about Toven's seat for last, but perhaps it was a better idea to start with that so the council members wouldn't wonder what he was doing there.

"Yes, I am aware of that." Toven shook his hand, said hello to Shai, who was still fussing with the equipment, and then sat down next to Kian. "Am I taking someone's seat?" he asked.

"We don't have assigned seating around the conference table. When we hold a meeting in the big assembly, each of us has our own throne. Well, we have only twelve. We will have to add two more. One for Kalugal and one for you."

Toven arched a brow. "A throne?"

Kian chuckled. "That's what I called the chairs Amanda commissioned for the assembly hall in the keep. They were an eyesore and made me feel ridiculous every time I had to sit in them. I think they were the major reason I called for so few meetings. We have less ostentatious seats in here, but the arrangement stayed the same. They are up on the podium, arranged in a semicircle and facing the audience." He glanced at his watch. "We have a few minutes until the meeting. I can show you if you wish."

"It can wait," Toven said. "I stopped at the lab before coming here, and I took a peek at the journal Kaia was working on." He glanced at Shai and raised an eyebrow in question.

"Shai knows everything. You can speak freely in front of him."

The god let out a breath. "That's good. I didn't know who I could confide in."

"Do you think you can help Kaia?"

Toven nodded. "As I said, I'm rusty with the language, and I'm not familiar with the scientific symbols. Kaia will have to bring me up to speed, which will slow her down, but after that's done, I believe I can help her progress faster. I told her and William that I would dedicate two hours a day to the project."

Kian had hoped for much more than that, but he would take what he could get.

"Thank you." He smiled at the god. "With your help, I believe we will get there faster."

Toven was about to say something when the door opened, and William walked in.

"I was just about to tell Kian about our conversation from earlier," Toven said.

"Which part?" William pulled out a chair on Kian's other side.

He didn't look surprised to see Toven there, so the god must have told him that he was applying for a seat on the council.

"About us not having the material and knowhow to create cyborgs."

"Oh, yes. That." William shifted in his seat. "The Odus are a fascinating combination of biological and mechanical parts, and they look remarkably human. The Odus we will build are not going to be so life-like. They will be very clearly machines."

"I think it's better that way," Toven looked at Kian. "You will have much less of a moral dilemma using this new breed of Odus for the clan's various purposes."

"Yeah, I guess so, although it shouldn't make a difference what material they are made from and what they look like. They can be made from metal and plastic, but if they can think independently and feel emotions like happiness and sadness or even fear or anger, they are sentient beings and should be treated as such."

"That's going to be a challenge," William said. "We are their creators, and we get to decide what traits they will have, what names they will have, and everything else about their lives. They can't be independent without learning responsibility, duty, empathy, and all the other things that keep society functioning."

"Like children." Toven leaned back. "But unlike children, they can overpower their creators with ease. You'd better incorporate robust safety features in their design."

"Naturally." William cast Toven an offended look. "I know what I'm doing."

"We need to come up with a cool name for them," Kian said to defuse the situation.

"Robodu?" Toven suggested.

"That's not bad." Kian turned to William. "What do you think?"

"How about Rombodu?" William's eyes sparkled with mischief. "Like Rambo, Rumba, and Odu combined."

"I like it." Kian clapped the guy on the back. "But it might be too long. How about Rodu?"

# Toven

Since they hadn't even deciphered the blueprints yet, the naming of the new Odus was premature, and Toven wondered whether it was Kian's way of making peace with his decision to build the new generation of intelligent butlers who could also act as soldiers and defend the clan.

"I propose to call them Obos until a better name presents itself," Toven said. "We are months away, most likely years, from being ready to build a prototype. I'm sure better names will present themselves along the way."

"I like Obo," William said. "It can have as many variations as an Odu. We can have an Okibo, Onibo, and so on."

Hearing a distant hum, Toven looked toward the door, which William had left open. "We have company, so let's change the subject."

Kian frowned. "Your hearing must be better than mine. Who's coming?"

"We will know in a moment. The elevator just stopped at this level, and now the doors are opening." As feminine voices reached his ears, he smiled. "Amanda, Edna, and Bridget."

"Kalugal is with them," Kian said.

"And so is Brandon," William added. "That's the entire core council except for Onegus."

"I didn't know that Onegus was a member," Toven said. "I worked with him during the Kra-ell rescue operation, and it never occurred to me that he was a council member."

"Onegus is part of the core council." Kian rose to his feet. "The Head Guardians participate when security issues are discussed, and what's on the agenda today is definitely a security issue."

As the group entered the room, they all cast curious glances at Toven.

"Good afternoon." Kian greeted each member with a handshake.

Amanda pulled him into a hug. "I'm on time for once. Aren't you proud of me?"

He chuckled.

As they exchanged greetings with Toven and William, Kalugal approached him with a calculating expression on his face. "I'm surprised to see you here. What's the occasion?"

"I want a seat on the council."

Kalugal forced a smile. "Well, that was a direct answer. What prompted your decision to seek a seat?"

"Same as you, I want to be in the know. I've proven my loyalty and worth to the clan." He turned to Kian. "By the way, you should offer Jade a seat as well. If you want the Kra-ell to become contributing members of the community, they need to be represented."

"It's too early for that." Kian walked over to the door to welcome the chief and his Head Guardians.

When everyone was seated, Shai closed the door, and Kian stood at the head of the table.

"Let's start with the simpler matter first. Toven wishes to become a member of the council, and naturally, I approve his request." He turned to Toven. "Would you like to say a few words?"

Toven rose to his feet. "I would like to thank everyone here and in the village for welcoming me into the community and making me feel at home. After most of my family and friends perished, I wandered the world, drifting from place to place, and for thousands of years, I haven't felt a connection to anyone or any place. I hadn't realized how important it was to me and how much I missed being part of a community. My family is here, my son, my daughter, and my grandchildren, and I want to take an active part in protecting them and ensuring their safety and prosperity. By being a member of the council, I will be one of the first to know about new problems and in the position to offer my help." He smiled. "That's my entire speech. I hope you will vote to include me."

Kian rose to his feet. "That was short, sweet, and to the point. Everyone in favor of granting Toven a seat on the council, please raise your hands."

Kalugal pursed his lips. "Hold on. Aren't you going to ask Toven whether he wants to stay for the vote or wait outside?"

Letting out a breath, Kian turned to Toven. "Do you want to stay?"

"Of course."

"That's what I thought." Kian turned to face the council. "Everyone in favor, please raise your hands."

The only one who hesitated for a split second was Kalugal, but he added his hand to the unanimous vote.

"You can put your hands down." Kian offered his hand to Toven. "Congratulations. Welcome to the council."

"Thank you." Toven pushed to his feet. "I thank all of you for voting in favor of my inclusion."

# Kalugal

K alugal wasn't happy, not because he had a problem with Toven being on the council but because his chances of getting another seat had just diminished significantly.

Next, they would invite Jade, and then he could forget about a seat for Phinas, Rufsur, or Jacki.

As the murmurs of congratulations subsided, Kian lifted his hand to get everyone's attention. "Now, for the main reason I called this meeting. I have news to share with you, some disturbing, some exciting, and some a combination of both. The ship that carried the Kra-ell settlers also carried the infamous Igor you've all heard about by now. Turns out that he wasn't just a random opportunist who used his unparalleled compulsion ability to prey on his fellow settlers, kill the males, and subjugate the females to a small group of his lackeys. He was sent by the Eternal King, the ruler of the gods, to eliminate his one legitimate heir—Ahn."

"Why?" Brandon asked.

"Ahn was a rebel who shamed his father by taking up the Kra-ell cause and helping the uprising. He was banished to Earth along with his coconspirators, but his father still feared his son's influence. Ahn was popular among the young gods, and if they decided to dethrone the old king, Ahn would have been their natural choice for replacing his father. Or so we think. Igor wasn't given explanations. He was just a tool created by the gods to fulfill a mission. But Igor is not a dumb machine, and he had a lot of time to think about the mission he was sent on. He came up with the explanation I've just given you, and although it's just speculation, it seems reasonable to me."

"I agree," Onegus said. "I cannot think of another reason for the Eternal King to send assassins to kill his heir."

"You mean to say that there is more than one?" Brandon asked.

Given the expressions of most of the council members, they already knew all the details, and the only one out of the loop was Brandon. But it didn't make sense for Kian to call a full council meeting just to fill in the media specialist on what was going on.

As Kian continued talking about the assassins that hadn't woken up yet but still might, Kalugal tuned him out to think about ways to still get that additional council seat he wanted.

"—the queen's twin children were smuggled onto the ship—"

That got Kalugal's full attention. "Hold on." He lifted his hand to stop Kian. "Rewind if you please for a moment. How did you get from assassins and deciphering alien signals to the queen's children?"

Kian cast him an annoyed look. "You should have listened more carefully. Jade was on the queen's guard before being chosen by the lottery to join the settler ship. She didn't know what the twins looked like because they were always veiled, but she recognized them by their posture and body language when they were brought to the pod next to hers. Naturally, that wasn't conclusive, but there were other hints that indicated to her that there was something off about the neighboring pod. The pods had room for twenty people each, but while all the other pods had three or four females to sixteen or seventeen males, the pod with the suspected twins had an equal number of females and males. Also, the tech tending to that pod was exhibiting signs of nervousness, sweating, and fidgeting, and since he was a god, that was unusual. Still, that was all circumstantial evidence, and Jade couldn't be sure about the duo's identity."

It was infuriating that Phinas hadn't told him about the twins. Jade had no doubt confided in him, but he'd chosen loyalty to his mate over loyalty to Kalugal. It stung, but it was understandable, especially if she'd asked him to keep the information confidential.

"Why would the queen smuggle her kids out?" Kalugal asked. "Was she afraid for their lives?"

Kian nodded. "She was."

"And why were they always veiled?" Brandon asked.

Again, Kalugal noticed that only he and Brandon were asking questions, and the rest of the council seemed to know the answers.

It was annoying that even as a member, he still felt like an outsider. Toven, who had just joined, seemed to know what was going on as well.

"They were acolytes," Kian said. "Dedicated to the service of the Mother of All Life, but the real reason for the veiling was so the people wouldn't recognize them for what they were—half gods and half Kra-ell—which was considered an abomination by both societies."

Kalugal frowned. "Is that more speculation?"

"No, that's actually fact. The Clan Mother got that information out of Igor's head. But that's not the most shocking part." Kian took a deep breath. "The twins' father was Ahn. They are Annani's half-siblings, and they are incredibly powerful. Since both their parents were extremely strong compellers, and since they were twins, they might be able to combine their powers. The Eternal King knew that his son had an affair with the Kra-ell queen, who, at the start of the rebellion, was still just the heir apparent. He suspected that the twins were his grandchildren, but he wasn't sure about it. He also found out about them being on the ship. Igor's task was to eliminate Ahn, put the twins on the throne of the Earthbound gods, and when they trusted him completely and lowered their guard, kill them too."

Kalugal grimaced. "That king was a nasty piece of work. My great-great-grandfather makes my deranged grandfather seem like a nice guy." He looked at Toven. "Right?"

The god shrugged. "I don't like to think about my genes. It's too depressing. I thought that Mortdh was crazy because his mother was a piece of work. Now I'm no longer sure of that. He might have inherited those traits from our father."

"So, what now?" Bridget asked. "We know that they are somewhere out there on the other side of the planet, and they are either dead or alive. What do we do to mitigate the risk?"

Kian glanced at Toven, then at William, and then back at Bridget. "We can't find them until their pods come back online. In the meantime, we shouldn't assume the worst about the twins, but we should ready our defenses as if we do."

"Meaning?" Kalugal asked.

"Meaning that I will schedule another council meeting when I figure that out."

# Vanessa

❦

anessa stretched her arms over her head and looked out the sliding doors. There was still some light outside, but it was fading fast, and if Mo-red hoped to get some more sunshine on his skin, she should wake him up now.

After two rounds of lovemaking, the first fast and wild, the second soft and loving, they had fallen asleep in the super comfortable king-sized bed, and Vanessa was still feeling the afterglow, languid, loose-limbed, and happy.

Getting out from under the covers to dip in the lap pool didn't seem very enticing, but Vanessa knew that Mo-red would want to catch those last sun rays of the day, and then he would probably like to stay outside and bask in the moonlight as well.

The poor guy had been locked up for so long, first on the ship on the way to Greenland and then in the keep. At least on the ship, he could look out the window and get some of the weak sunlight, but he hadn't been allowed outside on the deck, and then he'd been brought to the dungeon.

He'd been going crazy from the lack of fresh air and space to move. The excursions to the gym and the pool had been therapeutic for him, but the other prisoners hadn't enjoyed the same privileges.

It was time to get it over with one way or another, but even if Mo-red was spared, it would be devastating for her if the Kra-ell sentenced the others to death.

Vanessa had grown to like most of the males, and she didn't want them to die for something that wasn't really their fault.

But life was unfair, and she was old enough to know that. Mortals died prematurely, suffering was inevitable, and there was very little she or anyone else could do about it.

"Hey, sleepyhead." She kissed Mo-red's cheek. "Wake up. There is still light outside for you to enjoy."

Smiling, he opened his eyes and pulled her on top of his chest. "I don't remember ever feeling such contentment, and I don't want to move a centimeter."

"I know. I feel the same." Vanessa looked down at Mo-red's handsome face, her heart so full of love that it felt about to burst. "I love you." She lowered her head and kissed his lips. "But if we don't get out of bed now, you will miss the last minutes of sunlight."

"I don't care." His hands closed over her butt cheeks, and he arched up, grinding into her. "There will be more of it tomorrow. Besides, I have it right here."

"Sunshine?"

"Yes." He smiled. "You are my sunshine."

It was a sweet thing to say, but she'd seen his expression when he'd stepped on the terrace before. It reminded her of a nature show she'd seen a long time ago. A female chimpanzee had been released from captivity, and when she'd seen greenery for the first time, the look of awe and pure joy on her face had been heart-wrenching.

Perhaps Mo-red wasn't looking forward to the skinny-dipping, and that was why he was reluctant to step outside?

"We don't need to go to the pool if you don't want to. We can just sit outside on the loungers and watch the sunset over drinks. No water involved."

Mo-red chuckled. "I don't mind the water. In fact, I would love to give the large jacuzzi tub in the bathroom a try. We can both fit in there with room to spare, and we can enjoy drinks while sitting in warm, fragrant water."

It sounded lovely. But when had Mo-red seen the bathroom?

Had he woken up before her and gotten out of bed without her being any the wiser?

She must have blacked out again.

Mo-red's venom wasn't as potent as an immortal male's, so it didn't happen every time they made love, but his bites had a cumulative effect. When he bit her twice in a row, she got to experience the euphoric trip she'd heard so much about from other immortal females who'd been lucky enough to experience that with an immortal male.

In fact, she identified a syndrome that was specific to her community—bite envy. Those who had never experienced a venom bite envied those who had.

The thought of the string of orgasms she'd experienced before passing out brought a fresh flush of arousal, and in response, her feminine center warmed and moistened.

"I like the way you think." She rubbed herself over Mo-red's hard length. "We can fill the large tub with water, add some bubble bath, and I can give you a very thorough wash. When you are clean, I will wrap you in a big fluffy towel, and we will go outside and sip on drinks in the moonlight."

A sexy smirk lifted the corners of Mo-red's lips. "On one condition."

"Name it."

"I get to wash you just as thoroughly."

She smiled. "I'm counting on it. But I get to do it first."

# Mo-red

**V**anessa sat on the edge of the tub with her hand dangling in the water and looking like a painting of Aphrodite.

Hell, Venus had nothing on her.

If Mo-red had any artistic talent, he would have immortalized this moment by sketching her long elegant body, those full generous breasts, the round, heart-shaped ass, and the luxurious blond locks that framed a gorgeous, intelligent face.

How had he gotten so lucky?

What had he done to be gifted with such an incredible boon?

The truth was that he hadn't done anything to deserve Vanessa, but he would spend his life earning that boon by worshiping her and making her happy.

As he knelt on the floor in front of her, she shook her head. "Get in the tub, big guy. I promised to make you squeaky clean, and you are going to be good about it and let me do it."

Gazing longingly at the cleft he'd been adamant about licking, he leaned, gave the smooth flesh a quick kiss, and rose to his feet.

"I guess she-who-must-be-obeyed doesn't reference just the Clan Mother." He stepped into the tub and sat down in the shallow water.

Vanessa grinned at him. "Sometimes I like to be in charge, and sometimes I like you to take over. Now it's my turn."

"Yes, ma'am."

The truth was that even when her wrists were bound, and she was pinned under him, Vanessa was still in charge, and that was precisely as it should be. His pleasure was derived directly from hers, and therefore his task was to bring her as much of it as possible in any form she desired.

Leaning over, she cupped his cheek and kissed him on the lips. "You are sexy as hell when you say things like that."

"Yes, ma'am," he repeated with a grin.

Vanessa swung her legs over, and as she rose to her feet and leaned over to grab a washcloth, the sight of her backside made Mo-red salivate.

Turning around, she gave his body a thorough perusal, and the heat in her eyes made his shaft twitch and lift in greeting.

She smiled. "Wait your turn, Mr. Impatient. I will get to you soon." She blew him a kiss.

Mo-red swallowed. "He can't wait. He wants a real kiss."

"He'll get it soon."

As Mo-red's eyes roved over her perfect body, he couldn't decide what excited him more, her pale breasts that were tipped with pink nipples and begging for his kisses, or those full lips of hers that needed to be kissed as well or alternatively wrapped around his shaft.

Vanessa's eyes were sultry when she motioned for him to scoot forward so she could get behind him. He did as she demanded, but while he loved to feel her touch, he hated not being able to see her.

Maybe that had been her intention, a way to slow down the seduction, but his imagination was filling in the blanks, and with every swipe of the soapy washcloth over his back, he wondered where she would touch him next.

When she leaned against him to wash his chest, plastering her full breasts to his back, he closed his eyes and groaned.

Was she going to clean his shaft next?

He needed her to touch him more than he needed to take his next breath, and if she didn't do it soon, he was going to grip himself.

Except, she didn't touch him, and he nearly groaned in frustration.

Instead, she leaned away and freed his hair from its binding.

"Are you going to shampoo my hair?"

"I've been wanting to do it since the first time I saw you."

"Does it have to be now?"

"Yes." Vanessa laughed, and a moment later, her fingers were massaging shampoo into his scalp. "Patience, my love. Delayed gratification enhances pleasure."

He'd said the same words to her only a short time ago when he was eating her up and keeping her on edge without letting her climax.

"This is revenge, isn't it?"

"No way. I'm just repaying the favor," she said too sweetly.

"Then I guess I'm not allowed to touch myself."

"That's correct."

The feeling of her long fingers massaging his scalp was pleasant, and perhaps he could've focused on them and relaxed if she wasn't leaning against him and rubbing her breasts with their pebbled nipples over his back.

"You are a wicked female, Vanessa."

She laughed. "Let's rinse out your hair. Stand up, my love."

His legs were shaky when he obeyed her command, probably because all the blood was concentrated in his straining erection, which she avoided touching as she turned him around and coaxed him to brace his arms against the tiled wall.

"Don't move," she commanded as she turned on the shower head.

As the water hit his head, Vanessa gently rinsed the shampoo out of his hair and then knelt behind him and started working on his feet.

"This is pure torture."

"I disagree. This is pampering. Lift your other foot."

As she worked her way up his calves, the tension inside him grew unbearable. He fought the urge to turn around, grab her by the nape, and thrust his shaft into her mouth.

He knew she wouldn't object.

In fact, it would probably turn her on.

# Vanessa

Vanessa wondered how long Mo-red would last before he took over and fed her his shaft.

She was playing with fire, and it was exhilarating.

He was so adamant about giving her pleasure, but she wanted to give it too, and her guy needed to be tricked into letting go.

When he turned around, she stifled a smile and affected a mock stern expression. "Did I say it was okay for you to turn?"

"No, but I can't take it anymore." He gripped his shaft, wrapped his palm around her nape, and teased her lips with the tip. "Having you kneeling behind me just won't do. As you are already on your knees—"

He stopped talking as Vanessa extended her tongue and flicked it over the velvety head, which was already wet and not from water. When she lifted her hand and gripped him, he threw his head back and groaned.

"Look at me." She stroked him. "I want to see your face when I pleasure you."

His expression of ecstasy was priceless.

Locking eyes with him, she took his shaft into her mouth, sucking the length as deep as it would go.

Mo-red's eyes rolled back in his head, but he forced them to refocus on her, and his hand on the back of her neck tightened a fraction before he loosened his grip and caressed the skin under her hair.

Somehow, he'd regained control and was trying to be gentle, but that wasn't what Vanessa wanted. She wanted him to forget about everything and give himself up to pleasure.

Moving her head up and down his shaft, she reached behind him and gently massaged his testicles while staring into his eyes.

In moments, his hips started thrusting, but he was still in control, still doing his best to keep from ramming his shaft down her throat, and she was starting to doubt that she could coax him to let go.

Applying more pressure to his balls, she took him down even deeper.

Mo-red hissed, "Mother of All Life, Vanessa. If you don't stop, I'm going to come."

She was tempted to continue and make him come inside her mouth, but his hand on the nape of her neck tightened almost painfully, and he withdrew.

For a moment, they were at a stalemate, but then he dropped to his knees, wrapped his arms around her, and kissed her.

The kiss wasn't gentle. It was desperate and fast, and then she found herself pushed against the side of the tub with Mo-red behind her, his arousal poised at her entrance for a brief moment, testing her wetness, and then without warning, he slammed inside of her.

Vanessa's eyes rolled back in her head, and a throaty groan left her throat.

He felt so good, filling her up so perfectly, and as he withdrew and slammed back in over and over again, her moans and groans grew louder and more demanding.

Behind her, Mo-red's breathing grew heavier, and she knew he was getting close and tilted her head, offering him her neck.

As his fangs pierced her skin, she screamed his name and climaxed, and as he kept drinking from her, she kept climaxing. At some point, Mo-red's body went rigid, and as his seed exploded into her, she climaxed again.

Her vision darkened, and she expected to black out again, but when Mo-red retracted his fangs, licked the puncture wounds closed, and withdrew from her body, she was still fully conscious.

Turning her around, he folded her into his arms and kissed her softly. "I love you, my perfect mate."

"I love you too." She could barely keep her eyes open. "You didn't get me clean like you promised."

Mo-red chuckled. "The night is still young, my love."

"I'm joking. All I want is to get back into bed."

"Your wish is my command." He rose to his feet with her in his arms and stepped out of the tub.

Vanessa glanced at the soapy water that had spilled all around. "We've made a mess."

"We can clean it up tomorrow."

Holding her up with one arm, he snatched a towel from the stack and wrapped it around her while carrying her to the bedroom.

"I love how strong you are." She purred into his neck. "Heck, I love everything about you."

"I adore you, my Vanessa. And if you are up to it, I'll soon demonstrate how much."

She had a pretty good idea about what he was hinting at. "Mo-red, my love. You say the sweetest things."

# Gilbert

G ilbert was having the most bizarre and sexy dream. He knew he was dreaming because Karen would have never gotten naked in front of another man, not in private, and definitely not while Gilbert was watching her strip for another male.

He was too possessive and jealous to even fantasize about something like that, let alone get aroused by it, but this was a dream, so he could relax and enjoy the ride.

Right.

Gilbert could never understand swingers and how they could swap partners and then go home to their normal lives and their normal jobs like nothing unusual had happened.

He didn't want the other guy to look at Karen, and when the guy's partner began undressing and sashaying her boobs in front of him, all he wanted to do was to move her aside because she was blocking his view of Karen.

"Hey, handsome." The woman leaned over him, her big breasts filling his field of vision. "Don't you want to play with these beauties?" She lifted the big melons so her nipples were nearly poking at his eyes.

"Please, move aside," he tried to be polite. "I only want my wife."

"I'm not your wife," Karen said from somewhere behind the woman. "We never got married."

That couldn't be. They had five children together. The two daughters Karen had when they met and the three little ones they had together. Of course, they were married.

"What are you talking about? You gave me three babies."

"True, but I didn't want to marry you, remember?"

As he strained to remember, his chest felt heavy, like there was a sadness weighing on it. Why had Karen refused to marry him? Had he proposed, and she'd said no?

Disappointed at his indifference, the big-boobed woman huffed out a breath and joined her partner on the bed, straddling him and riding him for all she was worth.

Gilbert had seen his share of porn flicks, and they usually aroused him, but not this real-life performance. Or was it a dream life?

Yeah, this was definitely a dream.

He wanted to get up and go to Karen, but he couldn't move, and panic seized him. "Why can't I move? What's going on?"

"Take it easy, love." Karen was suddenly in front of his face, her beautiful body glowing like it was covered in diamond dust. "It's just a dream. That's why you can't move. It's sleep paralysis."

"Oh." He let out a relieved breath. "Do you love me?"

"Of course, I do. What kind of a question is that?"

"So why did you refuse to marry me?"

Her eyes turned sad. "I wanted to stay true to my late husband's memory, but that was a long time ago, before we had kids. You didn't ask me again."

"I'm asking now. Will you marry me? You don't have to change your last name. You can keep your first husband's name to honor him. But I want to be married to the mother of my children."

The other naked couple in the room was going at it like a couple of pros in one of the old porn movies that he used to watch as a young man.

Karen leaned over and kissed his forehead. "Yes. I will marry you, Gilbert. But first, you need to come back to me."

"I'm right here. You are touching me."

"Come back to me, Gilbert. I need you."

"I'm here!"

"Come back." Karen was crying now. He could hear it in her voice even though there were no tears in her eyes.

The dream didn't make sense, and it was no longer sexy or fun. It was scary. Why was Karen telling him to return to her when he was right there with her? And why was she crying?

Maybe something was wrong?

Were the kids okay?

He had to wake up right now.

The woman on the bed turned her head to look at him over her shoulder, and as she smiled, she bared a pair of monstrous fangs at him. "Come here, Gilbert. Come join us. I know you want to. Don't be shy."

Horrified, he stared at her fangs and glowing eyes. "What are you?"

"Your salvation." She blew him a kiss.

What the hell?

He was losing his bloody mind.

"Gilbert!" Karen's voice was urgent. "Do it again! Squeeze my hand!"

He wasn't even holding her hand. He was fisting his hands to protect her from the barracuda on the bed.

"Get out of here, Karen. Run! I will not let them come after you! I'll hold them back!"

He didn't know how he was going to do that when all he could do was clench his hands, but he would think of something. Maybe he could scream for help?

"Gilbert! Do it again!"

# Karen

Gilbert was squeezing Karen's hand so hard that she feared he was going to crush the delicate bones, but he wasn't waking up, and she was afraid to pull her hand out of his grip and sever the connection.

"Gilbert! Wake up."

The nurse rushed in, but Karen stopped her with her other hand. "Wait. I think he's trying to open his eyes."

As Gilbert's eyelids fluttered, his grip on her hand slackened, and a long moment passed during which she was afraid to breathe. Then his beautiful eyes popped open, and he looked at her with such terror that tears misted her eyes.

"It's me, sweetie. Did you have a nightmare?"

He just kept staring at her with wide eyes.

"Bridget is on her way," Gertrude said from behind her. "I'll leave you alone. Call me if you need me."

Wasn't she supposed to check Gilbert's vitals?

"What's going on, love?" She leaned down closer and kissed his forehead. "What got you so scared?"

The kiss must have calmed him because he let out a breath. "Are we married?"

The poor guy must be delirious. "No, sweetie, we are not. But it doesn't matter. We are it for each other, forever and ever, right?"

"Would you marry me?"

"If it's important to you, sure."

"You can keep your last name. I know you don't want to give it up."

The tears that were just a mist before solidified, and she had to wipe them away with the back of her hand. "I know. We talked about that before. What's important right now is that you are awake."

Nodding, Gilbert licked his lips, and she realized that he must be thirsty. He was hooked up to an IV, so he was not dehydrated, and she'd kept his lips moist, but his throat probably felt dry.

"I'll get you some water." She walked over to the sink, got a paper cup, and filled it up.

The nurse had told her that the water was filtered, so it should be okay to give it to Gilbert. She found a straw, pulled it out of its paper cover, and stuck it in the cup.

When she got back to the bed, the door opened, and Bridget walked in.

"Welcome back." She got to Gilbert in three strides. "How are you feeling?"

"Thirsty," Karen said. "Can I give him water?"

"Yes. Just small sips, though."

As soon as the straw touched Gilbert's lips, he latched on to it and sucked down much more than small sips.

"That's enough," Bridget said. "If you can hold it down for a few more minutes, Karen will give you more."

Reluctantly, he let go.

Already, he looked much better than in the first panicky moments. The gleam in his eyes was back, and his facial muscles were relaxed.

"How long was I out?"

"You passed out Monday morning, and this is Thursday."

"Three days," Gilbert said. "That's not bad, right? Did I grow?"

Karen chuckled. "No, you didn't. There have been no physical changes yet."

He looked disappointed. "Nothing? Not even more hair?"

"It has been only three days," Bridget said. "And you are not out of the woods yet. Let's see how long you stay awake."

He looked at the IV and then down at where the catheter line snaked from under the sheet.

Bridget followed his eyes. "Those are not going anywhere yet. If you manage to stay awake for the next eight hours, I might take them out." She stopped next to the instruments for a moment but didn't write anything down. "Everything looks good." She turned to smile at them. "I'll leave you two alone, but I'm not going back to the office building. I'll continue my work from my office here. Call me if you need anything."

"Thank you," Karen said.

When the doctor closed the door behind her, Karen brought the straw back to Gilbert's lips. "You looked terrified when you opened your eyes. Do you remember what scared you so?"

He nodded. "I dreamt that we were in a room with another couple and that we were all naked. The woman had huge boobs, and she was trying to distract me with them, and when I showed no interest, she climbed on top of her partner and rode him like a porn star. I was trying to talk to you and ask you to marry me, but she kept trying to get my attention, and then she had fangs and glowing eyes, and I told you to run, but you didn't. You kept saying come back to me, and I couldn't understand why you were saying that when I was right in front of you." He stopped his rapid monologue and frowned. "What's funny? Why are you laughing?"

Stifling her giggles, or rather trying to, Karen put the cup on the side table and took his hand. "It's all my fault. I had a crazy idea about us involving another couple in my induction instead of choosing just a male to help us. I thought it would be easier, and the truth is that it got me turned on. Anyway, I was telling you about my idea, and that must have prompted your nightmare."

"Did the female have fangs and glowing eyes?"

"Nope. I only said that she should be a clan member and that the guy should be one of Kalugal's men. There are many hookups going on in the village between the former Doomers and the clan ladies, but so far, there are no bonded couples, so they could actually do it with us. Anyway, your mind must have filled in the blanks."

"I guess. So now that I'm no longer unconscious, tell me your crazy idea in more detail."

"With pleasure." She climbed on the bed and lay down beside him. "Yesterday, Darlene came to visit us early in the morning, and she—"

# Gilbert

As the hours passed, Gilbert kept feeling better, but Bridget hadn't come back yet, and Gertrude was reluctant to take out his IV and the damn catheter without the doctor's permission.

The upside was that the nurse was not strict about him having too many visitors and pretended not to notice that there were more than two at a time in his room.

"I knew you'd be fine." Eric pulled a bottle of whiskey out of a paper bag and handed it to Darlene to hold while he pulled out a stack of small paper cups. "You did it so much faster than me. I was in a coma for two damn weeks, and here you are, awake and chipper after three days." He took the bottle from Darlene and filled the first cup.

"It's not a competition," Darlene said, handing the cup to Karen.

"I don't think Gilbert should have whiskey. Bridget said to be careful with how much water I gave him."

"He can take a lick." Eric filled another small cup. "He's immortal now. A few drops of alcohol are not going to make him sick, but they will improve his mood."

"My mood is fine," Gilbert grumbled. "I'm alive, which is all that matters."

So, he hadn't started growing new hair, and his saggy jowls were still just as bad as they had been before the start of his transition. Big deal. They would get better over time.

Maybe he was like Kaia, and his transition would be gradual.

Damn, he really hoped so. Immortality was awesome, but he would rather spend it looking like a thirty-year-old than a nearly fifty-year-old.

"Don't worry." Karen kissed the top of his head. "The hair will grow. Bridget told me that Turner was completely bald before his transition, and look at his hair now. It's almost as pretty as Jackson's."

"Speaking of Jackson." Darlene leaned closer to Karen with a conspiratorial look on her face. "Did you hear what his mother has done? She mated one of the Kra-ell prisoners. They had an official ceremony with the Clan Mother presiding over it and everything."

Karen frowned. "Isn't the goddess's presence in the village supposed to be a secret? Or is that over now?"

"No, it's still a secret. Kian sneaks her in and out of the keep so the Kra-ell won't see her." Darlene chuckled. "I heard that her disguise is a pair of tight jeans and a t-shirt."

"I would love to see that," Eric said. "I can't imagine the formidable Clan Mother wearing jeans."

"Right. Neither can I." Shaking her head, Karen turned to Darlene. "What I want to know is how come you are so well informed?"

Darlene shrugged. "It's this face." She circled her hand over it. "People like to talk to me. I heard about the wedding from Toven, who heard it from Annani herself. By the way, he's coming over with William and Kaia as soon as they are done working on whatever it is they are working on."

"I thought you knew everything that was going on." Eric put the bottle of whiskey back in the paper bag.

"Not everything. They are keeping Kaia's project very hush-hush, and I don't ask questions. I prefer not to know those kinds of things, and I would probably not understand them even if they were explained to me. I'm only interested in gossiping about personal stuff. It's much more fun."

"True." Karen lifted her paper cup. "To life, love, peace, and harmony."

"Amen." Gilbert lifted his cup to Karen's and touched the rim to hers.

The satisfying clink of glass on glass was missing, but the smile in Karen's eyes and on her lips more than compensated for it.

He barely wet his lips with the alcohol and put it aside.

"I envy you," Eric said. "When I woke up from my coma, I could barely move a muscle."

"Yeah, but you looked ten years younger while I still look the same."

"Not really." Darlene leaned away and pursed her lips. "Your skin has a healthy shine, and you look calmer. That nervous energy that was pulsing under the surface is gone."

"That has nothing to do with the transition." Gilbert took Karen's hand. "Or maybe it does in a roundabout way. Karen and I decided to get married as soon as possible, and that makes me feel good. We should have done that a long time ago."

Karen's expression was apologetic when she looked at him. "Not yet, my love. I want to transition first. We said that we would do it after both of us are immortal."

His heart sank. "That was before my transition. After the damn dreams you made me have, I decided that we should get married right away, and you agreed."

She shook her head. "You misunderstood. I meant for us to get married after my transition."

"Hold on." Eric lifted his hand. "What dreams?"

Karen's cheeks got red. "I was telling Gilbert about an idea I had for inducing my transition, and apparently he heard me, and it influenced his dreams, or rather nightmares."

Darlene smiled. "Was it by any chance my idea?"

"Not quite," Karen said. "I took it one step further."

# Karen

After Bridget had authorized Gertrude to unhook Gilbert from all the wires and tubes, Karen helped him into the bathroom despite his protests.

"I'm fine." He smiled. "But if you want to hop into the shower with me, I won't say no."

Well, it seemed that her man was back to his usual self—overconfident, boastful, and lustful. She loved all those things about him, but sometimes they could become irritating and overbearing.

"Our entire family is crammed into the waiting room, anxiously waiting for you to get ready for your test, including the boys and Idina. I don't think it's a good time for us to enjoy shower games."

He made a pouty face. "They can wait a few minutes longer."

Chuckling, Karen shook her head. "Just be done with it quickly, so we can do the test and go home. If you're okay here by yourself, I'll go out to the waiting room and say hi to everyone."

His bravado faltering, he braced a hand on the shower wall. "Stay. I'm not steady on my feet."

"No problem. Let me help you with the johnny."

As he turned around, she untied the strings and patted his naked butt. "This still looks as fine as ever."

He looked at her over his shoulder with the familiar smirk lifting his lips. "Are you sure about not joining me?"

"I'm sure." She leaned against the vanity and crossed her arms over her chest.

After his big talk, Gilbert ended up taking that shower sitting down on the bench, and when he was done, Karen helped him to towel dry and get dressed.

"I feel funny about getting back in that bed. Can't we do it out in the waiting room?"

"You wanted to be tested like all the other transitioning Dormants, and that's how they all did it. In the hospital bed."

Letting out an exasperated breath, he let her help him up to the bed, and when he lay down, he closed his eyes for a moment. "You know what? You were right. The shower used up whatever energy I had left, and I don't have enough to even sit up. All I want to do is lie down like a slab of beef."

Karen chuckled. "When will you learn that I'm always right?" She leaned and kissed his clean-shaven cheek. "And you are not a slab of beef. You are my beefcake."

That got a smile out of him. "I used to be your beefcake, and I hope to be again once I get my strength back. I intend to hit the gym every day."

He'd been promising to do it for years, but he'd never stuck to it for more than a couple of weeks at a time. There were always more urgent things to do than run on the treadmill or lift weights in the gym.

"I'll tell Bridget that you're ready and call the others in."

"Thank you." He took her hand and brought it to his lips. "For everything. You are my rock. My gift from the Fates."

"You're sweet." She kissed his forehead. "Now, let me go."

Gilbert always got super mushy when he wasn't feeling well. It was as if he was surprised anew each time that she took care of him and was grateful for it.

It was nice to be appreciated, but it also made her sad to think that he didn't expect to be taken care of. As the oldest child, he'd always looked after his younger siblings.

When she opened the door, she was greeted by excited sounds coming from the waiting room, and then it got suddenly quiet when they saw her standing in the doorway.

"Gilbert is ready for his test," Karen said. "I hope you can all fit in the room." She stretched on her toes to search for the doctor, but she couldn't even see the door to her office past the crowd. "Can someone call Bridget?"

"I'll get her," Orion said.

Kaia pushed through with Evan in her arms. "He wants to see Daddy."

"Of course, sweetie." Karen took the boy. "Where is Ryan?"

"Right here!" The crowd parted to let Cheryl and Idina through. Ryan was perched on Cheryl's hip, and Idina was on her other side, holding her hand.

"I want to go home." Idina cast angry looks at the adults around her. "Bring Daddy home too."

"I will, honey." Karen took her hand. "Let's go to Daddy's room and give him a kiss. He misses you so much."

Idina's lower lip quivered. "I miss him too."

"You saw him yesterday," Cheryl said. "You gave him a kiss."

"He didn't give me a kiss back. He was asleep."

"He's awake now," Karen said. "And he can't wait to see you."

# Gilbert

"Daddy!" Idina pulled her hand out of Karen's and ran to his bed.

Gilbert wasn't sure he had the strength to lift her, but he gritted his teeth, leaned over, grabbed his daughter under her arms, and hoisted her up onto the bed.

His vision swam, and he was instantly covered in sweat, but there she was, sitting on his chest, her big eyes luminous with unshed tears. She cupped his cheeks with her little hands and leaned in to give him a big, sloppy kiss.

"I was worried," she said with an accusing tone. "You were asleep, and you didn't wake up. Mommy said that you were sleeping very deeply because your body was changing, but you look the same."

His daughter was very astute.

"Daddy!" Ryan wailed from Cheryl's arms. "I want Daddy!"

"Bring them over." Gilbert patted the bed on both sides.

As soon as Karen and Cheryl put the boys down next to him, they both wrapped their little arms around his neck and put their cheeks next to his, sandwiching his face.

Idina laughed. "You look funny, Daddy."

He felt funny too. In fact, he was on the verge of tears.

Having his babies surround him with love was the best feeling in the world, and as he thought about how close he could have been to never seeing them again, a tear slid down his cheek.

Karen, his beautiful, smart mate, leaned down to kiss him, effectively shielding him from view, and wiped the tear away with her lips.

"Don't choke Daddy, boys. Ease up a little."

It took a long time and the promise of ice cream from the café for the children to let go of him so others could come to congratulate him, and Bridget could conduct the test.

As Cheryl and Kaia took the little ones out, Toven approached his bed. "I'm glad to see you on the other side, Gilbert. Welcome to the clan."

"I thought I was already a member."

"You were an honorary member," Kian said from behind Toven. "Now you are a full-fledged member."

"Does that mean I'm getting a share in the profits?"

For a moment, Kian looked unsure, but then he nodded. "I guess so."

"Just kidding." Gilbert smiled. "I'm grateful to be here, and getting a house with all the utilities and amenities for free is more than enough. When my children mate clan members, though, I will expect them to get a share."

Kaia was already getting it, and one day Cheryl would find an immortal to mate, and she would get it too.

Gilbert couldn't wait to meet the guy who would fall in love with Idina. That dude would have his hands full and then some.

Kian nodded. "The more the clan grows, the better, but it means that I need to work harder to produce more profits."

"Make room, people!" Bridget's voice carried over the crowd.

For a tiny female, she had a strong voice and a commanding tone that brooked no argument.

As people pushed against each other to make room for her, Gilbert craned his head to see if his children were back. It might be a little scary for them, and the boys might start crying, but he didn't want them to miss it.

Reading his expression, Bridget looked over her shoulder. "Make room for Gilbert's kids. They get a front-row view."

It was easier said than done, but somehow it was achieved. Kaia held Evan, Cheryl held Ryan, Karen held

Idina, and all three kids held a cone of ice cream that was melting over their little hands.

"I'd better hurry," Bridget murmured.

She took his hand, cleaned it with gauze, and lifted her little scalpel. "Ready?"

He nodded.

The cut was tiny and didn't hurt much, but as blood welled over it, Ryan started crying, and then Evan joined him.

Idina rolled her eyes. "They are such babies. There was more blood when I fell and scraped my knee. It's not a big deal."

Gilbert was so proud of his little girl and how brave she was.

"Look," Karen whispered. "It's already closing."

That was an exaggeration, but it was certainly healing faster than it had when he was still fully human. The blood stopped welling, and as Bridget wiped it away, the skin seemed to already start knitting itself together. Two minutes later, it was as if the cut had never been there.

Bridget lifted his hand so everyone could see. "Welcome to immortality, Gilbert."

# Vanessa

"It's started to drizzle," Vanessa murmured lazily. "We should go inside."

Mo-red smiled. "You have the umbrella to protect you, and I don't mind a few drops of water."

The double lounger they were sprawled over was half in the shade for her and half in the sun for him, and the symbolism wasn't lost on her. Her ancestors avoided the sun and preferred living underground, while the Kra-ell couldn't live without soaking it up.

She turned on her side to face him. "You don't mind when it's just a little drizzle, but you do mind when it's a lot of water. You couldn't wait to get out of the pool."

Alfie had brought them swimsuits after almost walking in on them naked the day before—a red bikini for her and swimming trunks for Mo-red. Where he got the trunks was easily explained, but she had no idea where he'd gotten the bikini, and he'd refused to say.

The top was a little too small for her ample breasts, but Mo-red wasn't complaining.

Her guy was too busy ogling.

"That's not a pool." He waved a hand at the lap pool. "It's a very large tub." He turned back to her and brushed his knuckles over her cheek. "But since you enjoy swimming, I will learn to enjoy it too."

She'd thought he would feel safer in the shallow pool, but evidently, it wasn't about fear of drowning but just a general aversion to prolonged immersion in water.

It must be instinctual to the Kra-ell.

"I don't want you to do anything that you are not comfortable with. I don't love swimming that much. I just thought that it would be fun. It's not like there is much else to do here except make love."

His lascivious smile stirred the embers of her desire. "That's fine with me."

They hadn't left the penthouse since they'd gotten there two days ago. To celebrate their mating and enjoy what could possibly be their last days together, Vanessa had canceled all of her remaining appointments.

The trial was tomorrow morning, so they didn't have much time left, and her relaxation was giving way to a steadily growing anxiety.

"Hey." He drew her closer to him. "Stop worrying. It's going to be okay."

She nodded. "With Kian's testimony, we have a good chance."

Mo-red's hand closed on her bikini-clad bottom. "Remember our deal. We are not talking about it until tomorrow."

He'd threatened to spank her if she brought up the trial instead of enjoying their short honeymoon, and he'd made good on that promise twice already.

Just thinking about it made her face flush and her nipples harden. Maybe she should keep talking just to make him do it again?

It had been very pleasurable.

Mindful of his superior strength, Mo-red was very careful with her, and it was a novelty to be handled that gently. She wasn't a dainty thing that human males perceived as fragile. No male she'd been with had felt as if he had to hold back.

On the one hand, she loved that Mo-red was gentle with her, but on the other hand, she wanted to see him lost in the throes of passion, unhinged and wild. But that was stupid. It might seem sexy in her head, but the truth was that she didn't want the male she loved to cause her real pain.

Games were fun, but limits were important, and they shouldn't be crossed.

Still, it pained her to think that Mo-red would always need to remain in control.

His soft lips brushed over her cheek. "Are you still thinking about the thing you shouldn't be thinking about?"

"No." She opened her eyes and smiled. "I was thinking about you having to always remain in control with me. Perhaps one day we will know how to enhance ourselves the way the gods enhanced Igor, and I could become as strong as a Kra-ell. Wouldn't that be fun?"

His face fell. "Am I not pleasing you?"

"Of course, you are." She cupped his cheek. "I'm worried about you not enjoying yourself to the fullest because you are afraid to hurt me."

"I enjoy myself tremendously. In fact, I've never enjoyed myself as much as I do with you. You are incomparable, my love."

Vanessa grinned.

If he were anyone else, she would have thought that he was exaggerating, but she'd learned that Mo-red didn't say anything he didn't mean. If she wasn't the best he'd ever had, he wouldn't have said that. He would have found some other way to compliment her.

"Tell me all the ways in which I am incomparable." She cuddled up even closer.

"How about I show you?" He took hold of her wrist and brought it up to his lips, kissing the pulse point.

He'd never bitten her there, only her neck. Was he going to do it now?

A shiver of anticipation mingled with a tinge of fear rushed through her. She wasn't afraid of his fangs, and the moment his venom entered her system, any pain she felt turned into pleasure, but there was always that first moment, and it was both scary and exhilarating.

Mo-red didn't bite her wrist, though. He kept kissing up her arm until his lips reached her neck.

# Mo-red

M o-red was determined not to squander Kian's generosity and use these scant precious days in this beautiful penthouse for anything other than enjoying his time with Vanessa.

There would be no more strategy talk and hypothesizing about what this, that or another witness would say.

The problem was that neither of them was the type of person who could easily turn off their mind and dissociate from reality.

The one time no errant thoughts intruded on their mated bliss was when they were consumed with passion.

Kissing across her cheek, then the corner of her lips, and finally her mouth, he pulled her on top of him.

She put her hands on his shoulders and flicked her tongue over the seam of his lips, and as he opened for her, she swooped in, sweeping her tongue against his.

Vanessa's ability to be dominant or submissive as the mood struck her was one of the many things he loved about her. There was never a dull moment with her, and nothing was predictable.

The only two rules they had for their games were that nothing was out of bounds between them and that nothing was ever forced.

Banding his arms around her, he flipped them around and gazed down at her. "My beautiful Vanessa."

He dipped his head and took her lips while reaching under her for the bra clasp.

The swimsuit, if one can call two small red triangles that, was hot, but he preferred when they both had been naked out on the terrace and constantly touching each other. The clothing, as scant as it was, created a barrier.

Once he'd bared Vanessa, he gazed down at her puckered nipples that seemed to be straining toward him, begging him to suck on them. He pressed kisses over the mounds first, teasing her with licks and nips that were dangerously close to her stiff peaks but avoiding touching them. When he finally dragged his tongue over one nipple, she cried out and arched up.

Gripping the top of his ponytail, she tugged his head closer.

He punished her impatience with a gentle nip and then rewarded her compliance by slipping his hand into her bikini bottom.

Wetness soaked his hand, making his shaft pulse with need.

"You're so ready for me."

"Always." She arched into his hand.

"I'm the luckiest male on this planet." He pulled her bikini bottom down her shapely thighs.

When she parted her legs for him, he moved between her knees and licked his lips.

Heavy-lidded glowing eyes gazed at him with a mixture of love and lust—the best combination a male could ever hope for—and as he lowered his head and gave her a gentle lick, she moaned, the sound sending a zing straight to his shaft.

"I love that talented tongue of yours," she murmured. "The things you can do with that thing should be illegal."

Smiling, he nipped her inner thigh. "Why is that?"

"Because they are just too wicked."

She loved it when he penetrated her with his tongue, but he wasn't done teasing her yet.

Rubbing just the tip over her clitoris, he elicited a groan from her, and then she was tugging on his ponytail, demanding more.

His swimming trunks were about to get ripped from the strain his shaft was putting on them, and since they were borrowed, he felt a little guilty about leaving them on, but not enough to get rid of them. The flimsy barrier they provided was the only thing keeping him from ramming into Vanessa's wet heat.

Instead, he gave her what she craved, delving into her entrance and tasting the sweet nectar of her arousal.

When he started fucking her with his stiffened tongue, Vanessa's strangled moans and undulating hips nearly undid him.

Unable to hold off any longer, he shoved the swimming trunks down and gripped his throbbing shaft.

"Mo-red," she husked. "I want you inside of me."

It was hard to answer when his tongue was deep inside of her and he was teasing her clit with his upper lip.

She gripped his head and rocked her hips, fucking his tongue as if it was his shaft.

He was about to come, but that was fine. He still hadn't broken the record of climaxes he'd boasted about, and it was now or perhaps never.

He might not get another chance.

# Vanessa

Vanessa was close, but so was Mo-red, and the sight of his weeping erection was mouth-watering.

"Turn around," she commanded. "I want you in my mouth."

He didn't need to be told twice. Turning her on her side, he somehow managed to maneuver his body to get his shaft in position without having to stop what he'd been doing with his tongue.

That was an impressive show of acrobatics that she couldn't emulate.

Well, she could compliment him later. Right now, she had a very big lollipop to lick. As she teasingly flicked her tongue over the slit, collecting a delectable drop of his seed, pleasure flooded her as if he had sunshine stored in it.

Hey, maybe he did. He'd been soaking up the sun for hours.

As she circled the crown with her tongue, she shuddered, and as she kissed down the side of his length, he groaned deep in his throat, and the vibrations traveled down his tongue into her core.

Her eyes nearly rolled back in her head from the pleasure.

If she were focused only on herself, she would have orgasmed, but her focus was split in two, which held her climax at bay.

Tightening her hand around the base of Mo-red's shaft, she took him deeper into her mouth and pumped him with her hand, but she didn't intend to let him come just yet.

The longer she could keep him on the precipice, the more intense his orgasm would be.

When she felt his shaft swelling and his tongue inside of her getting frantic, she eased off and waited until he slowed down his tonguing to increase the tempo again.

Mo-red groaned, sending more of those delicious vibrations into her sheath, but the note of frustration in his groan tempted her to let him come.

Well, maybe just a little longer.

There was power in bringing a strong male like him to his knees just with pleasure, and Vanessa reveled in it.

As his legs started quaking around her ears and his shaft swelled again in her mouth, she sank her nails into his buttocks and took him as deep as he would go.

He erupted, and she kept sucking until the last drop. She didn't stop when there was no more, though. She continued until she got him hard again.

Too focused on Mo-red, Vanessa hadn't orgasmed, but that was fine. It wasn't even night yet, and they had plenty of time to play.

He withdrew from her mouth and from her sheath at the same time, mounted her, and without a word, entered her with one swift thrust.

As pleasurable as what they were doing had been, nothing could compare to the feeling of him inside of her and his muscular chest pressed against hers.

It was a joining of flesh and soul.

As Mo-red clenched her body to his and thrust between her thighs, the coil inside of her wanted to spring free but couldn't. It had been wound too tightly for too long and was stuck in the locked position.

Not for long, though.

Sensing that she was stuck, Mo-red withdrew, flipped her around, and entered her from behind.

Pulling her bottom up to his pounding, he went fast and hard for a few moments and then bared her neck and struck.

Vanessa detonated like a firecracker, her climax taking her up to the clouds even before Mo-red's venom hit her system, but she didn't black out right away. Hovering just on the edge of euphoria, she enjoyed one climax after another until they were both spent and collapsed exhausted on the double lounger.

After a long moment of catching their breaths, Mo-red chuckled. "Maybe I will break that record today after all. What number orgasm was that?"

"I lost count." She tried to remember. "Seventh? Or was it eighth?"

He grinned. "That's five more to go. Are you up to it?"

She looked at the sky. "It's just started to get dark. We can easily squeeze five more in before tomorrow morning."

"I might not make it till morning, but I'll die a happy male."

She slapped his arm. "Don't talk like that."

He laughed. "I wasn't talking about the results of the trial. I was talking about dying from sexual exhaustion."

"I know. I just don't want to hear any talk about dying."

# Kian

Bad dreams had woken Kian before four in the morning, and he was too disturbed to go back to sleep. He couldn't remember what the dreams had been about, only that he'd woken up alarmed.

Next to him, Syssi was sleeping peacefully, and through the baby monitor he could hear Allegra's rhythmic breathing, but he still got up, threw his robe on, and walked over to his daughter's room to make sure that she was alright.

For long moments, he just stood next to her crib and watched her sleeping, but unlike the many other times he'd done the same thing, the sight of his sweet bundle of joy didn't help relieve his stress.

The next stop was his office. Turning his desktop on, he checked the security feed, and even though everything looked fine, he called the security office.

"Good morning, boss," the Guardian on duty answered. "This is Marco. Anything I can help you with?"

"I'm just checking whether you noticed anything out of order."

"No, boss. Everything is quiet as usual. Why? Did Syssi have a vision?" The guy sounded concerned.

"No, she didn't. I just had an uneasy feeling." He wasn't going to tell the Guardian that he was bothering him because of a bad dream. "Stay alert and let me know if anything seems even a little out of order."

"Will do, boss."

After ending the call, Kian checked his emails, and when he found no urgent problems there, he checked the news app. Finding no new major catastrophes reported, he closed his desktop computer, palmed his phone, and rose to his feet.

The device pinged with an incoming message as he was about to open the door.

Fully expecting the message to be bad news, he was relieved to see that it was from William and that it seemed only mildly urgent.

*Something came up. Call me when you can.*

William kept odd hours, waking up early to go swimming or just to jot down a new idea that came to him in a dream. As long as the message didn't say to call him immediately, it couldn't be too bad, right?

Still, he was awake, and so was William. Turning away from the door, Kian sat on the couch and placed the call.

"Good morning, William. Are you on your way to the pool?"

"Pool? Oh, no. I don't do that anymore. I was in bed when the automated system I set up to search for signals from the Kra-ell settler trackers sent a message to my phone." William's voice sounded strained, and it was obvious he was walking. "Three signals came online and immediately winked out. I'm heading to the lab to see what's going on. I hope it was a malfunction, but I doubt it."

Kian's sense of alarm intensified tenfold.

Was that the reason for the bad dream that had woken him up?

"It would be one hell of a coincidence if a pod came online right as we were about to put Igor in stasis."

Annani had been adamant that Igor wasn't broadcasting telepathically or otherwise, but what if he wasn't aware of doing so?

It wouldn't surprise Kian if the gods had installed the ability in Igor's subconscious.

"I don't think those signals came from the settlers," William said. "If a pod came online, we would have gotten twenty new signals, not just three."

"Perhaps the other seventeen are dead. The pods crash-landed. It's possible that some of them got partially damaged, keeping only some of the occupants alive."

"That actually makes sense. It would also explain why they immediately winked out. The three occupants could have revived for a moment, but since the pods weren't functioning well, they went back into stasis or died."

That would be a convenient explanation, and it would also ease Kian's mind, but it wasn't necessarily the correct one.

"I hope your system recorded the signals so we can find out where they came from."

"I'm sure it did, but I need the Odus to decipher it. I'm almost at the lab. Can you send Okidu over?"

"I don't know if Okidu can do it alone. I'll get Onidu as well. Do you want to meet us at my office or at the lab?"

There was a moment of hesitation, and then William said, "Your office. I'll double-check the equipment to make sure that it wasn't a glitch and bring the recording to your office for the Odus to decipher."

Kian chuckled. "Let me guess. Your lab looks like a war zone."

"Worse. It looks like an alien battlefield. I'll be in your office in an hour."

"If the signals come online again, let me know immediately."

"I will."

As Kian ended the call, a knock sounded on his office door, and as he opened it, he wasn't surprised to find Okidu standing in the hallway.

"Good morning, master." His butler bowed. "Would you like a cup of tea to help you fall asleep?"

"That would be lovely, thank you. But I'm not going back to bed. I need you to get Onidu and come with me to the office building in an hour."

His butler's raised brow was such a human expression that Kian wondered whether the two rebooted Odus had reached a new level of awareness.

"Did Master William's device detect new signals?"

Yup, his butler was certainly evolving. Not too long ago, he wouldn't have asked why Kian needed him and Onidu to accompany him to the office. He would have just done it, no questions asked.

Now, he was not only asking but also guessing the correct answer.

Kian wasn't sure how he felt about that, but right now, he did not have the bandwidth to dwell on the possible ramifications.

"Yes, it did. But they immediately winked out, so it might have been a glitch. William will meet us at my office and bring the recording with him. I need you and Onidu to be there to decipher it and tell us where the signals came from."

"Of course, master." Okidu dipped his head.

"Thank you."

It had been on the tip of Kian's tongue to ask whether Onidu's presence was at all necessary and whether Okidu could decipher the signals alone or needed his brother to do that, but he'd decided not to ask just yet.

It would be interesting to see whether Okidu would have enough autonomous thinking to offer the information himself.

"I shall make the tea." Okidu bowed again. "And I will notify Onidu to meet us at the office building." His butler went into the brief trance-like posture Kian had noticed before.

Apparently, he had to pause all other activities while communicating with his brother.

It was an odd programming decision, and Kian suspected that it was just one more safeguard to mitigate the potential risk the Odus represented.

# Mo-red

Mo-red shuffled his chained feet toward the bus waiting for him and the other prisoners, and as he climbed the stairs, he had a strong sense of déjà vu.

Not so long ago, he'd made the same shuffling climb into the airplane that had transported him from Greenland to the immortals' dungeon.

He remembered how despondent he'd felt, fearing it was the end, but things had turned out much better than he could have ever imagined. He'd met Vanessa, had fallen in love, and now they were mated.

After spending three days and nights with her at the luxurious penthouse, being shuffled into the bus with the other prisoners, his ankles and wrists chained once again, was like waking up from the best dream to a nightmare, but who knew? Maybe this trip would turn out much better than he expected as well.

"Do you know where they are taking us?" Madbar asked quietly.

Mo-red knew they were being taken to the village for the trial, but he didn't know where the village was. "It's where the rest of our people are. They will be our jury."

Pavel wasn't on duty when Mo-red had been escorted back to the dungeon and from there to the underground parking, where the bus had been waiting for them. His son was probably getting ready for the trial, perhaps even making a last effort to sway the opinions of those Kra-ell who were undecided.

Lusha had come up with that strategy, explaining that those whose hearts were filled with hate and the need for revenge couldn't be persuaded to change their minds, and those who were more merciful and willing to forgive wouldn't suddenly change their opinions and demand the prisoners' heads.

Only the undecided could be swayed either way, and the most effort should be spent on them.

The good news was that the number of haters and forgivers was nearly equal, so the few who were in between could tip the scale, and if the defense did its job right, the undecided would be more inclined to side with the forgivers.

Or so he hoped.

"You're lucky," Madbar said as they sat down. "No matter what happens, you're going to keep your head."

Evidently, the rumor about his and Vanessa's wedding had spread somehow, and he wondered who was responsible for the leak. Was it one of the Guardians, or was it Pavel?

"If our people are adamant about making me a head shorter, I don't think even my marriage to Vanessa will save me. The big boss wouldn't risk alienating the Kra-ell over this. He needs them to be in a cooperative mood."

Madbar cast him a sidelong glance. "He might anger his own people if he throws their therapist to the wolves. She is well liked, and so is her son, and he wouldn't do that to her."

Mo-red was glad to hear that. He'd been impressed with Jackson for many reasons, especially with how the young immortal was respectful toward his mother and doted on his mate.

"What did you hear about them?" he asked Madbar.

For some reason, people liked to talk to Madbar. Maybe it was because the guy didn't have too high an opinion of himself, was easygoing, and didn't appear too smart. He was also a gossip and asked a lot of questions.

"Vanessa is a legend among their people. The Guardians talk about her as if she's a saint." He cast Mo-red a smile. "They were shocked by her interest in you, and they speculate that you must be something special for her to fall for you. Naturally, I confirmed that for them." Madbar straightened in the seat. "I told them that you are an outstanding male and that Vanessa has good taste."

"That was nice of you."

Madbar shrugged. "What can I say? I'm a nice guy."

"What did they say about her son?"

"He's really young. Practically a kid, and yet he's been mated for a while and is a successful businessman. He started by managing one coffee shop and branched out into building his own commercial bakeries and supplying his goods to coffee shops and vending machines across the city. Rumors are that he's already a millionaire."

"That's impressive."

The guy was also movie-star handsome, but that he got from his mother.

Vanessa was gorgeous.

Mo-red's heart constricted with worry for her. If the trial didn't go as they hoped, she would be devastated.

"Tell me more," he said to Madbar. "I need something to distract me from the anxiety of what's awaiting us."

"Let's see." Madbar lifted his eyes to the ceiling. "What else did they say about Jackson? Oh yeah, he used to play in a rock band. He plays the guitar and is a good singer. Alfie said that it's a shame that he doesn't have time to keep the band going. He said it would be nice to have weekly performances in the village square."

Mo-red arched a brow. "Did the Guardian tell you about the village?"

"Yeah. Why? Is it supposed to be a secret that the immortals call their neighborhood a village?"

"That's the impression I got from Vanessa. That's why I never mentioned it." Mo-red glanced at the other prisoners over his shoulder, but they were all busy either talking among themselves or gazing out the window.

There were a total of nine, including Valstar, who had been downgraded from a high-risk prisoner to one of them.

There used to be ten, but Porgut had gotten released almost immediately. Well, released was the wrong term. They'd taken him out of the dungeon and allowed him to join the rest of the Kra-ell. The guy was a hybrid, and he'd been captured with Balboth and Korvel, who had also been with Igor when the compound had been liberated, and the only reason Igor had taken Porgut with him was that the kid looked so human that he could easily pass for one.

There had been no animosity toward Porgut, and he'd probably been accepted by the Kra-ell community with open arms, but there was a lot of hostility toward the nine males in shackles riding this bus.

## Kian

Kian tiptoed to the closet, going as quietly as he could so as not to wake up Syssi. He'd managed to leave the room without disturbing her sleep, but he wasn't as lucky on his way back.

"Where are you going?" she asked sleepily. "Why aren't you in bed?"

Changing direction, he walked to the bed and sat next to her. "I need to go to the office. William's alert system picked up three new signals, which winked out as soon as they came on, so there is no reason for alarm yet, but we need to investigate them and find out where they came from."

Her eyes wide open, she sat up in bed. "Do you think a pod came online?"

"That's one possible explanation." He didn't want to disturb her with his morbid hypothesis, especially since it was only a guess and he had nothing concrete to base it on.

"I hope they are okay. I'm worried that the signals stopped." She pushed a strand of hair behind her ear. "Someone might have killed them as soon as they woke up, but who? We have Igor in custody, and I doubt any of the others got the same ideas about eliminating the males."

"It was most likely a glitch." He leaned over and kissed her lips. "Go back to sleep, sweetness. Worrying about it will only make you tired. It's not like we can do anything about it other than make sure the village is safe."

Syssi nodded. "What bad timing for it to happen on the day of the trial."

He smiled. "It's never dull in our village, is it? It was supposed to be a peaceful sanctuary for our people."

"It is." She took his hand and brought it to her lips for a kiss. "Just regrettably not for you."

"As long as I can keep you, Allegra, and everyone safe, I don't mind what I have to do. Are you going to come to the assembly when it's time for Igor's entombment?"

She shook her head. "I'll watch it at home together with your mother and Alena."

The ceremony would be broadcast over the village's closed-circuit channel for the benefit of those who didn't want to be in the assembly room but still wanted to watch it.

He could use her support when it was time for him to give his testimony. Just knowing that she was in the audience would have made it easier, but the truth was that he preferred for her to stay home with a team of Guardians patrolling around the house to ensure his family's safety.

"Good. When I deliver my speech, I'll be thinking of you watching me and rooting for me."

"I'll come during the break."

He put a hand on her shoulder.

"Don't. All of the Kra-ell are going to be there, including the prisoners. The Guardians will be on full alert, but I'd still prefer for you to be away from the assembly hall."

"It's going to be fine." She leaned and kissed him. "Come back as soon as you can so you can catch an hour of sleep before the trial."

"I hope I can." He let out a breath. "I'm crossing my fingers for it to be a malfunction and for the Odus to tell me that the signals came from the middle of the ocean and not somewhere nearby."

"Good luck." She lay back down and pulled the blanket up to her chin. "If you can't come back right away, call me or leave me a message so I know what's going on."

"I will." He tucked the blanket around her, kissed her cheek, and headed to the closet.

Half an hour later, he walked out his front door and made his way to the office building. Okidu had left ahead of him with the promise of brewing coffee for everyone, and as Kian opened the door to his office, he was greeted by the most welcoming smell of the dark roast he favored.

"Good morning." He walked over to where William was sitting next to the conference table with his laptop open. "Did you find where the signals came from?"

The guy looked like he had fallen out of bed, which he probably had, with a rumpled white T-shirt that was three sizes too big on him, gray sweatpants, and a pair of blue Crocs on his bare feet.

"Good morning, boss." He took his glasses off and rubbed his nose. "I waited for you to get here." He cast a quick glance at the Odus. "I don't think they would have done anything without you being here."

"Right. Okidu is supposed to take orders only from Syssi and me, but lately, he's been more autonomous, so I keep forgetting that he's not capable of ignoring his base commands no matter how sentient he is."

William glanced at the Odu. "Being sentient doesn't guarantee autonomy. Compulsion is like a base command that overrides everything else."

Kian winced. "Don't remind me. After I deliver my testimony later, I'll try to forget what Igor did to me."

Okidu walked over with a mug, bowed, and put it in front of Kian. "Here is your coffee, master."

After William had gotten a mug from Onidu, Kian motioned at the laptop. "Let's hear it."

"There is nothing for us to hear," William said as he typed a few commands on the device. "It's not in our hearing range."

The Odus seemed to have no trouble hearing whatever the recording was playing. Frozen in their wordless communicating mode, they looked as if someone had pressed their turn-off switches, which made Kian uncomfortable.

He liked seeing them animated and sentient. He'd always thought of Okidu as a family member, never as a machine.

After Okidu's reboot, Kian had been worried for a while that his loyal butler would not be as loyal anymore, but Okidu had proven that those worries hadn't been warranted.

The question was what would happen when they started making a new type of Odu that was not as lifelike. What the clan could accomplish would look like robots from old sci-fi movies, but they would have the same neural networks as the original Odus, and the same capacity for sentience, just without the thousands of years of living with people who cared for them and made them feel like valued members of the family.

They wouldn't have the store of good memories that Okidu and Onidu possessed.

William would have to follow the original designer's plan and ensure that the new line of robotic servants would not be able to achieve sentience for thousands of years. The problem was that these robots would be treated as machines because of how they looked, and they wouldn't absorb the same good stuff his mother's Odus had taken in since they had come into her possession.

"Should I write down the coordinates?" Okidu asked after a moment.

"Please do." William handed him a sheet of paper and a mechanical pencil.

"Thank you, master." Okidu pulled the paper to him and scribbled a list of numbers in his neat handwriting. "Here you go, master." He handed William the page.

William checked the coordinates and brought up the map. "Chengdu, the capital of China's Sichuan province."

Kian frowned. "Isn't that near Lugu Lake?"

William enlarged the map. "It's as close to the lake as Los Angeles is to Las Vegas. It's about four hundred miles away."

Rubbing his temples, Kian wondered if he should be worried about it. Even if a pod had come online, China was far away, and by the time his people could get there to investigate, there would be no trace left of whoever those signals had belonged to.

"There isn't much we can do about it." Kian rapped his fingers on the conference table. "We have Igor to put into stasis and nine Kra-ell males to save from the guillotine, and I don't have the mental bandwidth to deal with this." He drank the rest of the coffee and put his mug down. "Let's go home and get some sleep. Hopefully, we will get no more signals, or at least no more today."

# Jade

The catacombs were several levels below the dungeon, and as Jade and Kagra followed Dalhu and Bhathian out of the elevator, Jade made a conscious effort to release the hilt of her sword, which she'd been clutching with a death grip.

"This place is giving me the creeps." Kagra chuckled. "Well, it makes sense. We are in a crypt, right?"

"We call it the catacombs," Bhathian said. "And yeah, it gives me the creeps too, but probably for a different reason. Hundreds of our enemies are buried here. The bastards are in stasis, but those of ours they killed are not, and that's not okay with me."

Jade gave him an appraising look. "So, you are not in agreement with the no-execution rule of the gods?"

He bared his fangs, then glanced at Dalhu and deflated. "Perhaps the Clan Mother is right. Not all of them are evil bastards, and even if one can be saved, we need to give them a chance."

Kagra tilted her head and gave Dalhu an appreciative once-over. "You were once a Doomer, right?"

He nodded. "I was, and back then, I deserved the title of an evil bastard even though I was trying to fight it. If not for Amanda, I would still be doing evil deeds and hating myself for them."

Bhathian clapped him on the back. "You've paid your dues. I'm surprised that you volunteered to do this, though. This place must bring back bad memories."

Dalhu shrugged. "Kian asked me if I was willing to be the one to put Igor in stasis, and I took it as a compliment. He wanted someone big and strong, and he thought of me." He puffed out his chest. "Or maybe I was chosen because I was the one who dispatched the last bad guy that needed dispatching."

Bhathian snorted. "Yeah. Thankfully, that bastard is not here. Although, if he was, I would have awakened him myself and tortured him for weeks or even months the same way he'd tortured Carol."

"Who's Carol?" Kagra asked.

As Bhathian told the story about the sadistic bastard who had kidnapped a clan female, Jade thought about Kian's choice of an executioner.

When Bhathian had shown up with Dalhu at the parking lot, Jade had assumed that the muscular Guardian would be the one to put Igor in stasis, and she'd assumed that Amanda's mate was just hitching a ride with them. Then he'd told her that he'd been chosen for the task, and she'd been wondering ever since about Kian's odd selection.

Why a civilian whose occupation was painting pretty landscapes?

Now, it made sense.

Apparently, Dalhu used to be the clan's enemy, and somehow, he'd not only become one of them, but he'd mated the goddess's daughter.

There was a story there that Jade was curious about, but she wasn't going to pry unless Dalhu volunteered to tell her.

As they entered a circular stone chamber, Dalhu let out a breath. "Yeah, this place doesn't bring back good memories. That being said, it was the best thing I've ever done, and I would do everything again in a heartbeat."

"Okay." Kagra put her hands on her hips and turned to glare at the two males. "Either you tell us the story or stop dropping hints. I can't take the suspense."

Dalhu chuckled. "It's a story everyone in the village knows. I'm surprised that no one told you yet."

"We are new here. So, what's the story?"

"You see that wall over there?" He pointed. "I got whipped there, and after that, I was put in stasis and entombed for a week. That was my atonement for killing a clan member who Amanda was very close to. She called him her nephew, but she called most clan members cousins or nieces and nephews. They are all related in one way or another."

Jade wouldn't have been more stunned if the cavern had suddenly collapsed on top of them.

"You killed Amanda's nephew?"

"Not with my own two hands, but I was the commander of the unit that did it. We were ordered to strike against the enemy in a way that would leave an impact, and that was what I did."

"How could she mate you after that?" Kagra asked. "Did she know it was you who had given the order?"

He nodded. "Vengeance is not always the right answer. If I could rewind time and change the past, I would, but I couldn't. All I could offer was for the victim's immediate family to take a pound of my flesh to earn their forgiveness. The whipping was the easy part. Being put in stasis was terrifying even though I knew it would be only for a week."

"Why?" Jade asked.

"It feels like death. The venom does not work instantaneously like anesthetic. I felt my heart slowing down over long minutes until I felt nothing at all." He rubbed a hand over his jaw. "I hope that those who pass over to the other side of the veil do not enter a dark void like the one I was in. I hope there are sights and sounds to welcome them."

"Of course, there are." Jade clapped him on the back. "Everyone goes to where they earned entrance. The fields of the brave are filled with beautiful flowers and grassy meadows. And even though the valley of the shamed is not a desired destination, it is not a dark void either. It's just a road that leads to a better job done in the next incarnation."

# Kian

Kian looked at the huge screen mounted on the far wall of the stage. The camera was on, showing the ceremonial chamber in the catacombs. Jade, Kagra, Dalhu, and Bhathian were already there, but the sound was muted for now, so their conversation was private.

Soon, Igor would be brought in, chained, and escorted by Guardians and pureblooded Kra-ell, all wearing earpieces. Kian had wanted him to wear a gag, but Jade had asked that it be removed to allow him to say some last words to his people, so it had been decided not to put it on him.

Kian found Jade's request curious, but he hadn't questioned it. Maybe she hoped he would reveal more things in an effort to save himself, or perhaps she wanted him to say goodbye to their daughter. Whatever her reasons were, this was her show, and she got to make the rules.

The nine prisoners were seated in a semicircle on the stage. The fancy council chairs had been removed, replaced by simple iron ones bolted to the concrete floor. The prisoners were chained to them, and they also had cuffs that could administer a neurotoxin that, when activated, would immobilize them instantaneously.

The chains were not really necessary, and they were more for show than a way to restrain the prisoners. It was a reminder for them not to attempt anything stupid, and it was also good for the Kra-ell filling the front rows to see them like that.

The back rows were taken by clan members, who had shown up in force. The event was being televised and broadcast on the village's closed-circuit channel, so they could have watched the proceedings from the comfort of their homes, but for some reason, they wanted to be there in person.

It was a spectacle.

Maybe it was for the better, forcing the Kra-ell to act in a more civilized and less bloodthirsty way. They were making an effort to impress their hosts, changing the way they greeted people and using 'please' and 'thank you' more often.

Perhaps showing mercy to their own would fall under the same umbrella of trying to adjust to their new community.

"Nice turnout," Amanda said from behind him. "The assembly hall is packed to capacity."

"It is." He turned to her. "Where is Evie?"

"I left her with Mother. She probably wouldn't have understood what was happening, but I didn't want her to see her daddy bite another male. Who knows what babies absorb and remember."

"Syssi decided to watch the proceedings from home for the same reason. She was worried that Allegra would get upset."

He would have liked her to be there when it was time to deliver his speech, but he knew it was not only because of their daughter that she was staying home. Syssi didn't handle things of this nature well. Igor more than deserved his fate, but it would still upset her to watch it and would affect her mood long after everyone else had forgotten about it.

And if, Fates forbid, the Kra-ell decided to execute the prisoners, it would devastate her.

Kian wished he could shield her and Allegra from all the ugliness of the world, and he did his best, but since that was impossible, the next best thing was to shower them with as much love and happiness as he could muster.

The problem was that he wasn't very good at this either. He was a moody guy with a lot on his mind who couldn't lighten up as often as he would have liked.

"I'm going to sit with Alena and Orion." Amanda gave him an assessing look. "Unless you want me to stay with you and provide moral support."

"Thank you, but I will be fine. I'm the master of ceremonies of this circus."

Given the look she gave him, he hadn't fooled her. "Syssi told me that you intend to testify. I know it's not easy to share traumatic experiences. I can't go on the stage with you and hold your hand, but you can look at me when you deliver your speech and pretend that there is no one else in the audience other than me."

"Thanks. I might do that."

He wasn't embarrassed about what Igor had done to him and the way it had made him feel, but he wasn't good at communicating his feelings either, so looking at Amanda's expressive face would give him good feedback.

"Do me a favor, though." He smiled at her.

"Anything."

"You know how bad I am at these kinds of things. If you think I'm doing poorly, give me the thumbs down, and if I'm doing well, give me the thumbs up."

Leaning over, she kissed his cheek. "You'll do fine. Just be yourself and don't worry about it. By now, even the Kraell know that you are not a touchy-feely type of guy and that you are not easily rattled. That will work to your advantage. Your story will be that much more impactful."

# Jade

Jade tensed and rechecked her earpieces as the clanking of chains on concrete announced Igor's arrival. Next to her, Kagra did the same.

Dalhu's expression was impassive, which probably reflected how he felt about what he needed to do. He had no personal quarrel with Igor, but he knew the things the male had done, so he had no reason to feel apprehensive or uncomfortable about it.

When Igor crossed the entry arch, he was flanked by two Guardians and two Kra-ell purebloods on each side. His face was a mask of indifference, but as he looked at her, it briefly changed into a look of pure hatred.

Fear scorched a path in her chest, but she doused it with a wave of satisfaction.

Finally, after over two decades, she was going to get her revenge. It wouldn't be as satisfying as the kind she'd imagined nearly every waking moment, but it was close enough.

Or had she imagined the baleful look?

Igor had never expressed extreme emotions before. He wasn't capable of them.

Or so he claimed.

Igor had claimed many things.

He looked at the sword that was hanging at her side in a fancy scabbard. Both had been gifts from Brundar and the finest she had ever owned.

"You are finally going to get your wish." His tone and expression had returned to their normal impassiveness. "After all the promises you made and the vows you took, you're going to kill me. Does your daughter know what a dishonorable mother she has?"

Had no one told him that he would be put in stasis?

She shifted her gaze to Pavel, who shook his head almost imperceptibly.

Apparently not.

She would thank Kian for it later. The moments of rage and terror Igor was experiencing were priceless.

Except, Drova was watching in the village, and she didn't need the added drama.

"I'm not your executioner, Igor." Jade sauntered over to him. "I wish I were, but I have vowed that you would not die by my hand nor by the hand of anyone under my control."

When he looked at Kagra, her second shook her head. "I'm not your executioner either. I'm just here to enjoy the show."

His eyes shifted to Dalhu, roaming over his big body, no doubt searching for a sword or an ax, but Dalhu had no weapons on him. Igor turned to give Bhathian a similar assessment. The Guardian had a gun strapped in a holster but no sword.

"You are not going to die today," Jade ended the game only because their daughter was watching. "You are going to be put in stasis, and if the immortals need your services in the future, they will wake you up. Although, I hope they never do."

He visibly relaxed. "Don't I get a trial?"

"You were found guilty and sentenced to death over two decades ago. Fortunately for you, and regrettably for me, you had something we needed to bargain with, so your sentence was reduced to indefinite stasis."

"I was just a soldier following orders. Do I deserve to die for that?"

When Dalhu shifted from foot to foot, Jade put a hand on his arm. "We've already established that you'd had no orders to indiscriminately kill Kra-ell males so more females would be available to you and your lackeys. You acted in self-interest."

"Save your breath, Igor," Kagra said. "Nothing you can say will change what is about to happen. Make your peace with it and say goodbye to your daughter."

Jade knew that he wasn't going to do that. Kagra probably hoped to demonstrate how little Igor cared for Drova.

Lifting his head to look at the camera, Igor smiled a chilly smile. "I guess you are all watching this and rejoicing, and I bet the immortals are filtering the sound to render my compulsion ability useless. But I don't need compulsion to see the future as clearly as you can see me from wherever you are watching. I want you to remember this day when you realize that Jade or any other leader you choose is much worse than I ever was. I was designed to think logically and not let emotions rule me. That meant that I didn't hold grudges, I didn't carry out vendettas, and I didn't prefer one person over another. You all had an equal chance to advance in my compound. That's not what awaits you in the future. When you wake up to that reality and realize your mistake, you know where to find me."

Gathering the patience to allow Igor to say his final words hadn't been easy, and Jade was proud of herself for keeping her composure and holding her tongue from lashing out at him.

When he finally was done, she stepped forward and unsheathed her sword. "For the crimes of murdering defenseless males, adults and children alike, you deserve to die by my hand." She lifted the weapon and slashed a shallow cut across his throat that started to close almost as soon as she lowered the weapon. "This was my Kra-ell symbolic execution." She took a step back and motioned for Dalhu to take her place. "I now transfer you into the custody of the clan."

# Mo-red

**M**o-red was surprised to see Pavel as one of the purebloods escorting Igor into the ceremonial chamber where Jade and Kagra were waiting for him.

His son hadn't told him that he would be participating in the ceremony, and Mo-red hoped it was because Pavel had wanted to surprise him and not because he just hadn't deemed him worthy of being notified.

Not that there had been time.

He and Vanessa had spent every moment since their wedding together until it was time to go. Vanessa had left first, and when he'd been taken to the dungeon, Pavel wasn't there.

Yeah, the most likely explanation was that Pavel hadn't gotten the chance to tell him. During the wedding, he probably hadn't known that he would be escorting Igor, and even if he had, he'd been so stunned by the appearance of the goddess that he must have forgotten.

But where was Vanessa?

Mo-red had hoped she would come to him when he arrived at the judgment hall, but she was nowhere to be seen. Lusha was there, translating what was being said to benefit the clan members sitting in the back rows.

There were so many.

Vanessa hadn't told him how many members were in her clan, and not wishing to put her in an uncomfortable position where she couldn't answer him, he hadn't asked. Then again, given how many Guardians they had sent to storm the compound, he should have known that there were at least several hundred of them.

Surely not everyone had arrived to see the trial.

When Madbar gasped, Mo-red returned to what was happening on the screen.

Jade held her sword to Igor's throat, and even though Vanessa had told him that Igor would be put in stasis and not executed, Mo-red got carried away with the theatrics, and seeing Jade slash across the monster's throat had his gut clenching not with worry or regret but with fear.

What if that was what awaited him?

"This was my Kra-ell symbolic execution." Jade took a step back. "I now transfer you into the custody of the clan."

The tall immortal standing behind her came forward, and he just looked into Igor's eyes for a moment.

They were about the same height, but the immortal was at least twice as wide and outweighed Igor by seventy kilos or more.

Not that it made a difference.

Despite the guy's intimidating physique, Igor was more than three times as strong, but he was chained, and the chains were held by two purebloods on either side of him. They were holding on tight and not giving him any slack.

"What are you looking at?" Igor asked in English. "Are you just going to stand there? Or are you going to do it?"

The immortal tilted his head. "During my over eight hundred years, I've seen my share of evil. I know what it looks like, and I know what it smells like. I wanted to make sure that you are not a case of mistaken identity."

Igor lifted a brow. "And? What do you think?"

The immortal smiled chillingly. "You are not."

Grinning, Igor turned his head to look at Jade. "You see? I'm not evil."

"That's not what I said." The immortal's voice was calm and quiet, but his fangs elongated, and his eyes blazed amber. "I said that you are not a case of mistaken identity. You are evil to your core." He grabbed Igor by the nape and sank his fangs into his neck.

Igor struggled, but the four purebloods holding his chains held on tight, limiting his range of movement to no more than a centimeter or two.

Whoever had designed the chain system had done an incredible job. Whenever Igor tried to move any body part, the entire system tightened even more, and now the chains were cutting into his muscles, restricting blood flow.

Not that it mattered; the venom the immortal was pumping into him was going to render him unconscious any moment now.

"How long does it take?" Madbar whispered.

Mo-red had no idea.

Kra-ell couldn't enter stasis without the help of a life pod. Only gods could, and according to Vanessa, the immortals could do that too.

Evidently, the gods had put in Igor enough godly genes to enable him to do that as well. If not, the venom would kill him, and no one would be overly disturbed by that.

When Igor slumped against his chains, the four young purebloods held him up for the immortal to keep pumping him with venom. At some point, the Guardian who had been standing behind the immortal tapped him on the shoulder, but the guy lifted his free hand to signal for the Guardian to step back.

It took another minute before the immortal retracted his fangs. He didn't lick the puncture wounds closed and watched as the skin knitted itself without his help.

"He still lives," the immortal announced.

The purebloods lifted Igor's flaccid body and carried it to a plain-looking sarcophagus that had been hidden from the camera up until now.

The Guardian with the big muscles unlocked Igor's chains, and the purebloods helped untangle him and put his body inside the sarcophagus.

It took the four of them and four immortals to lift the lid and secure it over the stone coffin, but that wasn't enough. They wrapped the casket with titanium chains and locked them.

After Jade and Kagra had inspected the sarcophagus and the chains, Jade lifted her face to the camera. "Even if the gods had gifted him with special powers of spontaneously awakening from stasis, he's not going anywhere." She tapped the coffin. "He's as good as dead."

# Kian

Kian wasn't a bloodthirsty Kra-ell, and he wasn't vindictive, or at least he liked to think that he wasn't, but watching the lid being placed over that sarcophagus and then the chains looping around it had been immensely satisfying.

The threat that Igor had represented had been like a black cloud hanging over his head, and now that it was gone, he felt lighter.

Annani could finally come out of hiding and move into her own house. Not that he wanted her to leave. Despite the lack of privacy, he loved having her over, but he hated that she had to sneak around the village of which she was the queen.

When it was all done, and Jade had said her final words, someone started clapping, and soon the entire assembly hall was filled with applause and cheers. Kian walked on stage and clapped along until the ruckus subsided.

"I don't know about you, but I thought that was well done."

More applause and cheers erupted, and even the prisoners on the stage stamped their feet to join in the celebration.

The only one in the entire assembly hall who was conflicted about Igor's fate was probably his daughter, and he hoped she had someone to lean on. Searching the crowd, he found her sitting next to Phinas and leaning on his shoulder. The guy had his arm around her and was saying something in her ear that made her smile.

Kian's heart swelled with something akin to gratitude, but he wasn't sure who he was grateful to—Phinas for taking care of the daughter of the female he loved, Kalugal for handpicking the best males he could find in Navuh's camp and organizing their escape, or maybe the Fates for bringing Jade and Phinas together.

When the audience quieted down, Kian addressed them again, "We will take a one-hour break to allow Jade and the others enough time to return to the village before we start the trial. Refreshments will be served in the gym, and you are all welcome to partake."

On his signal, several Guardians walked up on the stage, released the prisoners from the chairs they were bound to, and escorted them to a classroom that would serve as their break room. They had all been fed before leaving the dungeon, but they might be thirsty or need to visit the bathroom. He couldn't leave them chained up for the entire day.

When most of the audience had left, Kian saw Amanda heading his way and walked down the steps.

"What did you think about my Dalhu's performance?" she asked.

"I didn't know he was such a showman."

She laughed. "He's not. He meant every word he said. I spoke with him on the phone, and he told me that the dude smelled evil. I asked him what evil smells like, but he didn't know how to describe it."

Wrapping his arm around Amanda's shoulders, Kian walked her out to the hallway. "Maybe sniffing out evil is Dalhu's special talent."

"That's a cool talent to have." She lifted her hand and waved. "Syssi is here."

Kian followed Amanda's eyes, and as he saw Syssi walking down the hallway with Allegra in her arms, he let go of Amanda and shoved his way through the crowd to get to his wife and daughter.

"You're a sight for sore eyes." He kissed Syssi and took Allegra from her. "How is Daddy's little girl?"

"Daddy," Allegra said in the same tone she used for ice cream and gave him a sloppy kiss.

"I love you, too, sweetie." He kissed her on both cheeks and held her close to his chest. "You make Daddy so happy."

With a contented sigh, she put her head on his chest and pushed her tiny hand inside the lapel of his jacket.

His eyes threatened to roll back in his head from pure delight, but they had an audience, and he couldn't go all mushy over his little treasure.

"I thought you wanted to watch everything from home." He wrapped his other arm around Syssi. "What changed your mind?"

"I figured I could visit you during the break. The worst part is over, so I might stay for a few minutes when the trial starts." She turned to look up at him. "When are you planning to deliver your speech?"

"Lusha wants me to go first, right after her opening defense speech."

"That's a good plan. Who is leading the prosecution?"

"Jade."

Syssi frowned. "She said that she has no quarrel with these particular males and that she's leaving them to the other victims."

"That's all true, but she's still their leader, and that's her job. She will deliver the opening speech, but she doesn't plan on cross-examining the witnesses or doing any of the things that usually happen in a trial. No one is disputing the facts of what these males did. The defense's only job is to prove that they had no choice and that it is not right to punish them for what they were forced to do."

# Vanessa

As the prisoners were escorted off the stage, Vanessa looked at Lusha, who was writing furiously on her notepad. "I need to see Mo-red. Will you be okay here by yourself?"

The girl didn't even lift her head. "Yeah. You can go."

Vanessa gave Lusha another glance to allow her to change her mind, but she was absorbed in her last-minute notes.

They'd been watching the feed from the cameras at the ceremonial chamber and the assembly hall to gauge the crowd's response to Igor's punishment. Lusha must have seen something Vanessa hadn't because she started rewriting her opening speech when Kian announced the break.

"I won't be long," Vanessa said as she opened the door.

Mo-red and the others were in a classroom two doors down from the one she, Edna, and Lusha had commandeered for their use before the trial, and as she knocked on the door, a Guardian's face appeared in the door's window.

Smiling, he opened up for her. "Good morning, Vanessa."

It was almost noon, so technically, it was still morning, but it felt as if it was much later in the day. "Can I come in? I want to say hello to Mo-red."

"Sure." He motioned for her to go in. "I heard that congratulations are in order, so congratulations."

She ignored the slightly sarcastic tone, smiled, and continued toward Mo-red.

He opened his arms as she neared, and she walked right into them. "Are you okay?" she whispered as he cocooned her in his embrace.

"Now, I am. It hurts to be away from you."

She felt the same and wondered for the umpteenth time whether they had bonded or if it just powerful love. It wasn't supposed to be possible for them to bond, and she would even prefer a nonbonded relationship, but she couldn't deny what they both felt.

Cupping his cheek, she kissed him on the lips.

He stiffened but didn't let go of her. She knew that the Kra-ell were uncomfortable with public displays of affection, and they were not alone.

"It's okay. You can let go," she whispered.

"Never," he said out loud. "You are my mate, and I will hold on to you for as long as I can."

Someone clapped, probably one of the Guardians, and then others joined in.

It was embarrassing but kind of sweet.

"Well said," a Guardian told Mo-red. "Maybe there is hope for you after all."

Mo-red's smile was strained. "How's it looking out there?"

He knew his people better than she did, but perhaps he'd been too stressed to gauge their response.

"Lusha seems excited. So, she probably saw encouraging signs in the crowd. To me, they seemed almost impassive."

"They were putting on a front," Korvel said from behind her. "They were excited, and when it was done, most were disappointed that it wasn't a beheading. They were only marginally satisfied after Igor was put in the coffin and the heavy lid was put over it. We don't understand why Jade agreed to such a merciful punishment. He didn't deserve leniency. Did your boss demand that she put Igor in the clan's custody?

Vanessa was glad that Mo-red hadn't shared with the others what she'd told him in confidence, but perhaps it was time to inform the Kra-ell about the assassins and the twins and why they needed to keep Igor in stasis as a backup in case the Odus weren't able to decipher all the signals. A slightly modified version could work as well, but it wasn't her place to decide how much they were supposed to know.

It was Jade's decision.

Then again, they already knew some of it, so she could use that as an explanation.

"Igor knows how to find the other pods when they come online. We negotiated with him to tell us how he does it, so we will know when it happens, but we might need him to decipher the location. If Jade had beheaded him, everything he knew would have been lost forever. Jade was smart enough to realize that her need for vengeance wasn't worth the lives of the other settlers."

"Why would Igor know all that?" Madbar asked in heavily accented English. "Who is he?"

That was information that Vanessa couldn't share without an okay from Jade and probably also Kian. "Igor is a bad guy who worked for other bad guys. That's all I can tell you."

*Jade*

"You're quiet," Kagra whispered. "Are you okay?"

Jade shrugged. "I feel like a balloon that was pricked with a needle. It was full of hot air, floating up high, and now it's deflated." She forced a smile. "It's the adrenaline rush and the low that follows."

They were on the bus, heading back to the village. With Igor gone and the other prisoners already in there, there was no reason to leave anyone behind, and the bus was full of Guardians and Kra-ell.

Well, only six Kra-ell, including her and Kagra, and about a dozen Guardians including Dalhu, who wasn't officially on the force but seemed to be an honorary member.

The young males who had helped bring Igor to justice were in high spirits, talking excitedly about the trial and how they hoped their fathers and grandfathers would be exonerated because Igor's end would satisfy their mothers' and grandmothers' need for revenge.

Dalhu turned around. "I heard that stage actors get depressed when a show ends. They come down from the high."

"Speaking of acting, I liked your performance," Kagra said. "You were very impressive with all that smell of evil thing. Can you really do that? I mean, smell evil?"

"Sort of. I get an allergic reaction."

"Really?" Kagra made a face that indicated she thought he was joking.

"Yeah. My hands start twitching, and my fangs elongate even if the evil is not directed at me and makes no aggressive moves."

Bhathian chuckled. "You should have seen him when he took out the last evil dude. One of the best swordsmanship performances I've seen, and given that I've seen Brundar in action, that's saying something." The Guardian clapped Dalhu on the back. "And when that head rolled off, man, that was something."

Jade was curious to hear more, but perhaps some other day. She had too much on her mind for idle chitchat, and as the others continued talking about swords and missions, she tuned them out and closed her eyes.

She hoped Drova was okay and that Phinas was taking care of her.

He'd promised to look after the girl, and Jade had no doubt that he would do his best, but Drova was not easy to care for. She had a mile-long independent streak, and she might have pushed Phinas away.

Although, with Pavel unavailable, maybe she hadn't.

Jade sighed. Instead of worrying about things she had no control over, she should think about her trial opening statement.

She did not have much to say, so she hadn't even prepared a speech. There was no burning desire in her chest to see those males sentenced to death, but she had a duty to all her people, and those who'd been wronged needed someone to speak up for them.

Ironically, the most vocal vengeance seekers didn't want to act as prosecutors. They only wanted to be called to the witness stand and testify, or rather vent. They had been livid when she'd told them there was no need for them to testify because no one was disputing that the murders happened. Still, she might have to call one or two females to the witness stand to defuse their anger.

Besides, Lusha planned to have Pavel and others testify in defense of their fathers and grandfathers, and balance was needed.

The truth was that Jade was tired of it all, and if she could, she would go home, take a long shower, crawl into bed, and not come out for days.

When the bus pulled into its parking spot in the village's underground garage, she took a deep breath, rose to her feet, and squared her shoulders.

For a few more hours, she had to play the role of leader, and then she could collapse into Phinas's arms and let him take care of her.

"What are you smiling about?" Kagra asked.

"I'm thinking about the bath I will take once this trial is over."

Her second gave her a puzzled look. "Do you expect it to be over in one day?"

"I certainly hope so. We need to put this behind us so we can go on with our lives."

"This way, ladies," Bhathian led them to the elevators. "Everyone is still in the gym, and there are refreshments."

Jade gave him a lopsided smile. "Unless those refreshments include vodka, there is probably nothing for Kagra and me over there, and since we are about to start the trial, we should stay away from alcohol."

He shrugged. "Maybe they got blood in boxes with straws for you. You know, like tomato juice. It could be a nifty product for you. You could take it on trips, and no one would be any the wiser."

Jade wondered when Kian would allow her to leave the village unsupervised. At the moment, she had no wish to go anywhere, but once the trial was over and her people were settled, she could resume her business endeavors. She had no wish to go anywhere without Phinas, and he served Kalugal and couldn't come and go as he pleased, so there was that.

# Kian

K ian escorted Edna to her judge's bench. "The
stage is all yours."

"Thank you." She smiled, not looking at all
perturbed by the responsibility she was taking off his
hands.

Kian was glad to transfer the baton to Edna and let her
become the master of ceremonies from that point on.
Like Jade, he wanted this to be over with, so everyone
could return to living their lives. The Kra-ell needed to
find jobs to fill their days with, and he needed to get back
to taking care of business.

He nodded at Lusha and Jade as they got up on the stage
next.

During the break, Guardians prepared the place for the
trial. Edna's bench was on an elevated platform about a
foot above the stage. Below it, facing the semicircle of

prisoners, was a long desk with two chairs for Lusha and Jade.

When the time came, Vanessa, Kian, and the other witnesses would sit in the first row and be called upon.

Kian sat beside the therapist and watched her exchange looks and encouraging smiles with her mate while he was strapped to the chair.

"Do you really think that's necessary?" she asked quietly. "It sends the wrong message to the Kra-ell. It makes it look as if we are afraid of these males."

She had a point, but Kian wasn't sure that all of them were as harmless as Mo-red, and he couldn't chain some and not the others. That would really send the wrong message. Still, they all had security cuffs and could be disabled quickly.

That might be long enough to snap Edna's or Lusha's head. Edna wouldn't die from that, but Lusha would. Not that he thought any of them were that stupid, but desperate people sometimes did unpredictable things, and he didn't want to be responsible for that.

"I'm sorry, but I can't take the risk of one of them going nuts and attacking either Edna or Lusha, taking them hostage, or just harming them for the sake of vengeance."

"I profiled all of them, and none are cold-blooded killers."

Kian shook his head. "Until the jury votes, they remain chained."

When Jade and Lusha assumed their positions and the door to the assembly hall was closed, Edna used her gavel to get everyone's attention.

"My name is Edna," she began. "And I am the clan's judge. However, I will not judge these males; I will only guide the proceedings so this trial remains civilized and everyone who needs to be heard will be able to speak without being interrupted. The prosecution may present its case." She nodded at Jade.

The female wore the same leathers she'd worn to the crypt, the same combat boots, and the sword was still hanging at her side. She looked ready for war and made Kian question his decision to wear a suit to the trial.

"This trial wasn't my idea," Jade began in Kra-ell, and there was a slight delay as Lusha's translation came through Kian's earpieces. "Tom and Kian negotiated with me to allow it, and I grudgingly agreed because I owed them more than I could ever repay. It was especially difficult for me to agree that Valstar would also receive a trial instead of the swift execution I planned for him. But I have learned a few things since those first days of dealing with these descendants of the gods, who are all that their ancestors strove to be but never quite got to be." Jade paused as chuckles and murmurs started in the back rows where the immortals sat.

"Nice speech," Vanessa whispered. "But where is she going with it?"

Kian had a good idea, but he put a finger on his lips to shush her. Jade wasn't done.

"They are merciful to a fault," she said. "Their catacombs are full to bursting with their enemies, who are not dead, but in stasis because their leader is smart enough to realize that killing those males will just hasten the immortals' extinction." She glanced at the prisoners and then back at the Kra-ell sitting behind Kian. "For what those enemy warriors did to the clan, or planned to do and were defeated, they deserved to die ten times over, and yet, they were spared because of hope that one day they could be redeemed."

Someone behind him said something in Kra-ell, and a moment later, the translation sounded in his ear. "Our people can't go into stasis without a life pod, and our life pods are either lost or destroyed."

"I'm well aware of that," Jade said. "And that's not what I'm suggesting. I'm just showing you an example of doing things differently. I'm the prosecutor in this case, but since this is not a human trial or even an immortal trial, I can do whatever I please with my opening statement." She waved a hand at the accused. "These males killed our defenseless tribesmen on Igor's command. That's an undisputed fact. The defense will try to prove that they had no choice and were victims, like the rest of us. All I ask is that you listen and keep an open mind." She paused again and waved over the crowd. "There aren't many of us here, and we might be the only ones still alive on Earth. Think long and hard before deciding to have any more of us killed."

# Jade

J ade hadn't prepared the speech she'd delivered, but she was happy with what had come out of her mouth.

She was in a good mood after speaking to Drova and Phinas and seeing that her daughter was doing okay and looking like a weight had been lifted off her shoulders. It must have been difficult for her to anticipate her father's execution. Drova had hated Igor, but he had never abused her physically, so she didn't have any reason to want to see him dead.

Jade had told her he would be put in stasis and not killed, so the theatrics hadn't affected her, but it still must have been difficult.

With everything looking good on that front, Jade could focus on what she'd learned earlier in the clan's crypt and the impression it had left on her. She no longer felt vindictive, and it wasn't just because she'd finally gotten rid of Igor for good.

Dalhu's story of full acceptance by the clan despite what he had done was part of it, but what had left the most profound impression on Jade was the goddess's mercy toward her clan's enemies.

It had been obvious from Bhathian's tales that the leader of the clan who refused to execute the captured enemy soldiers wasn't Kian. She had gotten to know him well enough to figure out that he wouldn't have issued such a decree. His mother, the real head of the clan, had seen further than the immediate satisfaction of vengeance.

Jade shook her head.

Her admiration for the goddess was bordering on worship, and that was an affront to the Mother.

"Thanks for stealing my thunder," Lusha murmured as Jade sat down. "That was supposed to be my opening remarks." She got to her feet and walked over to address the assembly. "For those of you who don't know me, my name is Lusha, daughter of Iskar and Karina, and I am a human." She bowed theatrically with a small smile ghosting over her lips. "I'm sure that the irony of a human defending a bunch of purebloods is not lost on you, and you probably wonder why I bother?"

A few calls from the Kra-ell side confirmed Lusha's statement.

"Perhaps you think that they offered me a lot of money to do this?" She arched a brow and waited as several Kra-ell nodded.

"I'm not getting paid at all. I'm doing it for free. And do you know why?"

"Why?" Borga called from the audience.

"Because it's a great opportunity to show off."

As laughter erupted in the Kra-ell and the immortal areas of the crowd, Jade wondered what Lusha was doing. Since when did the defense attorney use the jury and the audience to make her opening speech?

Turning around, she glanced at Edna, but the judge seemed amused, and it didn't look like she was going to reprimand Lusha for her unorthodox delivery.

Smiling, Lusha lifted her hand and laid it over her chest. "Yes, I admit it, I'm a show-off, and I'm going to enjoy myself showing these haughty purebloods that in their darkest hours they need a human to save their necks." Jade watched on the big screen as Lusha's expression changed from amused to serious. "It's a lesson for all of us. In most situations, there is no real difference between us. Gods, immortals, purebloods, humans, and hybrids are all motivated by the same things." She lifted a finger. "We want our basic needs to be met." She lifted another. "We want to be safe." She lifted a third. "And we want the respect and appreciation of our community. That can only happen when people are judged based on merit and not the genes they were born with or their nutritional needs. But without free will, we can't judge people based on merit. Am I right? When a person's mind is subjugated to another's, neither good nor bad deeds should impact their merit score. Right? It's not their doing, not their decisions, and not their sacrifices."

"There is always wiggle room," a female from the audience said.

"Sometimes there is, and sometimes there isn't." Lusha walked over to the accused. "I'm going to prove to you that there was no wiggle room when it came to the big things, like to kill or let live. There was a tiny bit of wiggle room in some small things, and these males made good use of it. It wasn't much, but it was the best they could do under the circumstances, and they deserve credit for having the courage to disobey Igor even in the smallest of ways." She walked over to the edge of the stage and looked at the Kra-ell. "How many of you dared to disobey Igor?"

There were a few murmurs, but no one came forward.

That wasn't surprising.

Igor was smart, and the way he'd phrased his compulsion had left very little maneuvering room, if at all. Jade had a strong will and was a good compeller in her own right, so she could fight Igor's compulsion to some extent, finding loopholes and exploiting them to the fullest. But others weren't as strong or resourceful, and she didn't hold that against them.

People were born with different levels of ability. Some were destined to be leaders, while others were destined to follow, and there was no right or wrong about that. She'd never wanted to be a leader, but her attributes had made her one, so she had an obligation to use them for the greater good.

"Jade disobeyed Igor," Kagra said. "Without her, we wouldn't be here. I disobeyed too, but not to the same extent. I'm stubborn and willful, but I have nothing on Jade, and I wouldn't have been able to pull off what she did."

That was such unexpected praise from her second that Jade was lost for words, and all she managed was to dip her head in acknowledgment.

A grin split Lusha's face. "Jade is one of a kind in many ways. But despite being one of the few who could resist Igor's compulsion in small ways, she knows that if he had commanded her to kill her second or her daughter, she couldn't have resisted him. She would have done it." She turned to Jade. "Am I right?"

Jade nodded. "I would have fought the command with every fiber of my being, but I doubt I would have been able to resist for long. He would have kept pushing until my mind snapped, and then I would have taken my own life."

Lusha assumed a sad exaggerated expression. "No, you wouldn't have. Igor would have forbidden you to kill yourself, and you would have been forced to live with the guilt and the sorrow just like these males before you."

"Do they feel guilt and sorrow, though?" Rishana said from the crowd. "Or did they enjoy the fruits of what they had harvested by killing our males?"

Lusha looked like that was precisely the question she'd been waiting for. "Would it have mattered to you if Igor felt remorse for killing your males? If he went down on his knees and cried his eyes out, sobbing that he was sorry, would you have accepted a lesser punishment for him?"

The headshakes were unsurprising, and then Sheniya said, "He got a lesser punishment, and I still don't understand why Jade decided to show him mercy."

"It wasn't mercy," Jade said. "It was practicality. We need him in case the other pods come online. If we kill him, all he knows is lost. When he's in stasis, we can wake him up anytime we want and then put him back into his coffin."

# Kian

A Kra-ell female lifted her hand. "How come Igor knows how to find the other pods while no one else does?"

Kian had been expecting someone to ask that, and as Jade looked at him, he rose to his feet and climbed on the stage. He had intended to be the first to testify anyway, immediately after the opening statements, and Lusha had done such a fantastic job of delivering an entertaining performance that the script had to be adjusted very little for his part to come up next.

"I will answer that, as it concerns my ancestors." He'd chosen to speak vaguely about Igor's missions and their relation to him. "The Eternal King planned on assassinating his only heir, whom he had exiled to Earth for his part in the Kra-ell rebellion. The king smuggled Igor and an unspecified number of other enhanced assassins onto the settler ship. You know the rest. There was a malfunction, or maybe a sabotage, perpetrated by someone who wanted to thwart the king's plans, and the ship arrived seven thousand years behind schedule. In the meantime, the Earth-bound gods quarreled amongst themselves, and one of them dropped an advanced bomb on the rest while they were all assembled in the same building, doing Igor's job for him. Anyway, that's why Igor was equipped with the knowledge and ability to locate the other pods as soon as they went online. He was supposed to find the other assassins."

Kian had left Ahn, Annani, and the twins out of the story and the theory they'd come up with about the part the Eternal King's mate played in delaying the ship's arrival. Despite Vanessa's assurances, he wasn't sure that none of the Kra-ell in their midst were assassins.

For a long moment, there was a stunned silence, and then a barrage of questions ensued. Kian lifted his hand to stop them. "Suffice it to say that Igor found himself without a mission and improvised. We all know what he did, so there is no need to retell that story. We are here to determine the fate of these nine males, and I have a different tale for you, which is more relevant to their case."

The assembly hall fell quiet again, and the tension in the air was so heavy that he could practically taste it.

Remembering Amanda's advice to be himself and tell things like they happened, Kian took a deep breath. "I've spent many hours interrogating Igor and took all the necessary precautions. I wore earpieces that prevented the sound of his compulsion from traveling through my ears to my mind, and I ensured he couldn't grab me and yank those earpieces out. He was always behind bars or chained to the bed while I questioned him. But then we realized that we hadn't removed his tracker yet and that it needed to be done in case his handlers had a way of locating him. We didn't want the gods to send other assassins to finish the job. To do that, we had to put him into the MRI machine you are all familiar with now, and he had to go in without chains. We sedated him, took him into the parking garage, where a van with the device was waiting, and thought we had everything covered. We didn't account for his body's ability to neutralize the sedative. We did not know it was one of his enhancements."

"Did he try to escape?" asked one of the Kra-ell hybrids.

"He did. While he was in the van and supposedly drugged, I stayed outside with Jade and one of my body-guards. The doctor and my other bodyguard were inside. Igor neutralized the sedative, smashed the doctor's and the Guardian's heads against the MRI machine, leaped out of the van, and grabbed me."

Even though many in the audience already knew about the attack, gasps sounded all around.

"He pulled out my earpiece and ordered me to tell Jade and Brundar to drop their weapons and open the gate. I had no choice but to parrot the words he told me to say, and when Jade and Brundar didn't do as I commanded, he sank his fangs into my neck and started drinking my blood. Long story short, Jade leaped over, taking us both down, and then my bodyguard slashed Igor's throat."

Someone in the Kra-ell group started clapping, and then someone whistled and called out her name.

Kian let them express their admiration for their badass leader, and then lifted his hand and continued, "Igor's fangs tore out a big chunk of my neck, and I was in pain, but more than that, I was shaken to the core, and if you ask those who know me well, they will tell you that doesn't happen often."

A deathly silence spread over the assembly. It seemed as if everyone was holding their breath.

"I've been in some shitty situations that I had to claw myself and those with me out of, but I've never felt as helpless as I felt in those brief moments when Igor took over my will. I know this is nothing new to you because you've lived with it for so long, but it was terrifying to someone experiencing it for the first time. He told me not to move, and I couldn't even if my life depended on it. I was terrified that he would tell me to kill one of my bodyguards or both. They are like brothers to me, and if I was forced to do that, I knew I would not want to go on living and suffering the agony of guilt and remorse. But at the same time, I knew that he could just as easily prevent me from taking my own life, and that terrified me even more. I wouldn't want to spend immortality living with the pain of being forced to do something like that. It would be the worst hell anyone could have condemned me to."

Kian turned to face the accused. "These males didn't kill their best friends. They killed strangers, but they did so in the most disgraceful way imaginable to a Kra-ell. I do not doubt that they harbor enough shame and guilt to create their own hell or valley of the shamed among the living." He turned back to the audience. "If I had been forced to kill my best friend, would you have condemned me for it? Would his brother?" He looked from one harsh face to the next. "I think not."

# Vanessa

Kian had done so well that Vanessa was floating on a cloud of hope, but that soon evaporated as Jade called to the stage several of the older females who demanded to be heard.

They weren't as vehement as they had been in the interviews with her. However, they were still pretty full of hatred, vengeful, and unwilling to forgive.

Sheniya had said that a death penalty was warranted, but she echoed Jade's sentiment that it was not beneficial to the future of the Kra-ell on Earth. There were too few of them, and they needed genetic variety.

It wasn't a wholehearted endorsement, but it was better than what the others had said, and Vanessa held her fingers crossed.

When the prosecution was done, Lusha started calling up her witnesses.

Several other older females didn't want to see these males beheaded, and the children and grandchildren of the males testified on their behalf.

Borga hadn't been called to the stand, which was a good decision on Lusha's part, and then it was time for Toven's testimony to round up the defense.

He climbed up on the stand and looked at the rows filled with Kra-ell, making eye contact, smiling, and nodding. It was a great tactic to remind them that he knew them, that he had freed them from Igor's compulsion, and that he was their friend.

"My friends," he started. "Some of you know me as Tom, others know me as Toven, but you all know me as the guy whose compulsion ability made your liberation possible. So, you must agree that I know a thing or two about compulsion."

When murmurs of agreement sounded, Toven continued.

"All mind manipulation is vile and should be reserved only as a defensive measure, but compulsion is the worst because the person knows they are being forced to do things they don't want to do. It's not like hypnosis, which is more of a suggestion, and people will usually not obey a hypnotist's command to do something that goes against their core beliefs. Thralling is also more suggestive in nature, but on some people, it can be used in a similar way to compulsion."

Vanessa didn't know where he was going with that lecture about the different kinds of mind control. The Kra-ell were well versed in them and knew the differences.

"To free you from Igor's compulsion, I couldn't just remove it and free your minds. I had to override it with mine, which was extremely difficult. I couldn't have done it without the help of my mate, who is an enhancer. You've all met her." He smiled at Mia, and she waved her hand to greet them.

Toven moved a few feet to the right to stand closer to where Mia was sitting. "What I'm trying to say with my long-winded speech is that none of you could have resisted Igor's compulsion. What Kian said was right on the money. All of you, females and males alike, would have killed your children if Igor commanded you to do that. Thankfully, it didn't happen, but it was bound to at some point. Igor had the males of the other pods killed to even out the ratio of females to males. But he couldn't change the Kra-ell birth rate, and the next generation born to you was distributed along the normal Kra-ell ratio of about four males to one female. Before long, he would have culled the males to even up the numbers again. Can you imagine being commanded to kill them yourselves?"

Vanessa turned around and looked at the horrified expressions that even the Kra-ell couldn't suppress.

"I will not tell you to vote one way or another. I just want you to think about what I have just told you when you ponder the question of guilt and culpability. That's all I have to say." Toven turned around and walked down the stairs to sit at the edge of the first row next to Mia, who had parked her chair there.

Lusha got up and walked to the same spot Toven had stood on a moment ago. "Thank you, Toven." She clapped her hands. "We are all in your debt for freeing us from tyranny. It had not occurred to me before, but you are right. You saved us in the nick of time before Igor got any ideas about the young males of our community, whether pureblooded or hybrid."

# Mo-red

Toven's speech had resonated with Mo-red. He'd had the same fears about the future of his three sons, and he was pretty sure that he owed the gods for saving their lives.

He should offer Toven a life debt if he got free, but he needed Vanessa's permission to give it. As his mistress, she could forbid it.

Except, she would never do that. It wasn't her way, and he was so thankful for her that his heart was about to burst with love and appreciation. Throughout the trial he'd been watching her beautiful face as she listened to the various testimonies, and her expression had changed from hopeful to worried to hopeful again.

Lusha hadn't yet called any of the accused to the witness stand, and he wondered whether she would do that. She'd said that she wasn't sure and that it would depend on how the Kra-ell audience responded to the previous testimony. Lusha thanked Toven again, led the audience in a round of applause, and then addressed them again.

"I've debated whether to put these poor males on the stand so they would have a chance to defend themselves and plead their cases, but I think others have done an excellent job of doing it for them, and we don't need to put them through the ordeal. We've heard enough from both sides, and you have all the information to cast your vote. Since this involves the entire Kra-ell community, purebloods and hybrids alike, I want you all to be the jury, but I need you to approve this with a show of hands. Everyone who agrees that all Kra-ell should vote on this, please raise your hands."

Not everyone approved of Lusha's idea, but there were enough raised hands for a majority.

"Excellent." Lusha turned to Edna. "I transfer you into the capable hands of the clan's judge."

Edna rose to her feet and walked over to where Lusha had stood a moment ago.

"The testimony I've heard proves conclusively that the accused didn't have a choice and had to obey Igor's commands. They couldn't even choose their own death over killing others because they could not disobey. None of the testimony from those who lost loved ones has indicated that the accused derived pleasure from following Igor's command, and some even admitted that they saw the sorrow and revulsion in their eyes. The thing that you need to decide on is whether the accused deserve to die for being forced." She paused and took a couple of steps to the right. "The best parallel I found that might give you a different perspective on the issue was that some human cultures still execute rape victims. Do you think that is just?"

"It's not the same," Borga said.

"It is exactly the same. In those cultures, having a daughter or a sister who has been violated is shameful to her family. The victim is accused of encouraging the violation. Do you think that's the case?" Edna didn't wait for an answer. "To you, these males represent shame, a constant reminder of a terrible past, of watching help-lessly as your tribesmen were slaughtered. You'd rather get rid of them, so you never have to look upon their faces again and be reminded of your suffering. But is it just?"

Mo-red didn't like Edna's harsh speech, but he knew she was correct. Looking at the Kra-ell in the audience, he saw in their expressions that they realized that too.

Igor had turned them into broken people; even Vanessa couldn't put them back together. The damage was too extensive to fix.

"So, what do you suggest, Judge?" Sheniya asked. "That we let them go free as if nothing happened?"

Lusha rushed to Edna's side. "Community service is a win-win for everyone. The accused can redeem them-selves by serving the community."

Mo-red loved the suggestion.

He would muck out barns and sleep on a bed of nails if that would gain him redemption, not only in the eyes of others but his own. He was consumed by guilt even though he hadn't had a choice, and he would welcome anything that would lessen that guilt.

"What kind of community service?" Rishana asked.

Lusha spread her arms. "Anything that the community needs. Take care of the animals, work as busboys in the restaurant, tend to the plants, collect trash, and trim the bushes. There are dozens of tasks they could do."

"For how long?" Azar asked.

"For as long as the jury decides." Lusha moved to the center of the stage. "I suggest we all take a break and leave the jury here to deliberate among themselves. We will reconvene in an hour."

*Jade*

As the immortals left the assembly hall to give the Kra-ell privacy and the prisoners were taken to one of the classrooms, Jade stepped down from the stage and joined her people.

When the hall's doors closed and they were alone, arguments began almost immediately between those in favor of execution and those in favor of community service.

They would still be there in the morning or even the following night if she let it go on. Lusha was right, and those entrenched in their beliefs would not change their minds.

"People!" Jade lifted her hands. "Arguing is pointless. We will vote, and the minority will accept the majority's decision."

"I know what the majority will decide," Rishana spat. "And I disagree with their decision. I don't want these males in our lives. It's a new beginning for us, and I don't want to see their faces ever again and be reminded of being a victim and of everything I suffered."

It seemed that Lusha was right again, and it was about wanting to erase the past and the shame it evoked. Could the clan's therapist help eradicate those feelings?

Probably not.

By mating Mo-red, Vanessa had chosen which side she was on, and those who wanted to see him and the others dead wouldn't even talk to her.

As Rishana's supporters joined her protest, Jade lifted her hand again to silence them. "You need to decide how you want to live your lives. If you want our community to conduct itself democratically, you need to accept that the majority might not vote the way you like. If we return to our traditional roots, you will need to accept whatever decision I make, which doesn't really help you since I would vote with the majority. You might only achieve the desired results if we live in lawless anarchy, and everyone does whatever they please."

Rishana opened her mouth to argue, closed it, and opened it again. "Let's vote. I hope that I'm wrong and the majority will side with me."

"Good decision." Jade gave her a curt smile. "First, let's vote on execution versus community service. Suppose the majority chooses community service, as I predict it will. In that case, we will vote on how long and other particulars."

When Rishana and Sheniya nodded and sat back down, Kagra joined Jade facing their people.

"All in favor of community service, please raise your hands." Kagra lifted hers.

Jade joined her, and so did about eighty percent of their people. If the jury had been comprised solely of the original settler females, the result of the vote wouldn't have turned out so favorably for the accused.

"As you can see, the majority decided on community service, but don't put your hands down yet. I want Kagra to make an accurate count and record the results. I don't want anyone contesting the results in the future."

After the count was done, it was time to vote for the duration of the community service and what it would entail.

"At least thirty years," Sheniya said. "Not a day less."

"Fifty," Rishana suggested. "Given they have lorded it over some of us for over a century, that's only fair."

Soon everyone was suggesting a different number of years, and if Jade didn't stop it, they would keep arguing for hours, and she wanted this done.

She lifted her hand to stop the chatter. "Fifty years with an option of shortening the sentence for good behavior. I will decide on what that service will be according to the community's needs, including the clan. We owe them an enormous debt, and I don't have a problem with starting to repay it with the labor of these males."

"Who will decide on the question of shortening their sentence?" Pavel asked.

"For now, I decide. In the future, I hope we will have an elected council, and it will decide on the big issues. I don't intend to have a meeting about every little thing."

Her people were not ready for full democracy yet, and she didn't want to have to put everything to a vote. She liked how Kian ran things, and until she figured out her own way, she could start by emulating his style.

After several people murmured half-hearted protests, the majority voted to accept her proposal, and it was done.

When Kagra finished counting the votes, Jade smiled at her watch. "We've done it with five minutes to spare. Congratulations."

# Kian

The air was thick with anxious anticipation as they all waited for the accused to be returned and seated in their iron chairs.

Standing next to Jade, Kian was tempted to lean over and have her whisper in his ear her people's decision. She emitted no emotional scents as usual, and her expression was as guarded and impassive as always.

Regrettably, he would have to stifle his curiosity and wait to hear the voting results along with everyone else.

When all the prisoners were seated, and the assembly doors were closed, Jade turned around to face the accused. "Rejoice," she said in Kra-ell, and Lusha translated in his earpiece. "You were sentenced to community service. Fifty years of doing whatever you are told with the option to shorten it for exemplary behavior."

The Kra-ell were masters of the poker face, but the accused couldn't hide their relief. The release of tension was so obvious that even Kian, with his limited empathic ability, could see it and sense it.

Jade turned to him. "We owe you and your clan an enormous debt. Therefore, the accused will perform any tasks your community could benefit from. I'll ensure that they perform those duties to the best of their abilities."

"Thank you, Jade. But for now, let's release these males, so they can reunite with their children and grandchildren." He motioned for the Guardians to unchain the prisoners and turned to Lusha, who stood grinning on Jade's other side. "Congratulations to the defense team for a job well done."

She dipped her head. "Thank you. I couldn't have done it without Vanessa's help and your and Toven's testimony."

He turned to Edna. "Thank you for steering this trial in the right direction."

"My pleasure." She extended her hand to Jade. "Well done, Jade. I'm sure you had a lot to do with how your people voted. I know how difficult it is to let go of a vendetta, but you did it because it was the right thing to do and not just for the accused. It was the right thing to do for the future of your people."

"I agree." Kian turned to the prisoners. "Congratulations on the best outcome you could have hoped for. I wish you many happy years of service and welcome you into our community."

Mo-red, who had been freed first, pushed to his feet, walked over to Kian, and dipped his head. "You have my eternal gratitude. You made it clear that a life vow would make you uncomfortable, so I'm not going to make it, but I'm going to act as if I did."

Kian extended his hand. "For now, the only vow I need from you is to make Vanessa happy, but since you've already made that vow, we are good. Later, we will address what it means to be a village resident, and I will accept your oaths of loyalty then."

Mo-red put his hand over his chest. "I will defend the village and everyone in it with my life."

Kian nodded. It was as good as a life vow, just without using the vow word.

As Vanessa and Pavel rushed to congratulate Mo-red, the other former prisoners followed Mo-red's example, came to thank Kian, and offered him promises of gratitude.

He shook hands with them, smiling and nodding, but he felt uncomfortable. He hadn't done it to earn himself nine willing slaves. He had testified to prevent their deaths.

The last to approach him was Valstar, who looked as if he was ready to keel over. "Thank you." He turned his gaze to Jade. "And thank you. I've never expected to be given another chance, and I promise not to make you regret it in any way. I will make it my mission to prove that showing me mercy was a wise decision."

Jade nodded. "It was not mercy. Three experts told me that you were a victim, like the rest of us, and that you did your best under the circumstances. I trust these experts, but I've experienced your best and worst, so I'm not a hundred percent sold on that assessment, and I will be watching you closely."

Valstar smiled. "I expect nothing else." He bowed his head to her and then rushed to his daughter and granddaughter, who had joined the other families on the stage.

Turning to Jade, Kian let out a breath. "Thank the Fates, this is over. What's the next step?"

She shrugged. "We take them topside and show them the village?"

"Yeah, that's a good idea. Where are they going to stay? Did you have a chance to think about it?"

"For now, they can stay with their relatives. I'll speak with Ingrid about finding them lodging, but I don't want them to live together. I want to spread them among the rest of our community. It will take some maneuvering to get them settled with the right people who will keep an eye on them."

Kian arched a brow. "Are you still suspicious of them?"

"I'm cautious." She smiled. "I'm sure you can understand that."

"Naturally."

# Mo-red

Mo-red wondered how his legs were still supporting him. The wave of relief that had washed over him after Jade's announcement hadn't left yet and was still coursing through him, making him feel faint.

"You can come to stay with me, Alexi, and Jared," Pavel said.

Vanessa wrapped a possessive arm around Mo-red's middle. "Did you forget that we are mated? Your father is staying with me."

"Right." Pavel smiled sheepishly. "I didn't forget that. I forgot that your customs are different than ours."

Her hand squeezed Mo-red's thigh. "I suggest we beat the crowds and get to the elevators before everyone rushes out." She turned her face up and kissed his cheek. "I can't wait to show you the village."

Pavel fell into step with them on Mo-red's other side. "Yeah, you're going to love it. You used to complain about how cold it was in Karelia. We are in Southern California, where it is sunny three hundred and twenty days out of the year."

As they went down the steps of the stage, Borga blocked their way.

"Congratulations." She offered Mo-red her hand. "I'm glad the vote went your way." She glanced at Pavel. "I voted for the community service."

"I know," their son said. "I saw you."

"Thank you." Mo-red shook her hand. "I appreciate your support."

He knew it had been given grudgingly, but it was given, and that was all that mattered.

Borga nodded. "Sheniya and Rishana and some of the others are unhappy, and they will try to make your and your friends' lives miserable. I would watch my back if I were you." She looked both ways before leaning closer to him. "As much as we hated Igor's compulsion, it wasn't all bad. It prevented us from killing each other. I don't know how strong Toven's compulsion is and if it will protect you from other Kra-ell."

Vanessa's arm tightened around his waist. "Are you seriously suggesting that those females might take the law into their own hands and try to kill Mo-red and the others?"

Borga's smile was cold and vicious. "We are Kra-ell, and this is our way. Any of these females can legally and morally invoke her right to fight any males in a duel to the death or choose a male champion to issue the challenge for them."

"I'll speak to Jade about that," Vanessa said. "Any Kra-ell who wants to be part of our community needs to adopt new rules of conduct. This village is a sanctuary of peace and cooperation. It is not a place of violence, and such displays will not be tolerated."

Borga nodded. "Of course. But it's a transition period, and until new rules are made and enforced, it would be wise for Mo-red and the others to watch their backs."

"Thank you for the warning, Mother," Pavel said. "I will pass it on to the Guardians. Would you like to join us for a tour of the village?"

Her lips turned up in a mocking smile. "No, thank you." Borga shifted her gaze to Mo-red. "See you around."

Next to him, Vanessa was practically vibrating with either anger or irritation or a combination of both.

When Borga turned and walked away, Mo-red took Vanessa's hand and squeezed it lightly. "Don't take her too seriously. She just wanted to poke holes in my happiness."

"I know," Vanessa hissed. "I'm trying really hard to be understanding and sympathetic to her feelings, but she has just threatened my mate. I'm a mated immortal female first and a psychologist second." She cast Pavel an apologetic glance. "I'm sorry. I know that you care deeply for your mother."

"That's okay." Pavel resumed walking. "I think she meant well and wanted to warn my father of the negative feelings some of the other females still harbor, but her delivery could have used a little more finesse." He chuckled. "Except, very few of us even know what finesse means, let alone how to employ it. That's one of those cultural differences that we still need to work on."

Pavel's words were meant for Vanessa's ears, but Mo-red heard, and he knew Borga's warning shouldn't be taken lightly. The females who were unhappy with the majority vote were likely to try to get their vengeance.

As they reached the elevators, a large group of people was waiting to get in, most of them immortals. They were cordial, smiling, and congratulatory, but Mo-red also saw them glancing at his cuffs to reassure themselves that he was restrained. It would take time until he and the others could become trusted members of the community, and it would take a lot of work, but he was looking forward to all of it.

# Vanessa

Damn, Borga had rained on Vanessa's parade and had spoiled their joyful mood with threats disguised as warnings.

Instead of basking in the pleasure of their victory and the happy excitement of the surprise waiting for Mo-red at their house, Vanessa was now hyper-vigilant, and as the elevator doors opened at the pavilion level, she half expected assassins to jump them.

"Relax." Mo-red's thumb rubbed over hers. "Even if they are planning something, they won't dare do anything yet, and when they do, they won't ambush me. They will issue an official challenge."

"Are you sure?"

He shrugged. "It's not the Kra-ell way to stab someone in the back. The honorable thing to do is to face your opponent face to face in a duel. Still, given what I've done and how I've done it, they might rationalize that I don't deserve the courtesy of a fair fight."

At least he was being honest with her and wasn't trying to sugarcoat anything, but it was a reminder that the trial hadn't exonerated him and that he was guilty of everything he'd been accused of. He just hadn't been responsible for his actions.

"That's not very reassuring but thank you for being honest with me."

"Always, my love." Mo-red surprised her, saying the word with such ease and in his son's company. "I'll never tell you non-truths or half-truths. We are a team."

It felt good to hear him say that.

She rewarded him with a bright smile. "Yes, we are, and we are invincible. Those vindictive females will have to go through me to get to you, and I dare them to try."

Usually, she was a nonviolent, levelheaded person. Still, she was so angry right now that she fought back frustrated tears.

The stress of the trial, combined with her whirlwind romance with Mo-red, must have taken its toll and disturbed her equilibrium. The only other time she had cried at the drop of a hat was when she'd been pregnant with Jackson, but since there was no way that she was pregnant now, it must be the stress.

The Kra-ell males knew right away when conception happened, so Mo-red would have known if she'd conceived and told her.

He stopped in his tracks and turned to her. "Please, don't say things like that. These females are dangerous. I can handle them if they come at me, but only if you are out of harm's way."

Vanessa shook her head. "Let's not talk about that right now. I want to show you the village, and I want us to enjoy the walk to our home."

Our home. It felt so right to say that. Except, her house hadn't felt like her base for a long while now.

The sanctuary had become her home, but she couldn't take Mo-red there. Even if she could, she had promised to help the Kra-ell heal their traumas, so returning to the sanctuary full-time wasn't an option any time soon, if ever again.

Vanessa tried to ignore the small malicious voice in her head, whispering that she shouldn't help the females who sought to harm her mate, but she would take the high road and do the right thing even if it wasn't easy.

"What a beautiful place you have here," Mo-red's voice pulled her out of her head. "It's so green and sunny."

She hadn't been paying attention and hadn't registered that they had walked out of the pavilion and were standing in front of the village square.

"Sometimes it gets too sunny." She led their small group to the café, which was deserted because most of the clan had been in the assembly hall up until a few minutes ago.

Mo-red lifted his face to the sun and smiled. "I love it." He turned to look at her. "I don't think I've ever said love so many times."

"Or ever," Pavel said.

Lusha sighed. "I love it here too, and I don't want to go back to Safe Haven, but I can't stay here."

"Why not?" Pavel asked.

"The only humans in the village are the grandparents of Toven's mate and a few Dormants who are still awaiting transition. I'm not a Dormant, and I'll always be just human. There is nothing for me here." She smiled at him. "I should be among my own kind."

Pavel nodded. "I get it, but you're a celebrity now. Don't you want to stay and enjoy your fame for a while?"

Lusha chuckled. "Given that several of the Kra-ell females are very upset about the results of this trial, I don't know if I should. It might not be safe for me."

# Mo-red

Mo-red was glad they had left the assembly hall ahead of the crowd. The pathways meandering through the pastoral village were mostly devoid of people, and so far, they had only encountered one immortal female on the way to Vanessa's house.

She'd smiled, murmured congratulations, and hadn't seemed concerned or frightened about meeting a condemned criminal. Surprisingly, the immortals didn't view him and the other Kra-ell former prisoners any differently than the rest of their people.

Former prisoner. The words warmed his soul as much as the sun's rays warmed his skin.

He was free.

Sort of.

"This is the original phase of the village." Vanessa waved her arm around. "Since then, three more have been built.

Phase two was supposed to house clan members who currently live in different locations, but since they are not interested in moving in yet, or in the foreseeable future, that's where your people are staying. Kalugal and his men live in their own section, which was built after phase two, and phase three is where Kian, the council, and most of the Guardians live. It was completed only recently, and I was offered a house there, but since I was hardly ever home and stayed in the sanctuary most of the time, I decided to stay in the old village and save myself the hassle of moving." She smiled at him. "It must have been a premonition because you wouldn't have been allowed in phase three. It's a secure section inside the most secure location on this planet."

"Is it?" Lusha asked. "I mean, there must be safer places than this." She looked up at the sky. "How are you hiding from airplanes and satellites?"

Vanessa laughed. "Don't ask me. Our William is a true genius, and he designed a camouflaging system that makes us invisible from above. We also don't have any street lights at night, and all the windows have automatic shutters, so there is no visible light from the windows either. It's not a problem for immortals who have excellent night vision, but it is for the few humans who live here. On cloudy nights, they have to use small flashlights."

Lusha snorted. "Now you tell me? When you were staying with Mo-red at the keep, I was afraid to leave the house at night unless I had an escort. They must have thought I was afraid of the dark."

"I doubt that," Pavel said. "You fearlessly manipulated the audience during the trial. I don't know if I would have had the guts to turn the proceedings into an entertaining show, and even if I had the courage, I lack the skill."

Mo-red frowned.

He'd noticed before the appreciative looks Pavel had been sending Lusha's way, but he'd dismissed them as gratitude.

Could it be more than that?

Hopefully, his son wasn't infatuated with the human. She was a lovely girl, smart, friendly, and pretty, and if she were immortal or Kra-ell, she could have been perfect for Pavel. She could give him smart hybrid children, but she couldn't be his mate.

A couple of weeks ago, Mo-red wouldn't have thought it a problem, and he would have been glad to see Pavel interested in a female who was close to his age and who didn't carry any of Igor's cursed genes. But now that he knew what it felt like to have a mate, to love her with the ferocity of the sun, and to be loved in return with the same ferocity, he wanted no less for his sons.

Lusha smirked. "Yeah, I was good. I bet I could make a fortune out in the human world." She looked at Vanessa. "I just need to convince your boss that I'm not a security risk, so he will let me leave on my own."

"Give it time, Lusha." Vanessa turned into the walkway of one of the houses. "Kian is super careful, but he is not unreasonable."

Pavel didn't look happy about Lusha's aspirations. "Where would you go? And what about your family? Wouldn't you miss your mother at least?"

She shrugged. "I would come to visit. Most adult humans don't live near their parents. You are supposed to leave the nest and make a life for yourself."

Pavel shook his head. "I would love to leave for a little while to study at university, or to travel, or just to try new things, but once I have children, I will need a community to raise them."

Mo-red's heartbeat accelerated. "Are you planning on making me a grandfather?"

He couldn't wait.

A grandchild born free in the village would give him the opportunity to express all the feelings he'd had to stifle while his sons had been growing up in Igor's compound. He could hold the baby, bounce the toddler on his knees, and teach the child to hunt.

"Not anytime soon." Pavel clapped his back.

"It's not really up to you," Mo-red said. "The Mother decides when it's time."

"Then I hope she's not in a hurry either." Pavel climbed the steps to Vanessa's front porch.

"I would love a grandchild," Vanessa said. "But Jackson and Tessa are still so young. It will be a long time before I'm blessed with one."

She cast Mo-red a conspiratorial smile before opening the door, and his heart skipped a beat as he waited for her to say something that would make him the happiest male in the universe. Did she want to have a child with him?

Immortal fertility was extremely low, but they had a fertility doctor in the village who could help them conceive.

"Welcome home, my love." She kissed his cheek and motioned for him to go inside.

# Vanessa

Had Mo-red suspected something?

Vanessa couldn't decipher the look on his face, but his heart rate had suddenly accelerated, so perhaps he'd figured out where his other two sons had gone and why they hadn't escorted him on his first tour of the village.

Tessa and Jackson had left the assembly hall together with Vasily and Elias to prepare the surprise welcome party for Mo-red.

Well, it was more than a party.

In an act of pure optimism, the boys had ordered new clothing, toiletries, and books for their father, and they had rushed to their place to get the things to her house.

When Mo-red entered the primary bedroom, he would discover his things hanging in the closet and folded in the drawers and an entire shelf on her bookcase with titles he would be excited to read.

"Welcome home, Mo-red!" Tessa blew a kazoo whistle.

It must have served as the war horn. As the others joined their whistles to the cacophony and threw glitter bombs, Vanessa clapped her hands over her ears.

What had Tessa been thinking?

It would take her hours to clean up all the glitter, and she had better plans for Mo-red's first night in their house.

Standing in the middle of the living room, Mo-red looked shell-shocked. "When? How?"

"They rushed ahead of us." Vanessa led him to the couch.

"Time for a toast." Jackson walked over and handed them two glasses filled to the brim with whiskey.

"Indeed." Mo-red lifted his glass with a shaky hand. "I never expected a surprise like that. Thank you."

Her mate didn't like surprises, but she had a feeling that he loved this one.

Pavel grinned. "You've never gotten a good surprise before. It's about time you did." He lifted his glass. "To a long and happy life, Father. May we celebrate many more joyous occasions in our new home."

Mo-red lifted his glass. "To my beloved mate, to Lusha, to my amazing sons, and to Jackson and Tessa, may the Mother reward you all with her blessings." He clicked it with Vanessa's glass and then with everyone else in the room. "Jackson and Tessa, I want to thank you for welcoming me into your family and for arranging this beautiful welcome home party."

"It was our pleasure," Tessa said. "I'm so glad that everything turned out as well as we hoped."

"Tessa did most of the work," Jackson admitted. "I just brought the food for those who eat normal stuff."

Pavel nudged him with his elbow. "To us, blood is normal."

"I know." Jackson smiled at his new stepbrother. "It still doesn't make it any less gross." He made a gagging motion. "There are blood bags in the freezer."

Vanessa exchanged an amused look with Mo-red.

Since he'd started drinking from her, he rarely needed to supplement with animal blood. He claimed that hers was so rich only a little bit of it was needed to fulfill his nutritional needs.

Taking the half-full glass with her, Vanessa sagged against the couch cushions. She hadn't realized how tense her muscles had been until the tension started to abate. It felt as if she'd run a marathon or two.

It was over, they were home, and the only thing that still needed to be solved was what to do about her work in the sanctuary. She would have to divide her time between the Kra-ell and her girls, and that would require a commute to the sanctuary at least three times a week.

Mo-red leaned back next to her. "What are you thinking about?"

"The sanctuary. The person I left in charge is doing better than I could have ever hoped for, but she's not a psychologist, and she can't keep running the place without me. I will have to spend at least three to four days out of every week there, and I hate the thought of leaving you alone in the village."

Mo-red paled. "I don't want to be separated from you for so long. I'm not sure I will survive it."

"It's the bond," Tessa said. "In the beginning, it's impossible to be apart from your mate for more than a few hours, but it gets easier with time." She cast a loving look at Jackson. "Still difficult, but tolerable."

He chuckled. "It's not like I go anywhere without you. I never leave you for more than half a day."

Vanessa didn't bother to correct them. She and Mo-red couldn't be bonded, but it sure felt like they were. They were still a very new couple, and they were in love, but it was impossible to tell whether they had formed the mystical bond. Right now, they were still on a high from the victory and the enormous relief of no longer having an executioner's sword hovering over Mo-red's neck. But if the feelings persisted beyond a couple of months, she would have to reevaluate her beliefs.

Tessa pouted. "Half a day is twelve hours, and sometimes it feels like an eternity." She put her glass down on the coffee table and turned to Vanessa. "I talked with Ella and asked her if she and Julian were willing to move into the sanctuary for a while. You know, only until you are done helping the Kra-ell. Ella said that they would be glad to help and stay there for as long as they are needed."

Vanessa shook her head. "I appreciate the offer, but it won't work."

"Why not?" Tessa asked. "Julian is doing very well in the halfway house."

"He is, but those girls are on their way to full recovery and can tolerate having a male around them. The ones in the sanctuary are a different story. Besides, Julian is a medical doctor, not a therapist."

# Mo-red

T essa didn't back down after Vanessa's dismissal, and as Mo-red watched her square her shoulders and jut out her chin, he realized that her delicate appearance was misleading.

The young immortal had a backbone.

"I don't think Julian will have any trouble with the girls in the sanctuary. Ella is managing the fundraising activities for the charity that finances it, and the girls know her and trust her. They also know that she was a victim of trafficking herself, so they regard her as one of their own. When she presents Julian as her husband, they will not be afraid of him. Besides, he is so sweet that they would know he's trustworthy even without Ella vouching for him."

"Ella and Julian are not married," Jackson said. "So, she can't present him as her husband."

Tessa cast him a reproachful look. "You are not helping."

He lifted his hands. "All I'm saying is that she shouldn't lie to them. She can present him as her fiancé."

"That's not as good as a husband, but you are right. Ella shouldn't lie to the victims. They've been lied to and manipulated enough in their lives."

"Thank you." Jackson dipped his head in mock supplication. "I'm glad that you agree with me."

"I do, but I still think that Ella and Julian will do great managing the sanctuary."

Mo-red hoped that Tessa would succeed in convincing Vanessa because he truly couldn't imagine being without her for days on end. Whenever she had left for the village to conduct her interviews, he'd felt as if the cord connecting them was stretched taut, and the longer she stayed away, the stronger the pull was until it became unbearable.

"Julian is a sweetheart," Vanessa said. "And I'm sure that my girls will see that, if not right away, then with some gentle coaxing. But why put them through it? They are much more comfortable around women. Besides, Julian is not a psychologist, and they need me. I can't abandon them like that. I told them I would be back as soon as my emergency was over. Breaking my promise is out of the question."

"Can I come with you?" Mo-red asked. "If I let my hair loose, I will look more feminine and less threatening."

He'd heard the Guardians saying that the Kra-ell all looked the same to them and that they sometimes couldn't distinguish between the males and the females. He couldn't understand why they would think that, but perhaps it would work to his advantage.

Vanessa regarded him with an arched brow. "I don't think that will help much. You are six and a half feet tall, and although you are slim, your body is packed with muscle. They would need to be blind to think that you are feminine."

"I don't know whether to take that as a compliment or not."

She rolled her eyes. "Of course, it's a compliment. Do the Kra-ell males like it when people confuse them with females and vice versa?"

He chuckled. "We just think it's silly, because to us the differences are obvious. Do I look more threatening, though?"

"No. I think your females look scarier than the males. They are more openly aggressive." She puffed out her chest and assumed an angry expression. "Some of them walk with a bully-like swagger."

It was true, but it was a good thing. The females hadn't walked like that in Igor's compound, and now they were overcompensating for years of being subjugated.

"They are finally free," he said quietly. "Some are probably taking it too far, but after so long of living under Igor's thumb, they deserve some swagger. It's probably good for them."

"What about the eyes?" Tessa asked. "Will you cover them with sunglasses at all times? You can say that they are super-sensitive and that you have to wear protective glasses."

"Or I can forgo the glasses and claim that I was born with a deformity. That could gain me some sympathy, right?"

Vanessa sighed and put her hand on his thigh. "You can't come with me to the sanctuary. Kian will not allow you to leave the village anytime soon."

His spirits fell. "Yeah, I guess you are right." He took her hand and held it to his chest. "How long will you be gone?"

"I'll try to limit it to no more than ten hours a day. I will commute to the sanctuary, and given that it's over an hour's drive in each direction, I will probably be unable to make it any shorter than that."

Mo-red swallowed. "It's going to be difficult, but we will manage. I'm so grateful to be here that I really shouldn't complain about missing my mate while she's at work."

"Don't worry about it." Jackson refilled Mo-red's glass. "You will be so busy slaving away with whatever tasks you are assigned that time will fly by."

# Jade

As Jade made her way to the village square with Drova on one side and Phinas on the other, she didn't know how to start a conversation with her daughter.

Phinas was quiet, and so was Drova.

Casting furtive glances at her, Jade hoped to gauge her mood from her expression and her posture, but her daughter had mastered the Kra-ell impassive look and loose stance that revealed nothing.

Asking Drova whether she was okay would be met with a shrug, and asking her how she felt about her father's entombment would sound too much like the kind of questions the clan therapist asked.

"Are we going home?" Phinas asked.

"Not yet." Jade forced a smile at a group of hybrids. "I need to make sure that each one of the former prisoners has a place to stay tonight. But you can go ahead. I'll come home when I can."

Phinas gave her a loaded look. "Kagra can take care of the lodging arrangements. You and Drova should go home, get things off your chests, and if you need to get drunk to loosen up, I can hook you up with a steady supply of vodka with cranberry juice."

That got a grin out of her daughter. "I knew there was a reason I liked you."

He stopped and turned to her. "What, it wasn't my charming personality? You only appreciate me for my lax attitude toward underage booze consumption?"

"It's both." Drova threaded her arm through his and leaned her head on his shoulder. "You're okay."

Drova's public display of affection for Phinas was so shocking that Jade nearly stumbled. It was also more praise than Jade had ever heard from her daughter, and she was jealous but also pleased. Phinas had managed to win Drova's heart, which was a more difficult feat than making Jade fall in love with him.

She shook her head.

The word love still felt unnatural on her tongue or even in her mind, but she was growing used to it.

"I'll call Kagra." Jade pulled out her phone and called her second-in-command.

Kagra answered right away. "I've been looking for you. Where are you?"

"I'm at the village square, but I'm heading home with Phinas and Drova. Can you make sure that each of the prisoners has a place to stay tonight? I'll take care of a more permanent solution tomorrow."

"Sure. I was looking for Ingrid to ask her what else was available, but I couldn't find her. I don't think she was in the assembly hall."

Jade didn't know why so many clan members had shown up. It must be pretty dull in their village for them to seek thrills in a courtroom.

If she hadn't had to attend, she wouldn't have done so voluntarily.

"I'll call her tomorrow. Just take care of the sleeping arrangements for tonight."

"Will do, boss." Kagra ended the call.

When they got home, Phinas made good on his promise and poured cocktails for her and Drova and a shot of whiskey for himself.

"Come." Jade strode toward the couch and sat down. "We need to talk about your father."

Drova snorted. "Now you want to talk about him? Don't you think this is a little late? You should have asked me how I felt about it before you sentenced him to stasis and put him in a coffin."

Jade frowned. "I thought that stasis would be easier for you to stomach than an execution."

"It was, but you never asked my opinion about what should be done with him. You only told me that he would be put in stasis. I didn't know about the sarcophagus or the chains."

"I didn't know either," Jade admitted. "Kian is as good at sharing information as I am, which means he's really bad at it. He didn't tell me about the sarcophagus, but I thought it was a nice touch. That heavy lid and those chains are needed in case Igor's enhancements include the ability to spontaneously emerge from stasis."

"Yeah, I figured that was the reasoning behind them." Drova took a sip from her cocktail and grimaced. "That's not even tasty. Why do you drink it?

"I like it, and if you don't, don't drink it. You're too young for alcohol anyway."

"I'm not human, Mother. Their rules don't apply to us, and we don't have rules against drinking at any age."

That was true, and Jade added it to the long list of items she needed to address. Did she even care at what age young Kra-ell started drinking?

Not really. Drunkenness had never been a problem in her old compound or in Igor's. Kra-ell sometimes drank to excess, but it had never led to boisterous behavior like it did in humans. It only made them feel sick.

Shrugging, Drova took another sip. "I'll give it another chance."

"Ladies," Phinas said. "This conversation should be about feelings." He turned to Jade. "How do you feel about Igor's entombment?"

"Not as great as I thought I would," she admitted.

Drova grimaced. "You didn't get to chop off his head. That's why you are disappointed."

"No, that's not it." Jade brushed a stray strand of hair behind her ear. "I thought that the entombment would ease the pain, that it would fill the hole in my heart, but it didn't, and I don't think that chopping off his head would have done a better job of it. All I feel is exhaustion." She sighed. "But I'm glad this is behind us. We can finally bury the past and concentrate on building a future."

"Very good," Phinas approved. "Now, Drova. How do you feel about Igor's entombment?"

"Conflicted." She slanted a glance at Jade. "I didn't really hate him, you know. I resented him, and I stupidly hoped to one day hear him say that he was proud of me. And then I learned what a monster he really was, that he murdered my half-brothers and other males in cold blood, and I no longer wanted anything from him." She swiveled the ice cubes in her drink, watching the swirls they created. "The thing is, I still hoped for a miracle, for some logical explanation that would make sense to me." She smiled sadly. "It would have been nice if someone else could have been blamed for what he did, like his pod buddies that got to walk by blaming everything on him. But there was no one else to blame." She looked at Jade with eyes that suddenly seemed ancient. "When you are the leader, the buck stops with you."

Jade swallowed the lump in her throat her daughter's heartfelt admission created. "We could blame the gods who created him for how he turned out, but the bottom line was that he was a cold-hearted murderer, and we couldn't let him go because he was too dangerous."

As Drova closed her eyes, Jade thought she was fighting tears, but when she opened them, they were dry. "Do you think that the genetic mutations the gods put in him transferred to me?"

Jade shook her head. "You are not a cold killing machine, Drova. I think you got the genes Igor was born with, and not the mutations the gods put in him. Who knows? Perhaps at his core, he wasn't so bad."

# Annani

⚬⚬⚬

Annani sat next to her granddaughter at the dining table, entertaining the child while her mother directed the small army of five Odus in a choreographed dance of dinner preparations.

It was an important celebration, and Syssi had invited most of the family.

"Nini," Allegra said in a demanding tone. "Mo!"

"Yes, sweetie." Annani gave her another ripe strawberry. "You are making such a sweet mess."

Allegra's smart eyes were smiling as she stuck the fruit in her mouth, holding it by its stem and sucking, her slobber mingling with the juice and running down her chin and soaking her bib.

"You must be excited." Amanda sat down on Annani's other side. "You can finally move into your own house."

"I am, but I am also going to miss spending time with Allegra." She lifted a napkin and dabbed the baby's chin. "The truth is that I could have been in my home this entire time. The Kra-ell are not allowed in this section of the village, so none of them would have seen me. But it was fun staying with my family." She leaned closer to Amanda. "Perhaps now, I should stay with you for a couple of weeks."

"I would love that." Amanda glanced at Dalhu. "But my mate needs his tranquility to create, and there is none of that with you around."

Annani laughed. "I was just teasing. I will not do that to Dalhu again."

As Kalugal walked in with Jacki and Darius, Annani lifted her arms. "Give me this baby. I want to hold your beautiful little boy."

He was quite big for a three-month-old baby, and now that his colic was better, he was no longer fussy.

As Kalugal placed his son gently in Annani's arms, Allegra regarded him with a frown. "Bibi Didi."

"I think she means to say baby Darius." Syssi pulled out a chair on Allegra's other side and sat down.

"Bibi Didi!" Allegra repeated.

Darius turned his head to look at her and gave her a toothless smile.

There was nothing better in the world than holding a baby, and Annani did not care that it was instinctual, bred into humanoid species to ensure their survival. The same was true of sex, and that also gave her great pleasure. Not as much as what she had enjoyed with Khiann, but still good.

Life wasn't easy, and it was full of sorrow. One had to seek pleasure wherever it could be found to sweeten it.

"He's adorable," Amanda said. "Is the colic all gone?"

Jacki rocked her hand in the so-so gesture. "He still gets it, but not as frequently. It's mostly in the afternoons now, and he's finally sleeping for four hours straight at night. Kalugal and I are thinking about going on the trip to Egypt we've been planning for so long. We will take Shamash and several of the other men with us, so we will have plenty of help." She took in a dramatic breath. "I love the village, but I need to get out of here. I'm going crazy being stuck at home."

"You can come to work for me," Amanda offered. "We have a daycare set up in the university, so Darius will be right there next to you."

"Thank you for the offer, but I don't know anything about neuroscience."

"Pfft." Amanda waved a dismissive hand. "I can teach you all you need to know to conduct tests in a week. It could be fun for all of us to work together and, even better, for our children to be around each other."

Kalugal cleared his throat. "First of all, I don't want Jacki working on anything other than the charities she manages for us, and secondly, if we want our children to one day get romantically involved, we shouldn't raise them like siblings."

Turning toward Kalugal, Jacki cast him a glare. "You don't get to tell me what I can and cannot do. But you are right about the siblings thing."

Kian entered the room and sat across from Syssi. "They'll think of each other as siblings no matter what we do. Unless you move to Scotland, or send Darius to a boarding school."

"I'm never sending my son to boarding school, and I'm very comfortable here." Kalugal leaned back and draped his arm over the back of Jacki's chair. "When the time comes, we will come up with a solution."

Kian did not look like he had a problem with Allegra thinking of Darius as a brother or a cousin. In fact, he probably did not want to think about her being interested in boys at all.

"I am overjoyed with the results of the trial," Annani said to change the subject. "I am so pleased to see the Kra-ell changing their ways in such a short time. From a savage, autocratic, bloodthirsty society, they are changing into a democracy in front of our eyes."

Kian grimaced. "Not all of them. Some are not happy with the results of the trial. I expect trouble."

"What kind of trouble?" Amanda asked.

"I don't know. It's not going to be directed at us, but I'm concerned about the safety of the former prisoners. I told the Guardians to be alert."

"There is always something." Andrew sighed. "But then that's what makes life interesting, right?"

Kian chuckled. "I'm okay with a little boredom."

"Let's have a toast." Kalugal lifted his glass. "To our new integrated community."

# Kian

Kian lifted his glass and clinked it first with Syssi's and then with his mother's. "I just hope we will have at least a couple of weeks of peace." He looked at Alena. "We have a wedding cruise to plan."

To say that she didn't look enthusiastic was an understatement. Her forehead creased with a frown, she glanced at Orion and then returned her gaze to Kian. "If I didn't think that the other couples who want to get married on a ship would be disappointed, I would have told you to cancel the whole thing. It's too complicated to gather everyone in one place now, and we shouldn't leave the Kra-ell unsupervised in the village."

She was echoing Kian's sentiment, but he refused to let outside forces influence their plans. Well, they would always have to hide, but they should be able to have a damn vacation cruise if they wanted to.

"Can't we charter another ship?" Kalugal suggested. "We can load the Kra-ell on the other one and have a convoy. That should be fun. We could have a rope bridge between the ships, and the Kra-ell can demonstrate their superior physical abilities by going back and forth between the vessels."

Kian wasn't sure whether Kalugal was serious or not. It sounded like a joke to him, but his cousin's expression didn't reveal anything other than smug amusement about the idea he thought was clever.

"The Kra-ell are not fans of sea voyages," Syssi said. "But that's an interesting option." She turned to Kian. "What do you think?"

"I think that by the time we get around to doing it, Alena will have given birth. We are running out of time."

Alena shrugged. "I don't mind if the wedding is after I deliver. That way all of my children will be present."

"It shouldn't be complicated to charter a ship," Toven said. "We found one pretty easily in Europe when we needed a decoy. It doesn't have to be as fancy as the *Aurora*."

"We can play pirate games," Alena smiled at Kalugal. "The rope between the ships gave me the idea. We can even have costumes." She looked at Amanda. "I see the wheels in your head turning. What are your thoughts on the subject?"

Amanda shrugged. "You can always count me in for a party, but I was thinking about decorations, and I couldn't come up with anything that would fit a pirate theme other than chests filled with fake gold coins and jewelry."

"That's a good start," Nathalie said. "Phoenix would love it."

As the discussion continued, Kian snuck a quick look at his mother, verified that she was absorbed in the conversation, and pulled out his phone. Keeping it under the tablecloth, he leaned down and scrolled through his messages and emails.

He felt absurd about having to hide it from his mother, and he also felt crappy about the compulsion to check his phone at least once every hour.

What had he done before the invention of the internet?

Life had been simpler back then, but no less stressful. He'd had to wait for news to arrive via phone call, and before the invention of phones, via messenger.

The bottom line was that his life had always been about getting bad news. His mother chided him, saying that his pessimism was what courted trouble, but that wasn't true.

Kian wasn't a pessimist. He was a realist, and life was full of challenges.

When his phone vibrated in his hand, he wasn't really surprised as he read the message from William.

*The signals came on again, only two this time, and they winked out a few seconds later. I know that you are having a family dinner, and I don't want to impose, but since Okidu and Onidu are there, I could come over and have them listen to the recording. I'm curious whether the signals are coming from a different location this time, and it will only take a minute.*

Kian typed back. *Come over as soon as you can. This is important.*

William answered. *I'm leaving the lab now. I'll be there in twenty minutes.*

Annani narrowed her eyes at Kian. "You know my stance on phones at the dinner table."

"I know, and you are absolutely right." He put the phone back in his suit pocket. "But I'm not on the phone to disengage from the conversation and scroll through social media or read the news. I have to check my messages from time to time to make sure that there is nothing that requires my immediate attention."

Despite what he thought had been a sensible and courteous answer, Annani's reproachful look stayed put. "If something urgent comes up, I am sure the Guardians would call you, not send you a message or an email, and if your phone is off, they would know where to find you."

"Not always." Kian leaned back in his chair. "Sometimes they are not sure whether a matter needs my immediate attention or not, so they send me a message because they don't want to disturb me during a family dinner unless I deem it urgent."

His mother arched a brow. "Was the communication you received right now urgent?"

Kian smiled with satisfaction. "As a matter of fact, it was. William identified several alien signals this morning and again right now. He wants to check whether they are still coming from the same location, and he needs the Odus to help him decipher the signals."

# Vanessa

Vanessa hugged Jackson and then kissed Tessa's cheek. "Thank you again for everything. You've made Mo-red feel so welcome."

"It was my pleasure." Tessa waved at Mo-red, who was saying goodbye to his sons. "He's a good guy." She put a hand over her chest. "I feel it in here when someone is bad. It's like a sixth sense for evil, and there is none of it in Mo-red. I wish the two of you a long and happy life together."

"Thank you." Vanessa teared up again, and this time she actually had to wipe the tears away. "I don't know why I'm so hormonal."

Arching a brow, Tessa whispered, "Perhaps you are pregnant?"

"I wish, but Mo-red would have known if we had conceived. The Kra-ell males know immediately when their seed takes."

"I've heard about that, but I thought it was an urban legend." Tessa glanced at Jackson, who was busy texting. "Jackson is going to be a great dad, but he's so young, and I'm not ready yet. If it happens naturally, it happens, but we are not going to ask Merlin for his fertility potions just yet. Maybe in a few years."

"Take your time." Vanessa patted Tessa's slim shoulder. "There is no rush."

Pavel joined them by the door. "Jackson is texting his old band members to join us at the village square for an impromptu celebration. Do you want to come?"

That was a half-hearted invitation if Vanessa had ever heard one.

The young males had been chatting about Jackson's old band, and Pavel and his brothers had apparently managed to convince Jackson to jam together, but perhaps they didn't want their father to hear their attempts.

She looked at Mo-red. "Do you want to go?"

He shook his head. "I'm exhausted. I want to take a shower and get into bed." His lips quirked in a lopsided smile that told her sleep was not on his agenda.

She stifled a chuckle. "Yeah, I'm tired too."

As she'd suspected, Pavel didn't look overly disappointed, and a moment later, when Lusha came out of the bedroom wearing a sexy dress and high heels, Vanessa understood why.

Pavel didn't want his dad around when he was flirting with the human or perhaps hooking up with her.

They were both adults, so why not?

Lusha deserved to celebrate her victory, and Pavel was just the guy to celebrate with.

"You look so pretty." Vanessa gave the attorney an appreciative once-over.

Lusha smiled. "Thanks. Pavel convinced me to join him at the village square. Turns out he can play the drums, and he's going to jam with the guys."

"I'm going to suck." Pavel wrapped his arm around her middle. "I haven't played drums in ages."

Vanessa was surprised that he'd played at all. As far as she knew, Igor hadn't been at all interested in music. "Where did you learn how to drum?" she asked.

Pavel looked at Mo-red. "When I was a kid, I drummed on every surface, and my father got me a drumming course on CD and a pair of drumsticks. The rest of the instruments were improvised, and they sounded like crap, but I thought they were amazing."

"They were not bad," Mo-red said. "Especially given what you had to work with. You were quite inventive, and I was proud of you."

"Thank you." Pavel cast him a smile. "Are you ready?" he asked Lusha.

"I am." She waved at Vanessa. "Don't wait up for me."

"I won't."

Once everyone was gone and Vanessa closed the door, Mo-red pulled her into his arms and smashed his lips over hers.

Without missing a beat, she lifted her legs and wrapped them around his waist. Mo-red's big hands closed on her bottom, holding her up as he kept ravishing her mouth and walking toward their bedroom.

He kept kissing her until they were both starved for breath, and he had to let her come up for air.

"I couldn't wait to be alone with you." He sat on the bed with her in his arms. "I love my sons, but I couldn't wait for them to leave."

Vanessa smiled. "I love how easily you use the word love now."

He tightened his arms around her. "You taught me how to love."

She nuzzled him. "You've always known that." She peppered small kisses down the strong column of his neck. "You just needed a shock to the system to obliterate the false beliefs you grew up with, and a reboot to build new ones."

"I like that." He lifted her and spread her out on the bed. Hovering above her with a dreamy look in his huge eyes, he asked, "Will you do me the honor of one day becoming the mother of my child?"

For a moment, Vanessa thought that he was joking, but he was serious, looking at her with reverence in his eyes.

"Fates willing." Lifting her hand, she cupped his cheek. "Given how much I like your first three and how much I love mine, I can't wait to have one with you. I have no doubt that our child would be just as wonderful as his older siblings."

Mo-red grinned. "If the Mother wishes so, we might be blessed with a girl."

"That's not very likely, but I'll pray to the Fates to make it so. Can you imagine our four boys with a little sister?"

That dreamy look was back in his eyes. "Yes, in fact, I can."

# Syssi

Syssi smiled and chatted as if nothing had happened, while inside her worry was mounting.

Kian had told her about the signals when they had first appeared last night, or rather this morning, but he'd dismissed them because their appearance had been so short that it could have been a glitch and because they had been located so far away that it didn't make sense to even send someone to investigate.

But now they were back, once again coming online and then going offline only a moment later.

She had a strong feeling that their appearance was much more significant than Kian let on.

"So, what do you think?" Amanda asked.

Syssi had been listening to the discussion with only half an ear and contributing a word here and there. She didn't know which part Amanda was referring to.

"About what?"

"A different costume party for every night of the cruise. Each one will have a theme." Amanda's eyes sparkled with mischief. "It could be very naughty."

Kian regarded her with a frown. "There will be children present. You can't make it too outrageous."

"Right." She pouted but then brightened. "We can have the costume ball after midnight and not allow the kids to participate. The older children will babysit the little ones while the parents enjoy themselves."

Nathalie lifted her hand. "Count me in. I could use some naughty fun after all the stress of the trial. I didn't go to the assembly and watched it from home instead while demolishing a whole container of ice cream until the jury cast its vote. I was so relieved when they decided on community service. I couldn't have slept at night if those males had gotten executed."

Syssi wouldn't have been able to sleep either. She hadn't spent any time with the accused, and Kian had met only Mo-red during his mating ceremony with Vanessa, but that had been enough for him to solidify his position on the male's culpability or lack thereof.

Kian considered the love Vanessa felt for Mo-red and the support of his three sons proof that he was a good male.

"Thank the Fates." Annani lifted her wine glass and took a long sip. "I delved into Igor and Valstar's minds, and the difference was profound. Igor felt absolutely no remorse while Valstar was drowning in it. That is the difference between a sociopath and a decent male who finds himself in an impossible situation." She sighed. "Not that Valstar is all good. I've seen some shady spots in his mind, but none that deserved a death penalty."

The goddess did not support the death penalty for even the worst offenders, so her statement about Valstar was redundant, but no one dared to point it out.

"No one is a hundred percent pure-hearted," Kalugal said. "We all have shady spots on our psyche."

"All except for my wife." Kian leaned over and kissed the top of her head. "Syssi is an angel."

"I'm not." She rolled her eyes. "My spots might be small, but I have a few."

When the doorbell rang, and a moment later Okidu escorted William into the dining hall, Kian pushed to his feet to welcome him.

"Good evening, everyone." William tucked his laptop under his arm and bowed to Annani. "Forgive me for disturbing the family dinner, but we believe that this is important."

"You are forgiven." Annani waved magnanimously.

"Let's do this in my office." Kian motioned for Okidu and Onidu to follow him.

Syssi pushed to her feet. "Can I join?"

Kian looked surprised. "Of course."

Kalugal started to lift off his chair, but Jacki put a hand on his arm to stop him.

Syssi wouldn't have minded if he had joined, but apparently, Jacki wanted him to stay with her.

As they walked to the office, Kian put his arm around her waist. "I'm delighted to have you with me, but it's not like you to abandon your guests. Did you have one of your feelings?"

He knew her so well.

Syssi nodded. "It's just a general feeling of unease like a storm is brewing, but I don't know if it will blow away or mess things up for us."

He chuckled. "In my experience, it's safe to bet on the latter, and not only because I trust your premonitions. It's just the way it is."

"Fates, I hope not," William said as Kian opened the door. "I want some peace and quiet so I can help Kaia with the journals, and we can start manufacturing—" He cast a quick glance at the Odus. "You know what."

"Indeed." Kian motioned for the Odus to go ahead and for Syssi to take a seat on the couch.

William put his laptop on Kian's desk, flipped it open, and turned on the recording.

For a long moment, Okidu and Onidu looked like they were in a trance, and then Okidu took a post-it pad from Kian's desk and wrote several numbers on it.

"These signals are not the same as the others," the Odu said as he handed the note to William.

Kian frowned. "Do you mean different from the signals William recorded this morning?"

"They are different from the other ones we deciphered before. The ones that came from the Kra-ell trackers."

"In what way are they different?" William asked.

Okidu looked confused. "I do not know, master. I only know that they are different."

"Different technology?" Syssi offered. "Different encryption?"

When Okidu seemed even more confused, Syssi realized that he needed an example to understand what they were asking. "Is it like the difference between the limousine you drive and the clan bus? Both are vehicles, but they are not the same. Or is it like the difference between two limousines made by different manufacturers?"

He shook his head.

"I know." William lifted his hand. "Is it like the difference between the car you drove for Kian fifty years ago and the one you are driving now?"

A bright smile bloomed on the Odu's face. "Yes. This is that kind of difference."

Kian looked at William, then back at Okidu. "Which of the signals is the older car? The recent or the other ones?"

"The new ones, master."

The wheels in Syssi's mind started spinning. "If these signals are older technology, they could belong to the scouting team that was sent ahead of the settler ship. But all the scouts should be long dead by now."

"Maybe someone found their remains," William suggested.

"Check the coordinates." Kian waved a hand at the post-it note that William had glued to his laptop screen.

"Right." William brought up the world map. "Same as this morning. They are coming from the outskirts of Chengdu."

Syssi let out a breath. "That's good, right? They are still in the same area."

Kian frowned. "Let's get Kalugal in here." He pulled out his phone, typed up a text, and opened his office door.

A moment later, Kalugal's footsteps sounded down the hallway, and as he entered the office, he arched a brow. "What are my services needed for?"

Kian leaned against his desk. "The signals are coming from Chengdu, which is a four-hour drive from Lugu Lake. For China, it is practically next door. Okidu says that the signals are different than what the settlers' trackers emitted, and he thinks they are older technology.

Syssi suspects that they belonged to the scouts who were sent ahead of the settler ship, but they are supposed to be dead. My question to you is whether someone could have dug out their remains and found the trackers?"

"Not in my excavation site. Besides, we know from Jacki's vision that they cremated their dead. There wouldn't have been anything to dig out."

Raking his fingers through his hair, Kian groaned. "The trackers would have survived the fire. They are practically indestructible. But since they are tiny, someone would have to know what to look for to find them. The question is, who?" He looked at Syssi. "Do you have a premonition about that?"

She shook her head. "I don't, but I have a feeling that it's very important for us to find out who it is."

Kian nodded as if he'd expected her answer. "Then I guess we are sending a team to investigate in Chengdu."

"I will join them," Kalugal offered. "I need to check what's going on with my excavations near Lugu Lake. Maybe the two are connected."

"They are." Syssi put her hand on her stomach. "I feel it in my gut."

---

**THE ADVENTURE CONTINUES**
**GABI & URIEL'S STORY IS NEXT**

The Children of the Gods Book 74
**Dark Encounters of the Close Kind**

**Turn the page to read the preview—>**

---

**Join the *VIP Club***
To find out what's included in your free membership,
click HERE or flip to the last page.

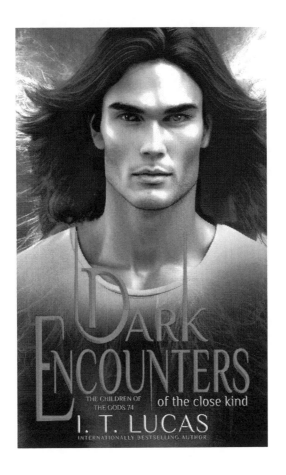

THE CHILDREN OF THE GODS 74

DARK ENCOUNTERS of the close kind

I. T. LUCAS

INTERNATIONALLY BESTSELLING AUTHOR

Convinced that her family is hiding a terrible secret from her, Gabi decides to pay them a surprise visit.

Something is very fishy about the stories her brothers have been telling her lately. Her niece, a nineteen-year-old prodigy with a Ph.D. in bioinformatics, has gotten engaged to a much older guy she met while working on some top-secret project, and if Gabi's older, overprotective brother's approval of the engagement wasn't suspicious enough, he also uprooted his family and moved to be closer to the couple.

What Gabi discovers when she gets to L.A. is wilder than anything she could have imagined. Her entire family possesses godly genes, her brothers and her niece have already turned immortal, and she could transition as soon as she finds an immortal male to induce her. Finding a suitable candidate in a village full of handsome immortals shouldn't be a problem, but Gabi's thoughts keep wandering to the gorgeous guy she met on her flight over.

Could Uriel be a lost descendant of the gods?

He certainly looks like them, but that doesn't mean that he's a good guy or that he's even immortal. He could be a descendant of a different god—a member of an enemy faction of immortals who seek to eradicate her family's adoptive clan, or what is more likely, he's just an extraordinarily good-looking human.

# GABI

"I'm sorry, Ms. Emerson." The gate attendant assumed a fake apologetic smile. "The flight has been canceled due to technical issues."

They had been having those issues for the past two hours, and every time Gabi had approached the desk, the attendant's answer had been that the problem was being worked on and that boarding should start shortly.

She had been afraid to stray away from the gate to use the bathroom or grab a cup of coffee, but when she'd finally dared a dash to the nearest coffee shop, the announcement about her flight had finally come—not that boarding was starting but that the flight had been canceled and the passengers should head to the customer service desk to make other arrangements.

It had been such a bad idea to book a flight straight from the conference to Los Angeles. She should have gone home, rested for a few days, and then hazarded another flight.

Except, Gabi knew that she wouldn't have done that. She would have chickened out.

"I just heard the announcement about my flight being canceled, and that's why I'm here. Can you please check if a seat is available on another flight to Los Angeles today?"

The woman affected another one of her fake smiles, but this one also had a condescending slant to it. "We don't handle flight bookings at the gate. You should go to the customer service desk."

There was a separate desk for that?

Gabi stifled a biting retort that would have felt awesome passing her lips but would have probably resulted in airport security escorting her away.

Her temper and her big mouth had gotten her in trouble before.

Still, she couldn't just let it go. "You could have told us that the flight might be canceled two hours ago, when you first announced that there would be a delay. Now, I'm probably not going to find a seat on another flight leaving today."

"My apologies, but I can only convey the information I receive, and until fifteen minutes ago, I was told that they were working on the problem. The customer service desk can help you book another flight, and if none work for you today, they will provide vouchers for hotel accommodations and meals."

Realizing that she wouldn't get any help from the woman, Gabi forced down a cuss word and took a long breath instead. "Can you point me toward the customer service desk?"

The gate attendant looked relieved at the prospect of finally being rid of her. "It's located in Terminal D, next to gate 98. Good luck, Ms. Emerson. And I apologize again for the inconvenience."

Practiced, empty words.

"Thanks," Gabi murmured as she grabbed the carry-on handle and rolled it in the direction the attendant had indicated.

Terminal D was at least a twenty-minute walk, and Gabi, for some unfathomable reason, was still wearing the high heels she'd put on for the last event of the conference this morning. She should have gotten a pair of flats from her carry-on while getting coffee, but she'd been in a rush, and she hadn't expected to have to march across the airport. She couldn't stop and do it now either, because with every minute she delayed, there was less chance of her getting a seat on a flight leaving today.

Perhaps the malfunction was a sign that she shouldn't go to Los Angeles.

Good God, she hated flying.

It made no difference to her that her brother was a pilot who owned a couple of jets and, until recently, had flown them for a living, and it didn't help that she knew that flying was statistically safer than driving. Gabi still preferred ground transportation.

If people were meant to fly, they would have been born with wings.

She should just give up on the idea of visiting her brothers, rent a car, and drive back home to Cleveland. It was only a five-hour drive from Toronto, and she could listen to an audiobook to pass the time.

No, she couldn't do that.

She wouldn't have a decent night's sleep until she found out what was going on with her brothers and her honorary adopted niece, and it wasn't as if she could drive all the way to Los Angeles to check on them.

Something was very fishy about the stories they had been telling her lately.

Her niece was a prodigy who had earned her PhD in bioinformatics at nineteen, but instead of accepting the teaching job that she'd been offered at Stanford, Kaia had abandoned her dreams, gotten engaged to some dude she'd met while working on a top-secret project and moved in with him.

The girl might be a genius, but she had zero life experience, and the last thing she should do was move in with a guy who was more than a decade older than her.

What Gabi found even more suspicious than Kaia's sudden engagement was that Karen and Gilbert had not only approved of her questionable life choices but had also moved to Los Angeles to be close to her, uprooting their family and leaving behind their beautiful house in the Bay Area. On top of that, Eric had fallen in love with a woman who worked for Kaia's fiancé, and he had joined the rest of the family in Los Angeles, giving up his executive jets chartering business.

At first, Gabi had been curious, then worried, and now she was panicking.

It wasn't like her brothers to act so impulsively, and Gilbert was the last guy on the planet who would have been okay with his honorary adopted daughter giving up her dreams for a guy.

Well, that was a slight exaggeration. There were probably more protective fathers and stepfathers out there, but despite the fact that Gilbert and Karen had never bothered to get married, and he had never officially adopted Karen's two daughters from her previous marriage, he was definitely up there with the worst of them.

Or was it the best of them?

Gabi should know.

Gilbert had always been more of a father than a brother to her, and when she couldn't get him on the phone for three days straight, she'd even called Kaia and Cheryl and tried to get them to spill the beans, but they had been as evasive as their mother, telling her the same story about a wonderful new business opportunity that Kaia's fiancé had offered Gilbert and Eric, and how it was keeping them both insanely busy.

Gabi wasn't buying it, so she'd booked the flight to L.A. right after the Nutrition, Fitness, and Health Management conference in Toronto was over. If she could have gotten out of attending it, she would have, but her ticket had been paid for months in advance, and attending the conference was important for her business.

Staying on top of the latest trends and learning about all the new research and discoveries was what her clients expected from her.

When Gilbert had finally called her, echoing the same crappy excuse Karen had given her about him being swamped with work, it had reinforced her decision to pay them a visit without advance notice.

Did they think that she was dumb?

Gabi felt tears misting her eyes.

What if Gilbert had a terminal illness, and that was why everyone had moved to Los Angeles, and Kaia had given up on her dreams?

What if that was where he was being treated?

But why keep her out of the loop? And couldn't Gilbert have come to Cleveland instead of Los Angeles? After all, the Mayo Clinic was there, mere minutes away from her home.

Except, Gilbert wouldn't have come to her hometown even if Mayo was the better option.

Her brothers treated her like a delicate piece of china that would break from the slightest touch, but she was their sister, and if Gilbert didn't have long to live, she needed to be by his side.

Did they think she wouldn't be able to handle it? That she would fall apart and cry her eyes out instead of being helpful and supportive?

Gabi could be brave if she needed to be.

God, she prayed it wasn't what she was thinking, and that Gilbert had just had a hair transplant or some other cosmetic procedure, and that was why he hadn't called her back and had asked Karen and the girls to cover for him.

Yeah, that was probably it.

Gabi had already lost her parents. She couldn't lose anyone else.

She wouldn't survive it.

Taking a fortifying breath, she wiped away the tears welling in her eyes, blew her nose on a tissue, and joined the long line of airline customers waiting to be helped at the service desk.

# KIAN

"Hello, Victor." Kian shook Turner's hand. "Thanks for coming."

The guy smiled. "I never say no to free food."

Next to him, Bridget chuckled. "Now look what you have done. You have given Kian the secret code." She lifted on her toes and kissed Kian's cheek. "If you want Victor's help, all you have to do is offer him a steak."

Kian doubted Turner would have enjoyed any steak Okidu had prepared. His butler sneered at anything produced on a grill, and if he cooked steak at all, it was in a pan or oven.

Turner, on the other hand, prided himself on being the best steak griller in the village, but his title was contested by Roni, who claimed that it belonged to him.

"I'm sorry to disappoint you, but Okidu is not serving steak for lunch."

Turner stopped and pretended to turn around. "Oh, well, I guess I have to go home and fire up the grill."

That was a rare display of humor for the guy, and Kian wondered whether Turner had been working on his people skills. It was also possible that he meant it literally.

"Don't be silly." Syssi gave Turner a brief hug. "Okidu made beef stroganoff. Wait until you taste it. You'll be licking your fingertips."

"I'm sure I will, but how would you know? Did you taste it?"

Yep. Turner was still as literal as usual.

Syssi shook her head. "I didn't have to. If the smells alone weren't mouth-watering enough to inform even a vegetarian like me, then Kalugal's frequent tasting and moaning were."

They needed to brainstorm the issue of the strange new signals that had popped up and immediately winked out twice so far, but Syssi hadn't wanted Kian to go to the office building on a Sunday, so she had invited everyone who could contribute to the brainstorming to lunch at their home.

Eighteen hours had passed since the last occurrence, so Kian's stress levels had decreased significantly, and he felt less urgency to send a team to investigate.

In fact, if not for Syssi's gut feeling about the importance of the occurrence, he might have been tempted to ignore the brief emergence of signals that had been supposedly emitted by alien trackers across the globe, but his wife's gut feelings were usually much more than a hunch, and ignoring them would be a mistake.

Ironically, what worried him the most about those new signals was that they were different from the ones emitted by the trackers that had been implanted in the Kra-ell settlers, meaning that they were not coming from the other assassins that Igor had told them about or the incredibly dangerous royal twins. Thankfully, it seemed that neither the assassins nor the twins had awakened from stasis. But the unknown source of the new signals was more concerning than a threat he'd already known about.

Okidu, who had deciphered the signals to identify their location, had said that they felt like an older model of those trackers, which probably meant that they belonged to earlier visitors to Earth.

Given that the settler ship had left Anumati seven thousand years ago, those trackers had to be even older than that. And since the signals were coming from Chengdu, the capital of China's Sichuan province and home to Lugu Lake and its Mosuo population, the assumption was that they had belonged to the scouting team that had been sent ahead of the settler ship to verify that Earth was suitable for the Kra-ell.

The problem with that theory was that there was no way any members of the original scouting team were still alive. The Kra-ell were long-lived compared to humans, but they were not immortal, and those males should have died out millennia ago. Furthermore, the Kra-ell cremated their dead, so there were no bodies for anyone to dig out either, and no one could have gotten the trackers out of the remains.

Could it be that the human descendants of those original Kra-ell males had kept the trackers, and they were now trying to activate them for some reason?

But if William, a genius who knew a thing or two about alien technology, couldn't break the trackers apart without destroying them, how could some humans in China manage that?

On top of that, the devices only worked when inside a living organism, so even if the descendants of the Kra-ell had kept them throughout the generations, they would have to know that live hosts were needed.

The only other possible option was that the scouts had managed to prolong their lives somehow, perhaps by staying in their stasis pods for hundreds of years at a time, and they were now starting to wake up, but something wasn't working right.

In the dining room, Kian pulled out a chair next to William. "I have a theory about the scouts and want to run it by you."

"Shoot."

"Do you think that the Kra-ell scouts could have used the stasis pods to stay alive longer? We know those pods could sustain life for thousands of years, so that's not a far-fetched scenario."

William exchanged knowing looks with his mate before returning his gaze to Kian. "Kaia and I talked about that last night. If I were in the scouts' shoes, that was what I would have done, and that also explains the discrepancy in what we assumed about them. For them to influence the Mosuo society, they must have been around during the time the Mosuo settled around Lugu Lake, and if the scouts arrived more than seven thousand years ago, they must have found a way to survive or left descendants who took it upon themselves to continue the tradition of their forefathers, and they were the ones who influenced the Mosuo."

"I had a vision about a cremating ceremony for one of the scouts," Jacki said. "And the subterranean chamber in which the ceremony was held was no older than fifteen hundred years." She turned to Kalugal. "Am I right?"

"Give or take a few hundred years. It's sometimes difficult to ascertain whether the most ancient occupants we can date used preexisting caverns or dug them out themselves."

"Anyway," Jacki continued. "If they could use the stasis pods to prolong their lives, why did some still die? They could have stayed in the pod for centuries at a time, woken up for a few days or weeks to check what was going on and whether the settler ship had arrived, and then gone back into stasis. They could have survived to this day."

"I really need to get to that pod," Kalugal said. "It's extremely difficult, and my team is basically digging by hand an inch at a time. I don't want anyone dying there because the scouts booby-trapped the site."

"Perhaps there is no pod there." Kian got to his feet and walked over to sit next to Syssi. "You just assume that a pod is causing the alien transmissions, but it might be something else."

"Right. Maybe it's an alien aircraft." Kalugal grinned. "That would be an even more exciting discovery than a pod."

"Not if the pod has live people in it." Annani floated into the room and waited for Kian to pull out a chair for her before sitting down. "I am much more interested in those lives than in the technology that brought them here."

# GABI

The customer service attendant looked like she'd been through the wringer, but she still managed a genuine apologetic expression for Gabi. "The only remaining direct flight to Los Angeles today is fully booked." She went back to her screen and kept typing. "Let me see if I can find you another way to get there."

Great. As if she needed two more takeoffs and landings.

"I hate flying," Gabi admitted. "I might not survive a flight with a stopover."

She should just give up.

No, she couldn't. She had to see Gilbert with her own eyes and hear him tell her he was okay.

"If you had gotten here fifteen minutes ago, I still had a couple of seats," the attendant murmured as she clicked on her keyboard. "Why did you wait so long?"

"I would have gotten here two hours earlier if the gate attendant at my original flight had told the truth about the flight being canceled and not delayed."

While waiting in line, Gabi had heard the other customers talking about how it was common practice. The airlines did it on purpose, so not everyone would storm the service desk at the same time, which explained why everyone else had gotten there ahead of her and she was the last one in line.

The woman's knowing smile confirmed the rumor. "I can put you on the first flight leaving for Los Angeles tomorrow morning and give you vouchers for a hotel and two meals."

"I don't want to stay overnight in the airport. I'm just going to rent a car and drive home to Cleveland."

She could go home, get some rest, and book a direct flight from there for the next day.

The attendant frowned at her screen. "It must be your lucky day, after all. I just had a cancellation in first class. I'm grabbing the seat for you." She typed furiously fast.

"Hold on." Gabi lifted her hand. "Do I have to pay for the upgrade?"

She rarely flew, so she didn't have any accumulated miles or preferred status or any of the other perks that airlines give to frequent travelers.

"It's a free special-circumstances upgrade." The woman lifted her head and gave her a conspiratorial smile. "I wrote down that it is an emergency. Your best friend is getting married tonight." She winked.

That was such an unexpected kindness that Gabi just gaped for a long moment. "Thank you," she finally croaked. "You're a miracle worker."

"Sometimes I am." The attendant handed Gabi the boarding pass. "Since you are flying first class, you also have access to the executive lounge. It's right across from here." She pointed at the opaque sliding doors across the aisle with the words Alliance Club engraved on them. "Enjoy."

"Thank you." Gabi snatched the pass. "You're the best airline employee I've ever encountered. If they send me a survey to fill in, I'm going to sing your praises."

"Thanks." The woman put up the closed sign on her desk. "Have a safe flight."

Gabi swallowed. The words safety and flight didn't belong together, not in her mind anyway, but since it was her lucky day, and she was flying first class and visiting the executive lounge for the first time, perhaps it was a sign that she was supposed to go to Los Angeles after all.

Rolling her carry-on, she sauntered over to the sliding doors and walked in as if she owned the place. The three-and-a-half-hour wait for the next flight didn't look so bad now when she could spend them having complimentary drinks at the bar.

The attendant took her boarding pass, scanned it, and handed it back, "Welcome to the club, Ms. Emerson."

"Thank you." Gabi rolled her carry-on straight to the bar and ordered a gin and tonic.

Since all the seats at the bar were taken, she took her drink to one of the round dining tables next to the buffet.

Come to think of it, she was a little peckish.

It had been a long time since she'd had breakfast, and she craved a salty snack along with her gin and tonic.

Hopefully, none of the conference attendees were in the club, or at least none of those who knew her, so she could indulge in peace.

A licensed nutritionist shouldn't consume alcohol and munch on pretzels in the middle of the day.

What kind of an example would she be setting?

Ugh, to hell with that.

She was a long way from home, and if anyone recognized her, she would pretend to be her own doppelgänger.

Putting the drink down, Gabi looked in the direction of the buffet, but her eyes didn't make it all the way to the food. They got snagged on three ridiculously good-looking men crowding one small table.

Had there been a model convention in Toronto she hadn't heard about?

Each of the guys could star in an ad for luxury cologne, cigars, whiskeys, watches, sports cars, or—

One of them must have felt her looking at him and turned toward her, taking her breath away.

The guy was unreal, with chiseled cheekbones that could cut granite and skin so smooth that it looked like his face was gold-plated. His eyes were dark, nearly black, but there was warmth in them as he looked at her.

He smiled, lifted his beer glass, and mouthed cheers.

Gabi swallowed. She couldn't take her eyes off him no matter how hard she tried, and she couldn't smile back or force her mouth to say cheers back to him either.

Damn, that was embarrassing.

It took a pinch to her inner arm to get her to stop staring, give him a slight nod of acknowledgment, and turn away.

Abandoning the idea of getting a snack because it meant passing by his table, Gabi sat down with her back to him, pulled out her phone, and pretended to read on it while sipping on her drink.

The book might have been written in Chinese for all she managed to read, and her stupid heart was racing as if she was a teenager with the hots for the most popular guy in the school cafeteria.

"Been there, done that, and I'm never doing that again," she murmured under her breath.

Gabi had married her prom king.

She'd snagged the hottest guy in school, married him after college, and divorced him five years later.

The problem with hot guys was that they were in high demand, and most didn't know how to say no, including her ex.

That had been eleven years ago, and she was still single, not because she lacked male attention but because she was a walking contradiction.

After divorcing Dylan, she'd vowed that if she got married again, it would be to a sweet nerd who attracted absolutely no female attention and would be hers and hers alone.

The problem with that was that she wasn't attracted to nice, nerdy men. She was drawn to the hot, bad boys who were bound to break her heart again.

# KIAN

As Okidu collected the empty plates, Turner leaned back and looked at Jacki. "The guy you saw in your vision didn't necessarily die of old age. He might have been killed in battle. The Kra-ell are not as fast healing as we are, and they can die from injuries that we can heal."

"True." Jacki nibbled on her lower lip. "But I thought about it, and there could be another explanation. They might have devised the idea of using the life pods only after several hundred years had passed and the settlers hadn't arrived. So, they were already old when they started using the pods."

"I don't think so." Kalugal draped his arm over the back of Jacki's chair. "The settler ship was supposed to take three hundred years to get to Earth, and in the meantime, the scouts had nothing to do. I bet they came up with the idea of using the pods early on, and I think they took turns in them. If it was me and my men, I would have assigned at least two to stay awake at any time in case something unexpected happened while the rest slept. When they realized that the ship wasn't coming, they might have decided that there was no point in waiting, and all got into the pods, probably in the hopes that someone would collect them at some point."

"What about communications with Anumati?" Syssi asked. "The scouts contacted the queen to tell her that Earth was habitable, so we know that they had the ability to communicate with home. But the question is how? Was there a god ship orbiting above the planet? Did they use the same satellites the exiled gods used before communications were severed? What were they told to do when it became clear that the ship wasn't coming?"

"Probably to go into the pods," Jacki said. "The queen would not have given up hope that her children were alive, and she would have told the scouts to sleep so they would be around when the twins finally arrived."

Kian had to admit that Jacki's assumption made sense. If Fates forbid his children were lost in space, he wouldn't have given up hope either and would have wanted the scouts to stay and wait for them.

The problem was that they were speculating, and by now they had so many ideas and possible scenarios that he had trouble keeping it all organized in his head.

"We should write down the sequence of events and all the good questions that are being raised. There are too many variables to keep track of."

Turner leaned down to pull his trusty yellow pad out of his satchel. "Let's do it now. What's our starting point?"

"Ahn and the Kra-ell queen have an affair," Syssi suggested. "The rebellion before that is less concerning to us. We need to determine the sequence of events from when the queen got pregnant with the twins."

"I agree." Turner wrote it down. "Next, the rebellion ends with a peace treaty, and Ahn and his cohorts are exiled to Earth. The queen is pregnant with his children, but we assume he doesn't know that. Does she know he's the father?"

Syssi pursed her lips. "The Kra-ell males know right away when a female is pregnant. The queen's consorts would have known it hadn't been one of them. How did she keep them from revealing her secret?"

"The vows," Kian said. "I'm sure the queen's consorts were bound by so many oaths of loyalty to her that they couldn't betray her even if they suspected that the father was a god, a big no-no in their society. Also, we know that the queen was a strong compeller. She might have compelled their silence."

"That wouldn't have been enough for her," Bridget said. "The Eternal King was the strongest compeller on the planet, and he could have overridden her compulsion and forced the truth out of her consorts. That's why the queen would never have trusted her consorts or anyone else with crucial information about her children. She probably lied to them, saying the father was a lowly Kra-ell male who she didn't want anyone to know about. Or even better, she could have commanded one of her consorts to claim that the children were his."

"And then had him killed," Turner said. "So, he couldn't be forced to reveal the truth."

Annani laughed, the sound breaking the somber mood that Turner's words had brought about. "We do not know what actually happened, and we are getting carried away with *Game of Thrones* types of scenarios. It is very entertaining, but we should stick to what we know or can make an educated guess about."

Syssi nodded. "I agree. The next item on the timeline is the decommission of the Odus, but since the exiled gods knew about that, we can assume that it happened before they were sent to Earth or shortly after."

"Probably before." Turner wrote it down. "That's why I always leave several empty lines between each item. Otherwise, things get messy."

Kian stifled a chuckle. "We wouldn't want that." He continued, "The peace treaty also included a Kra-ell settlement on Earth, but that's where it gets muddy. If Ahn knew about the terms of the treaty, he would have said something about expecting the Kra-ell's arrival, but he and the others said nothing about it. They never even mentioned the Kra-ell. Why is that?"

His mother shrugged. "They also never said that they were exiled. They did not even tell us they were from somewhere else in the universe. Khiann's father told Khiann and me in confidence about an ugly war a long time ago, but he talked in general terms and never mentioned the Kra-ell either." She looked at Toven. "What about you? Did Ekin or Mortdh tell you anything or at least hint at it?"

"Ekin did not like to talk about politics, and he never talked about the home planet. Mortdh, on the other hand, threw a lot of hints around, but I did not take him seriously. Even our own father said that Mortdh was a lunatic and that I should not listen to his rants. Now I'm starting to think that maybe my brother was not as crazy as everyone thought. He was power-hungry and lacked scruples, but that did not make him insane. Those two character traits describe ninety-nine percent of the world's leaders."

Annani shifted in her chair. "Insanity comes in different forms. Mortdh was smart, but he was crazy. Navuh told Areana things that no one else knew about his father, and it confirmed what everyone suspected about Mortdh. He was prone to fits of rage, he was a megalomaniac, he was violent, and he believed in patriarchy and the subjugation of females." She sighed. "He also believed that he was doing good things for the population under his rule and that they had nothing to complain about."

"Was he right?" Jacki asked.

"They were not hungry, and no one dared attack his region, but they were all his to do with as he pleased. He treated everyone as mindless slaves, as cattle—the immortals in his army, the immortal and dormant females in his harem, and the humans serving him."

"That was common back then," Jacki said. "Not that it was right, but that was how those in power treated everyone else in the ancient world." She snorted. "Heck, they still do. They are just more circumspect about it now."

She should know. Kalugal had built an empire by manipulating people's herd mentality to his advantage.

With everything that had been going on, Kian hadn't had time to look into Kalugal's social media company. Hopefully, his cousin wasn't doing anything overly nefarious.

As Okidu walked in with a tray loaded with desserts, Annani's mood brightened. "Let us take a break and enjoy these lovely sweets with tea."

"That's a wonderful idea." Syssi pushed to her feet. "Does anyone want a cappuccino?"

# GABI

Thankfully, the three hot guys hadn't stayed long in the club, or Gabi would have been starving by now.

Like a coward, she'd waited until they were gone to walk up to the buffet and load her plate with whatever junk food was offered. Well, most people would not call pasta with meatballs junk, but to a nutritionist, it was.

No one wanted advice about diet and fitness from an overweight or out-of-shape nutritionist. Heck, she would have no clients.

Nevertheless, it was free, and she was allowed to indulge once in a while. Just not too often. With a sigh, she put her fork down and pushed the plate away. It hadn't even been tasty.

What a waste of calories.

If she was sinning, she at least wanted to enjoy it.

Gabi softly chuckled as the impossibly gorgeous face of one of the three hunks popped into her mind's eye, the one she'd aptly nicknamed 'the devil.' The man was sin personified, and she wouldn't mind a tumble with either of his two buddies either.

No, that wasn't true.

They were just as gorgeous as her devil, but in a different way, and although they were nice to look at, she couldn't see herself naked with either of them.

Mr. Devil, however, was a different story. She could see herself doing a lot of naughty things with him.

Gabi sighed.

After the way she'd ignored his covert glances and his smiles when she'd caught him looking, it was pathetic of her to imagine herself doing anything with him. If she had given him the slightest indication that she was interested, he might have come over to her table and perhaps offered to buy her a drink.

He didn't seem like the shy type, but men these days were cautious about approaching women, and he was smart to stay away unless invited.

Not that she would have made a big deal of it if he had come over to talk to her uninvited, but she wouldn't have done anything more than talk, and if he wanted more, she would have politely declined.

Mr. Devil was too good-looking and too young for her.

Gabi knew that she looked incredible for a thirty-eight-year-old woman. She worked damn hard for it, and most people thought she was a decade younger, but she had experience and perspective that Mr. Devil most likely didn't have.

She shouldn't make assumptions based solely on his age and looks. Maybe he was a small business owner like her?

With the muscles he was packing, he could be a personal trainer. But had he ever been an overweight kid who the other kids made fun of?

Not likely.

Had he ever been cheated on by his girlfriend?

What woman in her right mind would replace that face and that body with another? Or what man, for that matter? Not that Gabi thought Mr. Devil swung that way. The looks he had given her had not been the platonic kind.

Whatever.

She should get going. The boarding for her flight had started several minutes ago, and although she had a first-class seat and could board without standing in line, she shouldn't delay too much.

With her luck, something would happen on the way to the gate, and she would miss her flight.

Gabi cleaned her table of the mess she'd made, pushed to her feet, and gripped the handle of her carry-on.

"Miss!" Someone called from behind her. "Miss!"

When she turned around, a man was pointing to the chair she had just vacated. "You forgot your purse."

"Thank you." She rushed back to retrieve it. "My passport and my boarding pass are in there." And her money and credit cards.

"You are welcome. Have a safe flight."

"You too." She smiled at him. "Thank you again. You are a lifesaver."

If the friendly man hadn't noticed the purse and called her, Gabi would have gotten all the way to the gate before realizing she'd left it behind. She would have been forced to run back to get it and would have missed her flight.

Was it lucky that the guy had noticed, though?

Or unlucky?

Was she supposed to be on that flight or not?

She was well aware that it wasn't smart to base her life decisions on what she thought was lucky or unlucky, and she shouldn't look for signs at every turn, but when someone was living in a state of constant fear, they clung to anything that could be a directional pointer in the chaos of life.

With panic seizing her lungs, Gabi forced her feet to keep moving. She was afraid of too many damn things, but her family needed her, and she needed to conquer these fears, at least for this one flight.

Hopefully, Gilbert and the rest of her family were fine, and she was panicking for nothing.

On the way back, though, she might rent a car and drive all the way home.

**ORDER DARK ENCOUNTERS OF THE CLOSE KIND TODAY!**

## Join the *VIP Club*

To find out what's included in your free membership,
click HERE or flip to the last page.

# Note

Dear reader,

I hope my stories have added a little joy to your day. If you have a moment to add some to mine, you can help spread the word about the Children Of The Gods series by telling your friends and penning a review. Your recommendations are the most powerful way to inspire new readers to explore the series.

Thank you,

Isabell

# Also by I. T. Lucas

## THE CHILDREN OF THE GODS ORIGINS
### 1: GODDESS'S CHOICE
### 2: GODDESS'S HOPE
## THE CHILDREN OF THE GODS
### DARK STRANGER
1: DARK STRANGER THE DREAM

2: DARK STRANGER REVEALED

3: DARK STRANGER IMMORTAL

### DARK ENEMY
4: DARK ENEMY TAKEN

5: DARK ENEMY CAPTIVE

6: DARK ENEMY REDEEMED

### KRI & MICHAEL'S STORY
6.5: MY DARK AMAZON

### DARK WARRIOR
7: DARK WARRIOR MINE

8: DARK WARRIOR'S PROMISE

9: DARK WARRIOR'S DESTINY

10: DARK WARRIOR'S LEGACY

### DARK GUARDIAN
11: DARK GUARDIAN FOUND

12: DARK GUARDIAN CRAVED

13: DARK GUARDIAN'S MATE

### DARK ANGEL
14: DARK ANGEL'S OBSESSION

15: DARK ANGEL'S SEDUCTION

16: DARK ANGEL'S SURRENDER

### DARK OPERATIVE

17: Dark Operative: A Shadow of Death
18: Dark Operative: A Glimmer of Hope
19: Dark Operative: The Dawn of Love

## Dark Survivor

20: Dark Survivor Awakened
21: Dark Survivor Echoes of Love
22: Dark Survivor Reunited

## Dark Widow

23: Dark Widow's Secret
24: Dark Widow's Curse
25: Dark Widow's Blessing

## Dark Dream

26: Dark Dream's Temptation
27: Dark Dream's Unraveling
28: Dark Dream's Trap

## Dark Prince

29: Dark Prince's Enigma
30: Dark Prince's Dilemma
31: Dark Prince's Agenda

## Dark Queen

32: Dark Queen's Quest
33: Dark Queen's Knight
34: Dark Queen's Army

## Dark Spy

35: Dark Spy Conscripted
36: Dark Spy's Mission
37: Dark Spy's Resolution

## Dark Overlord

38: Dark Overlord New Horizon
39: Dark Overlord's Wife
40: Dark Overlord's Clan

## Dark Choices

41: Dark Choices The Quandary

42: Dark Choices Paradigm Shift

43: Dark Choices The Accord

## Dark Secrets

44: Dark Secrets Resurgence

45: Dark Secrets Unveiled

46: Dark Secrets Absolved

## Dark Haven

47: Dark Haven Illusion

48: Dark Haven Unmasked

49: Dark Haven Found

## Dark Power

50: Dark Power Untamed

51: Dark Power Unleashed

52: Dark Power Convergence

## Dark Memories

53: Dark Memories Submerged

54: Dark Memories Emerge

55: Dark Memories Restored

## Dark Hunter

56: Dark Hunter's Query

57: Dark Hunter's Prey

58: Dark Hunter's Boon

## Dark God

59: Dark God's Avatar

60: Dark God's Reviviscence

61: Dark God Destinies Converge

## Dark Whispers

62: Dark Whispers From The Past

63: Dark Whispers From Afar

64: DARK WHISPERS FROM BEYOND
**DARK GAMBIT**
65: DARK GAMBIT THE PAWN
66: DARK GAMBIT THE PLAY
67: DARK GAMBIT RELIANCE
**DARK ALLIANCE**
68: DARK ALLIANCE KINDRED SOULS
69: DARK ALLIANCE TURBULENT WATERS
70: DARK ALLIANCE PERFECT STORM
**DARK HEALING**
71: DARK HEALING BLIND JUSTICE
72: DARK HEALING BLIND TRUST
73: DARK healing BLIND CURVE
**DARK ENCOUNTERS**
74: DARK ENCOUNTERS OF THE CLOSE KIND
75: DARK ENCOUNTERS OF THE UNEXPECTED KIND
76: DARK ENCOUNTERS OF THE FATED KIND
**DARK VOYAGE**
77: Dark Voyage Matters of the Heart

---

## PERFECT MATCH

VAMPIRE'S CONSORT
KING'S CHOSEN
CAPTAIN'S CONQUEST
THE THIEF WHO LOVED ME
MY MERMAN PRINCE
THE DRAGON KING
MY WEREWOLF ROMEO

---

## The Children of the Gods Series Sets

Books 1-3: Dark Stranger trilogy—Includes a bonus short story: **The Fates take a Vacation**

Books 4-6: Dark Enemy Trilogy —Includes a bonus short story—**The Fates' Post-Wedding Celebration**

Books 7-10: Dark Warrior Tetralogy

Books 11-13: Dark Guardian Trilogy

Books 14-16: Dark Angel Trilogy

Books 17-19: Dark Operative Trilogy

Books 20-22: Dark Survivor Trilogy

Books 23-25: Dark Widow Trilogy

Books 26-28: Dark Dream Trilogy

Books 29-31: Dark Prince Trilogy

Books 32-34: Dark Queen Trilogy

Books 35-37: Dark Spy Trilogy

Books 38-40: Dark Overlord Trilogy

Books 41-43: Dark Choices Trilogy

Books 44-46: Dark Secrets Trilogy

Books 47-49: Dark Haven Trilogy

Books 50-52: Dark Power Trilogy

Books 53-55: Dark Memories Trilogy

Books 56-58: Dark Hunter Trilogy

Books 59-61: Dark God Trilogy

Books 62-64: Dark Whispers Trilogy

Books 65-67: Dark Gambit Trilogy

Books 68-70: Dark Alliance Trilogy

Books 71-73: Dark healing Trilogy

## MEGA SETS

### INCLUDE CHARACTER LISTS

The Children of the Gods: Books 1-6
The Children of the Gods: Books 6.5-10

Perfect Match Bundle 1

## CHECK OUT THE SPECIALS ON
ITLUCAS.COM
(https://itlucas.com/specials)

# FOR EXCLUSIVE PEEKS AT UPCOMING RELEASES & A FREE I. T. LUCAS COMPANION BOOK

Join my *VIP Club* and gain access to the VIP portal at itlucas.com

## To Join, go to:
http://eepurl.com/blMTpD

Find out more details about what's included with your free membership on the book's last page.

---

# TRY THE CHILDREN OF THE GODS SERIES ON
## <u>AUDIBLE</u>
2 FREE audiobooks with your new Audible subscription!

# FOR EXCLUSIVE PEEKS AT UPCOMING RELEASES & A FREE COMPANION BOOK

JOIN MY *VIP CLUB* AND GAIN ACCESS TO THE VIP PORTAL AT ITLUCAS.COM
TO JOIN, GO TO:
http://eepurl.com/blMTpD

## INCLUDED IN YOUR FREE MEMBERSHIP:

## YOUR VIP PORTAL

- READ PREVIEW CHAPTERS OF UPCOMING RELEASES.
- LISTEN TO GODDESS'S CHOICE NARRATION BY CHARLES LAWRENCE
- EXCLUSIVE CONTENT OFFERED ONLY TO MY VIPs.

## FREE I.T. LUCAS COMPANION INCLUDES:

- GODDESS'S CHOICE PART I
- PERFECT MATCH: VAMPIRE'S CONSORT (A STANDALONE NOVELLA)
- INTERVIEW Q & A
- CHARACTER CHARTS

IF YOU'RE ALREADY A SUBSCRIBER, AND YOU ARE NOT GETTING MY EMAILS, YOUR PROVIDER IS

SENDING THEM TO YOUR JUNK FOLDER, AND YOU ARE MISSING OUT ON **IMPORTANT UPDATES, SIDE CHARACTERS' PORTRAITS, ADDITIONAL CONTENT, AND OTHER GOODIES.** TO FIX THAT, ADD isabell@itlucas.com TO YOUR EMAIL CONTACTS OR YOUR EMAIL VIP LIST.

**Check out the specials at
https://www.itlucas.com/specials**

Made in the USA
Las Vegas, NV
14 November 2023